With great humility, I dedicate this book to the children of East Prussia who were lost and orphaned as the Red Army advanced through their land during the final battles of Hitler's war. The children became known as the Wolf Children of the Eastern Front.

Few remain alive today to tell their story.

For further reading of their tragic lives, I recommend the book *The Wolf Children of the Eastern Front* by Sonya Winterberg, with Kirstin Lieff and preface by John Kay (frontman of "Steppenwolf").

I hope I do not appear to make light of their suffering.

## MAP OF GERMANY
## 1946

# PART ONE

## Helen

# 1

It was never going to be easy. It was never going to be the way it was.

They spend the night in a small *Gásthaus* close to the river. The sun is fading and darkness threatens to envelop the cobbled towpath as they walk along the riverbank. Her husband holds baby Karl tightly inside his camelhair coat, a gift from Major Mackenzie and his wife. A north-easterly wind has brought a fresh blast of cold air and islets of snow now lace the frozen waters of the Pegnitz. They walk briskly, the cold stinging their cheeks; it is not the weather for a gentle stroll. Helen can feel the icy damp creeping through the thin soles of her shoes; there had been no time to consider her own needs in the hurried departure from Normandy, nor those of their baby son. But the major's wife has been generous and their son has sufficient clothing for this time at least. Their eyes meet and her heart contracts with love; she has waited so long for this, throughout the many months when she had believed him to be dead on the battlefields of France and Belgium, with the snow drifting softy over his mutilated body.

They return to the *Gásthaus* where the *Gástgeber* has prepared a meal for them. She is an elderly lady who lost her sons on the Eastern Front and her husband in the RAF bombing of the city. She is very attentive to the needs of the family and insists on addressing Karl as General von Werstein. He does not encourage this, but neither does he correct her. The woman still feels pride in her sons' sacrifice for the Fatherland and there will be few ways of honouring them now Germany is a defeated nation. She should be allowed to have her memories and her pride. That her sons' lives were lost in a war waged by corrupt fanatics and sadists is no fault of theirs, or hers.

Their son is able to join them in the simple meal *Bratkartoffeln*. After he has eaten his fill, Helen opens her blouse and puts him to her breast. She feels her husband's eyes on her; he has not seen her nurse their son until now. She closes her eyes as she feels tears prickling, tears she suppressed during the days of the trial. But she hears him sob and looks up to see that he is crying. His tears flow without restraint down his face and onto the plate of food he has consumed so little of. She places their child into the baby carriage and puts her arms around her husband, silently soothing him.

After a while his tears stop and he says, 'I have missed so much. How can I live knowing how much I have missed, how much we have lost?'

She kisses him and holds him close to her. After a while, she rises to take the infant to bathe him and then rocks him to sleep in the wooden cradle the major's wife has loaned them. She returns to her husband and taking his hand, leads him to the bedroom. She undresses him slowly, kissing every part of his body as it is revealed. His battle scars are still raw and he is leaner than before, what flesh there was is now the muscle of combat, and his skin is the pallor of months of confinement in a prison cell. She undresses, holding his gaze as she does so. And then they are together, his hands seeking her, his lips on hers, on her breasts and on that part of her which in his absence has delivered their son. All he thought he had lost is now found and she is holding him, never wanting to let him go, not again, not ever.

Later they talk of how they will live; both wish to return to France, to the Château des Tilleuls which is now hers to do with as she wishes. But Germans are not welcome in France at this time, and she is considered a collaborator by some. Nor do they feel they can go to her home in Berwickshire. The neighbours who welcomed her return to Foulden in 1944 will perhaps not be so welcoming once they know of the identity of her husband, the father of her child. Their men have not returned from the battlefields of Europe and beyond. They are grieving and their grief will take a generation to be assuaged. Nor can they go to his former home; Prussia no longer exists and his estates are now forfeited, lost to the Soviet occupying forces. His family have been driven from their homes and he has had no news of them since the end of the war. They have become citizens of nowhere.

## 2

The following evening they are invited to supper by Major Mackenzie and his wife, Edith. After the meal, Edith takes Helen to the drawing room for coffee, leaving the two men at the table with cigars and the port bottle.

Later, as they make to leave, with baby Karl asleep in her arms, the major touches her husband lightly on the back in a gesture of encouragement, 'Well, think about it, my friend. You could make a real difference there. Patton spoke highly of you. Of course, if he were alive he would have represented you in person, but he left letters attesting to your character. What happens after the war is won can be more important than the war itself. As Montgomery himself said to the troops on VE Day "We have won the German war. Let us now win the peace". The fact that you were held in high esteem as an honourable soldier, and of course a general, will help in the transition of Germany from Hitler's Nazi *Reich t*o democracy. We need to give Germans hope for the future.'

As they lie together that night he tells her of the major's proposal. They are to move to Bonn, which is in the British zone of occupation. When she asks why Bonn and not Berlin, he explains that while the Allies hope eventually to make Berlin the capital of a reunified Germany, this is not possible at the present time due to the Soviet occupation of the centre and east of Germany, where Berlin is situated. Berlin itself had been divided into four sectors of occupation by the Allies at the Potsdam Conference in 1945. The Americans, under President Roosevelt, had believed Stalin would work peacefully with the Allies to ensure the transition of Germany into a functioning democratic state. Churchill had expressed no such confidence, and described Stalin as "a devil", predicting he would hold on to as much territory in Germany as he could and bring it under Soviet control. President Roosevelt's successor, President Truman, was in accord with Churchill. Thus, in the face of potential intransigence by Stalin, and even a land grab by the Soviets, Bonn will be the temporary centre of the institutions which will lay the foundations of the new German state. To have chosen the major cities of Hamburg or Frankfurt would have implied a permanent capital in the west of Germany and weaken support for the country's reunification.

'And what is to be your role in this?'

'I will tell you more tomorrow, but for now, *Liebchen,* I want to make love to my beloved wife.'

'I am still cautious of your wounds and do not want to cause you pain.'

'My wounds are nothing compared to the pain I suffered when I was apart from you.'

She rolls over onto him and holds him close between her thighs. He is so much thinner and the scars on his chest and abdomen are more visible in this position. This induces such a sense of compassion and anguish that for a moment he seems alien to her: he had always been the strong one, a leader of men, and also an enigma whose gentle irony caused her so much doubt and uncertainty in the days of war and occupation. Now she feels it is he who needs her protection.

Later she reflects on other women, the wives and lovers of the returned and defeated German army, whether they feel this need to protect their men: the men who had fought for the cause of

Hitler's Thousand Year *Reich* and are now reduced to beggars; supplicants of the victorious Allies' charity. But what they had done was evil, and more horror was revealed by the day: the atrocities in the East, the betrayals and deportation of neighbours to the horrors of the camps, the massacre of innocent civilians throughout Europe, such as that at Oradour-sur-Glane. These murders had continued long after the perpetrators knew the war to be lost. Germans appear to be reluctant to accept responsibility for the crimes against humanity committed during the twelve years of Hitler's rule, so much so that they now consider themselves to be victims.

## 3

February 1946
Bonn, Germany


They arrive in the snow of the coldest winter in living memory.

Major Mackenzie has explained that their accommodation will be provided through the British Control Commission. Karl will be subjected to interrogation to prove his *Persilschein*. This is a colloquialism for the assessment of his possible collaboration with the Nazi regime; his "cleanliness" will be determined by a *Fragebogen*, 133 questions which will determine his degree of association with the Nazis.

In the British Zone, the *Fragebogen* is only applied to persons applying for positions of responsibility, as in Law or Medicine. There is a significant shortage of expertise in both professions: so many Jewish doctors and lawyers were murdered during the Nazi years, and the professions tainted by Nazi ideology.

'The Americans are applying the *Fragebogen* to all and sundry and it has become a bureaucratic nightmare for them, especially as they are categorising the Germans into degrees of guilt. We are trying to be more flexible and more inclusive of the Germans. We need their cooperation to rebuild the country, particularly the industrial zone, which we have been allocated.'

'My husband was exonerated at his trial. Surely he has already proved that he was never a Nazi, and had no part in the persecution of Jews, or other victims of the Hitler regime.'

The major assures her this is merely a formality; neither she nor Karl should be worried about its outcome.

'Churchill is no longer in command but he still has influence. He never trusted Stalin and feels that war with the Soviet Union is inevitable. He believes Stalin will not honour the terms of Yalta and Potsdam, and will seek to extend and maintain his sphere of influence over the whole of Germany, as well as the countries which suffered under Nazi occupation: the Baltic States, Poland, Czechoslovakia, Hungary and the Balkans. German forces are disarmed and disbanded, but this situation will not last and there will eventually be a need for a German military. Churchill feels they would provide reinforcements in the event of war with the Soviet Union. *Persilschein* teenagers will not lead the troops into battle, but former generals such as your husband will; a degree of continuity must be identifiable.

'But there are other obstacles to overcome. There is starvation and a total breakdown of society. Fortunately, there has been no organised armed resistance to defeat and occupation, apart from a few troublemakers they call "Werewolf brigades". Germany has been utterly defeated and the Nazi regime discredited, and the majority of Germans have accepted this. We need respected Germans, such as your husband, to help in the process of reconciliation; the "winning of the peace" as Monty put it. Even more importantly, we must ensure that our peace and the conditions in our zones of occupation are more favourable than in the Soviet Zone. Your husband will be working as an administrator, as well as a potential military officer.'

They are invited to the home of Colonel Quentin Oakley. This is a requisitioned villa on the banks of the Rhine. It withstood the Allied bombing raids and maintains its magnificence behind an avenue of linden trees. The colonel's wife, Sybil, is courteous, but is clearly bewildered to be hosting a former German general and his wife. Helen knows she must maintain her oath of secrecy with regard to her time during the occupation of France and her involvement in D-Day. She will not attempt to justify her situation.

The conversation inevitably drifts to domestic issues. Their children, two sons at Eton and a daughter, Susan, "a difficult child, *entre nous*", will not be joining them in Germany. Susan attends a girls' school in Eastbourne, East Sussex, but has recently been withdrawn from her previous school, Granville House, also in Eastbourne.

'Of course, as soon as we discovered the school had been attended by the wife of a war criminal, who is being hunted for his crimes, we immediately moved her to Moira House, which fortunately is also in Eastbourne. Surely you have heard of Otto von Wächter and his wife Charlotte?'

Helen considers this. She has no knowledge of either of them, but she will enquire of her husband when she has the opportunity. Perhaps Sybil is of the opinion that she and her husband are of similar ilk to the Von Wächters. She struggles to remember a phrase; English has not been her first language for many years. Then she remembers it, "*Birds of a feather flock together*". This is how she and Karl will be regarded within the British community in Bonn. Sybil appears to sense Helen's discomfiture and attempts to turn the conversation back to domestic issues. The war had been a difficult time for the family, with her husband rarely given leave from the war office, the privations of rationing, and lack of domestic help at their home in Surrey.

'My dear, I did not know how to boil an egg when Mabel left our service to join the Wrens.'

She asks Helen how she will occupy her time while her husband is at work. She recommends the British Families Shop, NAAFI, explaining that the store sells goods and organises recreational activities for British servicemen and their families. She also invites her to join the British Women's Association of which she is the chairwoman.

'We meet twice a week for coffee and a good chinwag. There is always a bottle of gin at the ready and we take turns in hosting our meetings. Ostensibly we are planning charity events, helping the refugees and so on, but really it is an opportunity to snoop at each other's houses, assess who has appropriated the best and so on.'

Helen is shocked by this admission, and is determined not to join in any such meetings or *soi-disant* charity events. She understands that these military wives are living in houses requisitioned from German families, many of whom have been summarily evicted onto the streets. She and Karl have been given an abandoned apartment in a bomb-damaged block near the centre of Bonn. Their neighbours are all German women who work clearing the rubble from the ruined streets. Many are widows, but there are others who hope for the return of their husbands and lovers. These "*Trümmerfrauen*" leave early in the morning with their children to sort through the rubble of the bombed buildings. They form bucket chains, passing the bricks and stones from hand to hand onto the street, where it is again sorted and cleaned by their children. It is dirty and exhausting work. It is also traumatic: bones and body parts are frequently discovered among the rubble. But they have no choice as their entitlement to rations of food, which they consider to be near starvation level, is dependent on this work.

Sybil is astonished when Helen informs her that she intends to continue her medical studies at the university in Bonn. A local girl, a neighbour, will care for baby Karl while she is attending lectures, and she hopes German friends in Paris will join them as soon as the apartment is adequately heated and water supplies to the building are fully restored. Sybil offers to take Helen to the

NAAFI shop the following day. Her driver will collect Helen and baby Karl from their apartment building at 11 .a m.

They return to their apartment and her husband struggles to light the *Kachelöfen*. The stove survived the bombing raids which blew out the windows of the apartment and demolished much of the building. It is their only source of heat. Helen admires its craftsmanship and has taken pride in polishing the ochre tiles which absorb the heat of the fire within and should provide a gentle and consistent warmth. Their neighbours are generous and pleased to assist "The General" and his family. They leave wood salvaged from the rubble by their door, but tonight the wood is damp due to the snowmelt that covers it. Eventually the stove is lit and they bed down around it, wrapping themselves in the quilts and blankets the British Control Commission have provided. Although they have hammered large pieces of wood across the shattered window frames and filled the spaces between the slats with sacking salvaged from a potato lorry, icy draughts continue to seep through the apartment and they shiver as a milky frost settles on their clothing and bedding. They hold their son tightly between them, fearing that he will succumb to the same cold that has killed so many infants in this harshest of winters.

They have been promised a bed, a table and chairs and, within a few weeks, a bathroom and kitchen. At present they are collecting water from a standpipe in the street and waste buckets are provided in the hallways of the building. Helen takes her turn with the other women in emptying these. The standpipe often freezes up and the waste buckets have a layer of ice over them by the morning. It is a source of humour among her neighbours that the smell is contained by the ice. She is now able to communicate in German with her neighbours, and they in turn enjoy the opportunity to learn English from her.

Helen waits outside the apartment block, shivering in the

shabby coat she has worn since she departed from Normandy. Baby Karl is wrapped in a quilt and his plump hands pull at her long hair as she holds him close to her. After a short time, a chauffeur-driven black Mercedes car pulls up. Sybil winds down the window and invites Helen to get into the car. There are two other women with her, both are smartly dressed and smoking the distinctive Lucky Strike cigarettes. She is offered one but politely declines; she dislikes the smell and worries that the smoke could affect her child's lungs. He was coughing a few days ago. She is anxious that the cold and dust are the cause, and cigarette smoke would make him worse. It is at moments such as these that Helen misses the fresh air of her Berwickshire home, where their child would thrive in the attention of his grandparents, a warm house and the prospect of summer days on the lawns around the house. She imagines him kicking his legs in delight as Papa pushes him on the swing that hangs from the lower branches of the oak tree next to the drive, the same swing she enjoyed as a child.

They arrive at the NAAFI building. It is an unprepossessing structure on two floors. Sybil explains that household utensils and small items of furniture can be found on the ground floor, food and drink are on the first floor along with clothing for all ages and toys for the children.

'Plenty of gin but not much to go with it. The coffee and tea are the real thing. Thank goodness for the colonies. My sister is in Kenya, one of the Happy Valley set. They wanted for nothing during the war; a jolly good time was had by all, except for the odd murder by a jealous husband.'

Helen has no idea what Sybil is talking about, nor does she care. There are plenty of people in Britain who enjoyed a good war. Sybil excuses herself and joins her friends who are making their way up the stairs. Helen counts her vouchers. She has enough to buy some much-needed kitchen knives, a frying pan and soup bowls. The tiny cooking range in the apartment has only one hot plate and soup and bread are all she has managed to serve from it. Her husband never complains but often teases her with memories of the omelette she prepared for him late one night at the *château*. She remembers the moment he took her arm to steady her as she carried the tray out of the library. She remembers the reassuring warmth of his hand and the effect it had on her. These memories provoke a wave of love for him; he has suffered so much since those days. She will do all she can to keep the family together.

She pays for the goods and asks the counter assistant to look after them while she looks for clothing for her child. She also leaves the eiderdown, so baby Karl is able to wrap his arms around her neck and his legs around her hips. She climbs the stairs and hears the clipped accents of Sybil and her friends.

'I have no idea why she has been allowed such privileges. All I know is that she married a German officer, a general no less, during the occupation of France. I understand she is half-French, but we know what happened to collaborators, the women anyway: they were shaved and paraded naked around the towns where they had betrayed their countrymen.'

'That makes her no more than a whore, a camp follower. And you had to entertain them? My dear, how dreadful for you. Whatever did you find to talk about?'

At that moment baby Karl shrieks with delight at the brightly coloured toys he has spotted close to the top of the stairs. The women turn around abruptly; it is clear that Helen has overheard their conversation. But the sudden silence is broken by a loud male voice from the other side of the store.

'*Wae* if it *isna* Helen. I *canna* believe it! Come, Morag, *ye* must meet the *lassie* who saved *ma* life.'

A young man in the uniform of a lance corporal is approaching her, and with him is a young woman holding a baby. Helen is astounded; the three women equally so. It is Iain, one of the young soldiers she hid in the secret room in the early years of the occupation of France.

He looks around the room and announces, 'This *lassie* saved *ma* life, along with *ma pal*. She saved others *tae*, at the risk to her own life. *And a'* happen *te ken* that she did *mair* than that but she's *tae* modest *ta* talk *aboot* it, and bound *te* secrecy.'

Helen finds herself in the embrace of both Iain and "Morag". Their "*wean*", Jamie, is the same age as baby Karl. Iain loudly asserts that without Helen his family would not be here today. The effect on the counter assistants is immediate. Helen is plied with tea, sugar and coffee. Eggs, cheese and ham are put into bags, baby Karl is given woollen pants and jumpers, and she a fur-lined coat and boots.

Karl is given a brightly coloured spinning top and he and Jamie sit on the floor together while Morag shows them how it works. Both are enchanted by the strange toy and clap their hands in excitement. Sybil and her friends leave without acknowledging the reunion.

Iain explains that he and his family have a small apartment in the British Army barracks on the outskirts of Bonn. Fraser is in Hamburg with his wife. They are expecting their first child, who will be born in Germany. Iain will make sure they contact Helen and her family. He insists that he will drive her and baby Karl home in his military vehicle.

She is embarrassed by the dilapidated state of her apartment but Iain embraces her as he takes his leave. He has noticed the welcome she receives from her neighbours.

'By living here *ye're* helping us win the peace as Monty said we must *dae*. Promise me *ye'll* ask us if *ye* need any help, *ye* and *yer* man and the *wee one*.'

She kisses him farewell and unpacks her parcels. She shares the tea, coffee and sugar among her neighbours, and keeps sufficient eggs, cheese and ham to make an omelette for her husband that night.

# PART TWO

## Karl

# 4

June 1940
Paris, France

As a Prussian whose duty is to defend the Fatherland, I bitterly resented the order. Military Command decided I should be given an administrative posting until my wife, Sophia, recovered her health, and until my division was required for whichever military operation the *Führer* next ordered. I had commanded a *Panzer* division in Poland and was elevated to the rank of general soon after our victory; promotion comes swiftly in times of war.

We marched triumphantly into Paris on the 14th of June. Loudspeakers, in German-accented French, informed the people of Paris that a curfew was being imposed from 8 p.m. that evening. The French government had fled, declaring Paris to be an "open city". There was to be no resistance. The city would therefore be spared destruction.

My battle-weary men were given leave to enjoy the delights of Paris. They shopped for perfume and silk stockings for their wives and girlfriends at home, and enjoyed the company of young women who, to the disapproval of many of their French compatriots, were happy to be accompanied to bars and restaurants by handsome, smartly uniformed young soldiers.

An invitation to Maxims was issued to all commanding officers and I spent the evening in the company of *Oberstleutnant* Hans Schulz, who I learned was to be the *Oberfeldkommandur* of the Calvados region of Normandy. His headquarters would be in Caen, close to the town where I would be his subordinate, as *Feldkommandur*.

My sense of humiliation, that an officer of lower military rank was to be my superior, was soon overcome as Hans referred to me as General von Werstein when introducing me to our hosts and was good-humoured and attentive at all times. We were joined by several women, including those who were to accompany Hans and myself to Normandy as our personal secretaries. We were to choose between the women. Hans immediately selected the most attractive: two girls from Alsace, a region that had alternated between German and French control over the centuries and where fluency in both languages was common among the population. I sensed disappointment on their behalf as both girls, Adalie and Lisette, had been very flirtatious towards me during the course of the evening.

In the early hours of the morning, Hans took the two girls to rooms upstairs and encouraged me to accompany them. Exhaustion and elation at our victory overcame my reserve. I was not a man to bed a woman lightly, but Adalie took my arm and led me into one of the rooms. She was beautiful and impossible to resist. I took her roughly, exorcising the trauma of battlefields, and the devils which had beset me since the Polish campaign.

I awoke as the early morning sun filtered through the lace curtains. My sense of shame was such that I could not bear to look at myself in the mirror as I hastily shaved and washed. Adalie slept until midday. I brought her coffee and pastries and informed her the night could not be repeated; my duty was to my wife and to my command. My humiliation was intensified by the look of anger and disappointment that crossed her face; I understood immediately that she was a woman who would not accept rejection. I spoke of this with Hans, and he was astounded

I should have such scruples. He also informed me that Adalie's father had powerful connections in the Nazi party; she could be a dangerous enemy. It would be in my interest to keep her entertained, at least while we were in Paris.

It was not difficult, and she proved to be a pleasurable distraction from the dark memories of my time in Poland.

Two weeks later I left Paris and, together with my adjutant, secretaries and a detail of guards and orderlies, set out to take up my command at the Château des Tilleuls in the town of Sainte Geneviève-sur-Orne.

## 5

I had been informed that the *château* was owned by a wealthy Jewish family. There had been no sighting of them since the fall of France and thus I avoided the unpleasantness of evicting them; I knew how defenceless they would now be. I had also been informed that the *château* had a housekeeper, who could be replaced by another of my choosing.

The gardens were in good order; a large rose bush covered a wall some distance from the entrance and the gentle breeze carried its exquisite scent across the drive, where my detail waited in their vehicles.

I rang the doorbell, noting that the ring had recently been cleaned and oiled, and within a few seconds the door was opened by a young woman. After greeting me formally, she introduced herself as Gabrielle Doucet and explained she had been placed in charge of the *château* when the owners left. She informed me she had no knowledge of their whereabouts, and expressed discontent that she had not been paid for her services.

I was not convinced by her story but, more importantly, I was gripped by an overwhelming sense of recognition and a deep attraction. She evoked a childhood memory of someone my mother took me to visit when I was very young. It is my earliest childhood memory and I was no more than three years of age at the time: an old lady, who took my hand into her own and, looking into my eyes, spoke words I did not understand. But my mother wrote them down and translated them into the High German we spoke at home *"gheibh thu i agus aithnichidh tu i"* which she explained meant "you will find her and know her". I remember asking my mother what this strange language was and the meaning of the words, but my mother would not speak of it and dismissed my confusion as of no importance. I understood this lady died soon after.

Many years later, long after my marriage to Sophia, I found by chance the paper with the words my mother had written, along with the translation. I sought my mother out and questioned her again as to the language of the words and their meaning. My mother was greatly surprised by my curiosity and by my memory of the circumstances of that time. She explained she had been concerned that the contract of marriage between the two families Von Werstein and Karstein might be threatened if I had taken the words to heart, and perhaps doubted my destiny: to go the *Kriegsakademie* in Berlin as a *Fahnenjunker* and, having studied the basics of command, graduate as an officer. I would then go on to study law. Marriage to Sophia, whom I had known from childhood, would follow. This was my birthright and my destiny, and it was the path I had dutifully followed.

My mother went on to explain that the old lady was her grandmother and she was her favourite grandchild. She had asked to see my mother and me when she realised she was close to death. My great-grandmother had been Scots by birth and ancestry. She was credited with "second sight" and rarely spoke Gaelic. My mother confessed that the Von Blumenthal family had insisted she spoke only German or English when she came to Prussia as a young bride of eighteen years of age. Nevertheless, she had taken pleasure in teaching my mother the language of the country of her birth; although my mother claimed to have forgotten most of what she had learned during those far-off days.

I realised I had been so engrossed in this memory that I had not lifted my eyes from the young woman. *Fräulein* Gabrielle appeared to be nervous under my gaze, but her look of disdain when she spoke of her previous employers persuaded me no more than the newly peroxided hair. I overcame my discomposure by doing the Hitler salute, which she ignored, but expressed pleasure when I informed her that her role as housekeeper would continue and I would not neglect her payment.

She proved to be hard-working and efficient, allocating bedrooms to my adjutant, guards and secretaries and recommending the library as an office. To my great pleasure, I noted a magnificent Bösendorfer piano in the bay of the window of the library and an assortment of cellos close to it. The family who had taken flight from the *château* had been musicians; we could have made music together in other circumstances. My cook arrived later that day and she spent time showing him the vast cooking range and store cupboards of utensils. Later that day she knocked on the library door and was admitted by Lotti, one of my two secretaries. I gestured to her to take the chair on the other side of my desk, onto which I was placing photographs of my beloved Sophia and our three children: Alexander, Leon and Maria-Sophia.

I looked up at her, and could not look away. This made her self-conscious and she touched her hair and tried to avoid my gaze. She requested leave to attend mass on the anniversary of her deceased grandmother. The speed at which she declined my offer of an escort intensified my sense of incredulity at her attempts to dissemble, but I felt no animosity or threat on her part.

# 6

During the weeks that followed, I overheard the crude comments of the guards with regard to her physical attractions. I could not dispute their observations or deny her beauty, nor could any of us refute her efforts to make our lives at the *château* as pleasant and comfortable as possible in war-time. My cook was charmed by her ability to help in the kitchen and her advice on how best to purchase our requirements without unduly antagonising the local population. She also knew how to cook and prepared supper for me and my men on my late-night return from Germany. I did not believe her story regarding the cook's absence but respected the spontaneous loyalty of her excuse. And I now knew how easily she could lie.

The afternoon I heard her playing the piano confirmed my suspicions that *Fräulein* Gabrielle was more than a servant whose remuneration had been neglected.

I had observed her frequent ventures into the woods behind the *château* and the cook had noted the disappearance of food from the pantry. I retraced her steps one evening and found a pleasant clearing in the woods where I noticed the brambles and brushwood had recently been disturbed. There was a rusty grill under the brambles, which I suspected had been deliberately concealed. I sat there for some time enjoying a cigarette. Sophia did not approve of smoking, and I rarely indulged in what appeared to be an addiction among my soldiers. But it was a tranquil place to sit for a while and ponder on the girl Gabrielle, who so intrigued me.

She was playing the piano accompaniment to the *Arpeggione Sonata*. This had been a favourite of mine since my cello teacher first played it to me when I was ten years of age. I was determined to learn it and, despite his protestations that it would be beyond my ability, I performed it at the Königsberg Spring Festival the following year. I received a standing ovation and as a reward my proud parents purchased a magnificent Schönbach Markneukirchen cello, my first full-size instrument, and the one I took with me to the *Kriegsschule* when I began my military training as a cadet the following year.

I had startled her and she stopped playing at once. Her face flushed and she made to stand up from the piano, but I gestured her to remain seated and selected the Guadagnini cello I had found among the cellos which lined the wall behind the piano. I chose a bow, applied rosin, and with her help tuned the cello to the piano.

'So we shall begin, shall we not, *Fräulein?*'

She played well despite her embarrassment, which caused her to occasionally mistime an entry and stumble over the notes. At the end of the final movement, I invited her to take a bow with me, as though we were performing before an audience. I took her arm and felt as though a bolt of electricity ran through me. At that moment I knew this young woman, barely more than a girl, was the one foretold to me years ago by my great-grandmother.

I noted how pale her arm was and yet warm to my touch. The blush on her face reminded me of my cousin's daughter, Isolde, who had red-gold hair. I looked at her arm, before gently and reluctantly letting it fall to her side; the fine hairs were red-gold in the shaft of sunlight that suddenly illuminated the room. The peroxide hair was a disguise; I was determined to discover who Gabrielle Doucet really was and, with that determination, the resolve to protect her.

My suggestion that we perform in front of officers at the garrison in Caen was met with dismay and a plausible excuse. I had noticed how simply she dressed; I had seen peasant women in such clothes. I made it clear that there could be no dissent; *Fräulein* Gabrielle would be attired as befitted the accompanist of a general. The following day we were driven to the salon of Caen's most exclusive *couturier*.

The *couturière* selected the gowns and *Fräulein* Gabrielle was instructed to wear them for my approval. It was clear to both the *couturière* and I that *"mademoiselle"* did not enjoy disporting herself in this way. She showed no interest in the beautiful gowns that were put on her and made an expression of extreme distaste at one of them: a blue velvet gown cut low at the bust and revealing most of her breasts. We both laughed at this and, to my shame, I enjoyed the flush of anger that crossed her face when I informed the *couturière* that I would purchase this gown. I instructed that the gown, along with one in green silk and some lingerie, be delivered to the *château* that evening.

She sat sullenly beside me in the staff car, but I did not wish to engage her in conversation. My thoughts drifted to the memory of her in the gowns she had so reluctantly worn for my approval. I wanted to revisit the images and delight in them. I realised I was in love with this young woman, and with the realisation came an overwhelming sense of shame. I had betrayed my wife while in Paris with the girl from Alsace and now I was lusting after another. This tormented me. When we drew up outside the door of the *château*, I left the car abruptly. I needed to distance myself from her, for a while at least.

The recital exceeded all my expectations. The great hall of

the Château de Caen was filled with my fellow officers and their guests. I noted the speculative and appraising scrutiny that followed Gabrielle into the hall and onto the stage. The Brahms was well received, but the *Arpeggione Sonata* earned a standing ovation. The audience called for an encore and, after a quick nod between us, we reprised the final movement of the *Arpeggione Sonata*. During the final bow, Gabrielle fainted on the stage. My adjutant packed the cello and music while I carried her to the staff car. She remained unconscious throughout the drive to the *château* and as I carried her to her bedroom.

I noted how frugal the room was. There were no photographs of doting "*Maman* and Papa", and, apart from a crucifix above her bed, there were no ornaments or pictures that could reveal her interests or pastimes. I placed her on the narrow bed and looked into the small chest of drawers beside the wall opposite her bed. It was empty, save for the ornate package containing the lingerie I had ordered. This had been pushed, unopened, to the back of a drawer. A simple cotton nightdress hung over the end of the bed. I undressed her, but sensed for a moment that her eyes opened and met my gaze. I carefully put the nightdress over her and covered her with bed linen and an eiderdown. I went down to the kitchen and filled a glass with water, which I took up and placed on the nightstand beside her bed.

The following day I was obliged to host a lunch party for Hans and his two secretaries. Adalie was at her most seductive and Hans encouraged her in this; perhaps it suited him to be an *agent provocateur* to assuage his conscience at his infidelity to his wife and family in Koln. Both girls delighted in asserting their authority over Gabrielle, whose duty it was to serve them. I found this repugnant but could not express my displeasure. To my guests, Gabrielle was a servant, a citizen of a country humiliated by the victorious German *Reich*.

Following the lunch, it was my duty to accompany Hans and the women to Caen, where a ceremony had been arranged to honour those of my division who had fallen in the battle for France. There was to be a supper party following this and Hans was disappointed when I excused myself as being exhausted from the recital the previous evening. I returned to the *château* and made my way to the kitchen to inform the cook that my adjutant would need supper that night. As I entered the passageway to the kitchen, I was surprised by Gabrielle making her way out. She shied away from me, but I gently took her arm and drew her to me. She did not resist and clung to me sobbing as I picked her up and carried her to my room. I removed her clothing; her natural modesty in crossing her arms over her undergarments caused me to smile.

'My dear *Fräulein,* I already have experience of this with you.' I knew she would be a virgin and was gentle with her.

She responded to my caress and fondling, and even the sharp pain she felt as I entered her did not prevent her from expressing pleasure in my lovemaking. She cried when it was over and clung to me. After a while, she smiled and spoke a phrase in English. When I queried this, she responded in French.

My thoughts turned to Hamlet. *So, my darling Fräulein, there is far more to you than was dreamt of in my imagination.* I made love to her again. This time it was easier for her and her passion matched my own. I knew I could never let her go.

# 7

My work, as explained to me by Colonel Oakley, was to support rebuilding the public functions that had collapsed with Germany's defeat. The old order which had held Germany together during the Hitler years was gone. In its place was chaos: cities were in ruins and millions of people were trying to return to the homes they had been bombed out of or evacuated from. Released forced labourers, prisoners from the concentration camps and former prisoners of war joined the starving, desperate people who were crossing Germany at this time, in search of what remained of their homes and families.

There were also thousands of Germans from East Prussia, most of them women and children, who had fled as the Red Army approached their towns and lands. Amongst these could be my own family. I had received no news of them but feared the worst. I knew that wealthy landowners, *Junkers* such as my family, were shot, their goods stolen and their houses set on fire. Women and girls were raped, regardless of age. I feared for my mother and sisters-in law. Most of all, I feared for my beloved daughter, Maria-Sophia, who at nine years of age could have suffered such a fate, as well as her eight-year-old cousin, Johanna. My sons and their male cousins could have been shot or sent east to the *gulags*. The Red Cross was unable to find any trace of them, and I despaired of ever seeing them again.

People talked of this time as a "time of wolves" in which people had become as vicious predators towards others. This could not be said of my wife, Helen. She accepted the dilapidated apartment in the bomb-damaged building with equanimity, and immediately set about making it into a comfortable home for us. She shared whatever food she had from the British shop with our "*Trümmerfrauen*" neighbours, and equally shared in the daily tasks of getting water from the standpipes and emptying the waste buckets. I was proud of her. She was aware of the luxurious circumstances enjoyed by the colonel's wife and many other military families, but she was content with what we had. All she wanted was for us to be together as a family.

The British supplied the basic necessities to maintain the population, but they quickly found themselves having to rely on German administrators to assist them in rebuilding the shattered economy, and in the distribution of food and housing for the homeless and the refugees. Many of these administrators were former Nazis and this was causing outrage among the citizens of the countries which had been occupied by the Nazi regime or forced to go to war against it. They felt those responsible should be brought to justice and shown no clemency. The Nuremberg tribunals had achieved some semblance of justice in so far as many of the principal perpetrators of Nazi atrocities had been tried and executed. Equally many, however, had escaped justice, either by fleeing to South America or, by disguising their identities, been absorbed in the multitude of people who had drifted back to their pre-war lives. There was fear that in this chaos these Nazis could re-emerge as a force to be contended with, as a fourth *Reich*, or at the very least avoid detection and punishment. It was the role of the *Fragebogen* to determine who among these people could be accepted into administrative positions.

I had studied law, but the British accepted that I'd had no role in the Nazi judicial system. My diploma had been in Weimar Constitutional Law and my doctoral thesis on the protection of the rights of the individual within the republic. For a while I believed this would be my future role in the new Germany; most of the former judiciary had sworn allegiance to Hitler and permitted the abuse of justice by the Nazi administration. During my *Fragebogen*, it was made clear to me by Major Harrison, the intelligence officer who interrogated me, that while I would have a role in the judiciary, my true role would be to assist in identifying those senior Nazis who were still on the run in the British and American zones and bring them to justice. In return, my family would be allowed to live in the British Zone, albeit in meagre circumstances as a cover for my activities; former *Wehrmacht* generals could not seem to be living as victors.

Major Harrison smiled as he laid out the terms of my employment, 'Your wife must not be told of this; it is necessary in times such as these to make deals with the devil.'

'But the devil can take many forms and have his charms.'

'As you well know, Werstein.'

## 8

We were to meet monthly at his office at Allied Military Command.

Major Harrison did not waste any time with formalities. He did not stand up when I entered the room but lit a cigarette and waved at the chair opposite his desk. He addressed me as *Herr Doktor* Werstein, which was how I would be known in the office, validating applications for the judiciary.

'But you will be considered as no more than what we Brits call a "pen pusher", a low-grade civil servant, a "cog in the wheel". A bit of a come down I would say for a former general, and a lord of the manor from what I've heard.'

He stubbed out his cigarette and lit another. The man seemed unable to hold a conversation without a cigarette in his mouth.

'I assume you understand my figure of speech?'

'I am familiar with the metaphors and how they apply to my lowly status.'

'You are an arrogant man. Were it not for orders from a higher authority, I would have you assigned to "Operation Coal Scuttle".

'My just desserts for the dark crimes of my country.'

'We know how the Nazis' judicial system worked. It supported the regime and destroyed democracy. It ordered the sterilisation and murder of the crippled and mentally unfit; those who were not considered acceptable to the *Reich*. It imprisoned and ordered the murder of any who were opposed to Hitler's regime and was, eventually, responsible for the murder of millions of Jews, Gypsies and all those considered to be racially inferior.'

'I was never a Nazi. I was a soldier. I did not have any role in the judiciary during Hitler's *Reich.*'

'But you knew what was happening, didn't you? Or were you so preoccupied with commanding the serfs on your lands, or playing the cello, that you could ignore what was happening in Germany?'

'None of us, and I mean in particular those of us in the East Prussian lands, ever anticipated that a crude corporal from an inbred Austrian family could rise to such power and become the leader of our country. But we could not ignore him when we were called to fight for our country, under his leadership. Consider for one moment, Major, and I ask this respectfully, how would it be in Britain, or the United States, if such a man came to power and demanded allegiance? We could not control the judiciary, we could not control the intelligence services or their torturers, but we were obligated to fight for our country, as our ancestors had done for centuries, for better or for worse.'

The major lit another cigarette from the stub of the previous one.

'You put forward a good argument for "turning a blind eye".'

'My wife would say that I have a talent for that.'

He smiled. He was a man who should smile more; the deep furrows of his brow relaxed and opened eyes that I could imagine were congenial amongst those he loved, perhaps in the presence of children or grandchildren. I thought again of my own family and what was once our home.

'Of course, your wife; I have heard of her exploits. But you are quite a man for the ladies, aren't you, *Herr* Werstein? A handsome bastard like you must have them falling at your feet.'

'I am faithful to my wife.'

'But it was not always so. We shall return to that presently, but for now, we will discuss your public role, as a minor official in the Department of Legal Reconstruction.'

He explained that under the terms of the Potsdam Agreement, each zone of occupation was permitted its own policy for legal reconstruction. All, however, agreed that the system must be rid of the influence of National Socialism, expunging Nazi dogma from the legal codes and excluding all those who had been deeply involved in the Nazi regime. The British wished the Germans to be actively involved in reconstructing their own administration of justice.

'You will be expected to read the dossiers carefully and determine the suitability of the applicants. You will be part of a team of bilingual secretaries and others who have been cleared by *Fragebogen*.'

The ash dropped from his cigarette onto the desk; he swept it to the floor with a flip of his hairy wrist. He saw my look of distaste.

'We say ash is good for the carpet.' He lit another cigarette from the stub.

'Before I dismiss you, I would like you to look at some photographs and give me your... opinion on them.'

I took the photographs. There were six, all enlarged sufficiently to identify the subjects.

'Who took these photographs?'

'The rooms in which you and your erstwhile colleague Hans Schulz entertained your women were under surveillance; bugged is the word we use. It was an easy matter to place Minox cameras behind the washstands and set them on timers.'

'I cannot imagine what use these photographs are to British Intelligence. I was not married to Helen at that time; we had not met each other. She may be distressed by them. The woman, Adalie Franck, was often a guest at the *château* and my wife, in her guise as the housekeeper, had to serve her. I can explain all of this to her. What is your interest in them?'

'It could be argued that the photographs postdate your marriage to Helen. There is no detail in the photographs other than you and the woman enjoying each other in a bed. Who could prove the whereabouts of this bed, or indeed when you were in it?'

'So you are blackmailing me, but for what purpose?'

'Because Adalie Franck and her companion Lisette Meyer were recruited by Himmler's SD before the fall of France and were responsible for the deaths of many of our SOE agents in Normandy. Meyer is dead but Adalie Franck is still active.'

'Active? There is no SD. It died with Himmler.'

I had known that both girls were SD agents, but it suited me to feign ignorance, for the present time at least.

'Adalie Franck has been working for "ODESSA", which is the code name for the organised escape routes by which former war criminals, members of the SS in particular, are evading capture. We also call them "ratlines" or "*Die Spinne*".'

He went on to explain that, long before the end of the war, senior Nazis were anticipating eventual defeat. They planned to escape by crossing into neutral Spain, Switzerland and Portugal, and from there by ship to South America. Argentina was a favoured destination as the Perón government was sympathetic to the Nazi regime. While many senior Nazis had been tried at Nuremberg, and been sentenced to death, others were still on the run, often supported by former female agents of the SD.

'Adolf Eichmann was captured by the British but he escaped from the detention centre with the help of an agent disguised as a nurse. That agent we learned was Adalie Franck. Josef Mengele, the so-called Auschwitz Angel of Death, escaped in similar circumstances. There are many others on the run whom we wish to find and bring to justice. However, Adalie Franck has been "turned" and is now working for British Intelligence.'

I wondered at his naivety. Adalie Franck was adept at deception; she could be working for several intelligence agencies and each would believe in her integrity.

'And what is my part in this hunt for war criminals?'

'I should have thought that would be obvious. Adalie Franck will be delighted to discover that her former lover is in Hamburg, where you will be required to spend much of your time. I have no doubt that she will be more than happy to collaborate with you. She will know of the trial, and your exoneration, and will assume that your lowly administrative job at the judiciary is on account of your British wife; although at this point we are not certain she knows your wife's identity.'

I was unsure of the direction his conversation was taking.

'I do not understand what relevance this has to my work as a "pen-pusher" in the judiciary.'

'I am instructing you to encourage the "attentions" of Adalie Franck in order to find a certain war criminal for us. As for Eichmann and Mengele, we fear we may have lost them; we will leave it to Wiesenthal to find them. There is one particular fish we need to catch before the Soviets get to him, a certain Otto Altmann. He was deputy commandant at Majdanek Concentration Camp and had a reputation for extreme brutality. As you well know, such a command would normally be given to thugs and those of low education, but he was well-educated and studied engineering at Koln University. He was also an associate of Wernher von Braun and a scientist by the name of Manfred von Ardenne, and has worked with both of them on certain projects.

'You need not concern yourself with Braun or Ardenne; I am

sure you Prussian nobles stick together like glue, as we say, and you may well know more about them than we need to discuss for the moment. But we know that Altmann is on the run and we need to get him before he disappears... as so many others have. You will join Adalie Franck in the hunt for Altmann. She knows the routes of *Die Spinne* and ODESSA. You were an acquaintance of Altmann and will recognise him regardless of any disguises he may take. She will need your help.'

I remembered the stub of the sixth finger on his left hand. He would put tape over it when he played the piano as it impeded his performance. I also remembered the crescent-shaped scar on the back of his neck, where one of the Canaris family cats had clawed him.

He stubbed out the remains of his cigarette.

'I could say "set a thief to catch a thief".'

'And if I refuse?'

'Your lovely wife will find some very revealing photographs in her mailbox, and your lives in Bonn will be made extremely difficult. I can assure you.'

# 9

December 1941
Normandy, France

I arrived in the snow drifts that covered most of Europe. The train track between Strasbourg and Caen had been blown up by the Resistance, but the small airfield at Strasbourg was open. After the short flight to Carpiquet, an aerodrome close to Caen, I was met by the guards who had remained at the garrison when I left Normandy many months ago. Together we drove to Château des Tilleuls.

Save for a light in an upstairs room, the *château* was in darkness. I rang the bell and the door was opened at once by Emilia. My cook stood beside her and both helped me out of my snow-covered boots and coat. The cook went at once to light the kitchen range, while Emilia stood shivering and in distress before me.

I asked for Gabrielle. Emilia's hands were shaking as she led me up to the nursery where she explained Gabrielle had moved after... she hesitated at that point and said no more until we reached the door.

She was unconscious and her skin the pallor I had seen so often on the battlefield as men died from their wounds. Lotti was beside her, bathing her and attempting to get her to drink. The cook came into the room and took me aside. He informed me that Gabrielle was on the point of death, despite their efforts to

41

make her well. When I asked why no doctors had been called to the *château*, he explained the circumstances of her illness. Lotti spoke up for the cook and explained that he had saved Gabrielle's life from haemorrhage. The infection had occurred later and they had done all they could to save her. I dismissed them from the room and removed the covers from her body.

She was emaciated and her vagina oozed foul-smelling pus. She showed signs of fever, but now her body was cooling; I knew this to happen towards the end of life as the vital organs strived to maintain their function. I immediately sent my guards to the military hospital in Caen, ordering them to bring physicians to the *château*. I bathed her and tried to give her the tisanes the cook prepared. The physicians arrived soon after. They informed me her life could only be saved by the precious penicillin now available at the hospital. They wanted to remove her immediately to the hospital, but I would have none of it; she would be cared for at the *château* and by me alone. They returned and she had the first injection. I kept vigil by her bed through the days that followed, injecting the penicillin three times every day. By the end of the third day, she showed signs of recovery. I was able to give her some of the soups and tisanes the cook brought to me. I was weak with hunger and exhaustion but would not leave her side. I brought the cello into the room and played the *Arpeggione Sonata*. There came the day when she moved her head towards the sound and her eyes opened. Then I knew she would live.

The cook asked to speak to me the following day. I thanked him for all he had done for my beloved but was anxious to know how much Lotti and Emilia now knew about her.

'Both your secretaries are loyal to you. They believe Gabrielle is French but that she has family in Scotland. They were not suspicious when she spoke in English during her delirium. I knew of Gabrielle's work here at the *château* and that you were aware of it but did not wish to be confronted by it. I have been feeding her "guests" and will continue to do so until she is well again. There is a problem with regard to the *Oberfeldkommandur's* secretaries. My mistress has informed me both are agents of the SD and I am concerned for Helen... Gabrielle's safety, should they discover her identity and her activities. One of them, Adalie, is still bitter following your rejection of her after Paris.'

'How do you know of this?'

'My mistress is in a local resistance group. They had no part in the plot to kill the *Oberfeldkommandur;* their purpose is the protection of life and not its destruction. They help Jews and others escape arrest by the *gendarmes* and *Gestapo*. Resistance groups in Paris informed them of your posting here and...of your time with Adalie. They know that Adalie and Lisette were recruited by the SD.'

'And now I am part of this and compromised by my much regretted dalliance with Adalie.'

'If you love Helen, as I know you do, you must protect her. She has suffered much in your absence. She is brave and loyal, but I fear for her. You may have to make compromises to protect her.'

'I have already decided that I should marry her. Surely that is enough.'

'I will discuss this with my mistress, but the marriage must be secret. Adalie must not know that Gabrielle is more than a servant. It may also mean that Adalie should be encouraged in her flirtations.'

'Are you telling me I should bed her?'

'That is for you to decide. To protect her you will also need the group's codes. They use the lines from an English poet called Kipling, about smugglers.'

'I know it. I have studied his works.'

'Then that is all I can tell you. If you wish to dismiss me from your service for activities inconsistent with my role at the *château* you may do so. I am already indebted to you for saving the lives of my parents. Their lives were more precious than my own.'

'You have saved the life of someone equally precious to me. It is I who is in your debt.'

We shook hands and I returned to my beloved.

# PART THREE

## Helen

## 10

April 1946
Bonn, Germany

Helen accepts Morag's offer to care for their son on the days she
will attend lectures at the university medical school. Karl and
Jamie are old enough to attend the nursery at the barracks which
is well-equipped and has trained nurses in attendance. This is
particularly reassuring as their child continues to have bouts of
coughing and wheezing which she attributes to the dust inside
and outside their home. The barracks are situated on the outskirts
of the city in a wooded area known as Venusberg, above the banks
of the Rhine, where the air is fresh. Their son will enjoy playing
outdoors and will have companionship. The barracks are close
to the recently relocated university medical school where she will
be studying. Iain has arranged for a staff car to collect them from
their home and return them in the evening.

Bombing raids had left the original university buildings in
ruins, but a building in Venusberg owned by the university has
survived and it is here that she is enrolled as a medical student
under the auspices of Professor Johannes Steudel. She knows she
is very privileged. In this early post-war period, it is extremely
difficult to gain admission to medical school, even by former
medical students; so many in the profession and student body had
been tainted by National Socialism.

She knows of the so-called "mercy killing", the murder of

at least 70,000 innocent people, including children, who were considered mentally and physically unfit to live in Hitler's *Reich*. Many believe the numbers of those killed are far in excess of that figure and include victims in Poland and the former Protectorate of Bohemia and Moravia, under the command of Reinhard Heydrich. She also knows that from 1933 forced sterilisation was practised on those deemed racially inferior or whose families were considered to have known hereditary physical or mental defects. While only a modest percentage of doctors administered the killings, by gas or lethal injection, many more were equally guilty as they gave their patients into the hands of the killers.

At this time the Allies insist that the *Fragebogen* is applied to all former physicians and medical school lecturers and, consequently, there is a shortage of *Persilschein* doctors and teaching staff. A number of British and American doctors are employed as lecturers at the university and many of her lectures will be in English; she would struggle in those lectures given by German professors despite her progress in the language. She was interviewed by Professor Steudel and informed that in October she will be entered into the third year of training, and after six months she will be a trainee doctor in a hospital with patients to care for. For the present time, she will attend lectures until the summer recess.

Their family situation is also much improved. The British Control Commission has installed a kitchen and bathroom in their apartment. Work has begun restoring the parts of the building which had suffered the worst of the bomb damage. Most of their neighbours now have water supply and sanitation in their apartments, and those that do not have been welcomed by Helen and Karl to use the facilities in their apartment. This also applies to their kitchen, where they now have an electric stove with three hot plates. She organises a cooking rota for their neighbours, which ensures every family has at least one hot meal a day, albeit within the constraints of rationing.

To the great joy of some, missing husbands, lovers and sons are returning from prison camps and battlefields after long treks across the devastated continent. For others, there is either uncertainty or confirmation of their deaths. Of those who return, many have lost limbs, their sight, and some their minds. She is awakened during the night by the screams and ravings of these men in neighbouring apartments; men haunted by visions of battles, trauma and atrocities they had witnessed or participated in.

Helen and Karl now have a bed and their son a cot in his own small bedroom. They are able to resume lovemaking which has hitherto been restricted in concern for disturbing their child. Her husband's battle wounds have healed, leaving only faint scars. He looks as before, as he did at Château des Tilleuls. She had feared he would find her different; pregnancy and childbirth leave their mark on a woman, but he assures her that he finds her more beautiful and desirable than ever. He takes delight in teasing and provoking her to desire him more, to use his body for her pleasure as well as his own. She knows him to be very experienced with women and occasionally feels the need to know of these other women, how he enjoyed them and they him; but then she remembers Svetlana and does not wish to know.

They are anxious to avoid a pregnancy at this time. The potential for public health disasters remains. The destruction of water supply and sewage systems has caused the spread of infectious diseases. The lack of medical supplies and the overcrowding in whatever accommodation can be found is proving catastrophic throughout Germany. Malnutrition, the proliferation of lice, rats, flies and mosquitoes, and the rotting corpses which are still to be found under the rubble, exacerbates the precarious situation. It is not a world they feel another child should be born into, not yet anyway. She has her medical studies and Karl is busy at the office for the judiciary. He is required to travel to other cities within the British zone of occupation. These visits require him to stay overnight or even for days at a time. She finds this situation difficult; she misses him and without the kindness of their neighbours, who entertain their son while she writes up her lecture notes and essays each evening, she would struggle to continue at the university.

Lotti and Emilia have written to her; both are working as translators and secretaries in the French Zone, in the southwest of Germany. The terms of the Yalta and Potsdam conferences divided Germany into three zones of occupation: American, British and Soviet. General de Gaulle had been outraged by his exclusion from both conferences, and denial of a zone of occupation. Eventually, it was decided the French would be allocated those regions which border France. It was a common adage that the French got the wine and the British the ruins.

Her friends had struggled to be accepted by the French authorities; fraternisation with Germans had been strictly forbidden. But, as both have family connections to Alsace and Lorraine, they were eventually employed by the occupiers and are now engaged to be married to army officers. They hope Karl and Helen can be guests at their respective weddings later in the year. There are no secrets between them now: both friends have long been aware of Helen's true identity and marvelled at her enterprise in secreting the Jewish families and others evading capture during the years at Château des Tilleuls.

There is also news from France. Damian and Amelie are now grandparents to a grandson, Martin, who was born to Agathe in March. The farm continues to prosper with the help of Raisa and her daughters. Raisa's family now own a small house in the village but visit the *château* regularly to keep it in good order. Raisa is organising transit documents as she wishes to bring the Guadagnini cello to Bonn. Karl will be delighted to be reunited with it. All they need is a piano and she has made enquiries among their neighbours. They know of one that survived the bombing of an adjacent building and will bring it to the apartment.

## 11

June 1946
Bonn, Germany

*Darling Daughter,*

*We were most relieved and happy to learn of your husband's exoneration. You are now together as a family, although we appreciate that this will not have been without tribulation. The trial was not reported in the newssheets and wireless, so it is unlikely anyone known to you will be aware of it.*

*We are pleased you and your family are settling to life in Bonn and that you are able to continue your medical studies there. We understand the Provost spoke by telephone to Professor Steudel and was told your time of study in Edinburgh has been taken into account and that many of your classes will be in English. Nevertheless, we are sure you will be making every effort to learn German; you could not have a better teacher than your husband. We are looking forward to visiting you at Christmas and holding our grandson again.*

*Now we must tell you of an extraordinary coincidence. Two weeks ago we received a letter from my cousin, Angus Gordon. A Prussian lady has been in contact with the Gordon family, claiming kinship and with a terrible tale to tell. She was forced to leave her home in north-eastern Germany in January 1945 as the Russian army advanced westward. Fearing arrest, or worse, she and a maidservant joined thousands of others in crossing the frozen lagoon of the River*

*Vistula in an attempt to board a refugee ship, all the while being strafed by Soviet aircraft. She and her maidservant boarded a ship, the Wilhelm Gustloff, which set sail, but was then attacked by a Soviet plane. The ship began to sink and although nine thousand lives were lost including that of her maidservant, several passengers managed to get onto lifeboats, including this lady. The lifeboats had to break through the ice floes, and some made the journey into the open sea. They were picked up by a returning merchant navy vessel, one of the Arctic Convoy vessels which had been delivering supplies to the Soviet Union. They were landed at Loch Ewe in the Northwest Highlands and from there taken to an internment camp on the Isle of Man. The lady attempted to claim the protection of the British government on account of her Scottish heritage. Following V-E Day, Angus was contacted by the Home Office and tasked with verifying the lady's story, which he has done. The lady's name is Countess Luisa von Werstein, which is coincidence enough, but her maiden name was Luisa von Blumenthal. Angus went through his ancestry and Burkes Peerage and noted that the lady's grandmother was Lady Isobel Agnes Gordon, the youngest daughter of the 4th Earl of Gordon, who married Count Otto von Blumenthal in 1847. Angus arranged for the lady to be released from internment and travel to Berwickshire as his guest.*

*Of course we were most intrigued by this and immediately went to visit. You can imagine our surprise when we discovered that the lady is in fact the mother of your husband, Karl, and therefore your mother-in-law and, of course, kin by marriage to* Maman *and me as well as my distant cousin. The lady became quite emotional when the connection was explained to her and to discover that her son is alive and well in Bonn. She hopes to be united with you all as soon as travel arrangements can be made.*

*Meanwhile, we have invited Luisa to stay in our home, where she has now been for three days. She and* Maman *spend a great deal of time chatting over tea in the orchard. The lady speaks excellent French which, as you can imagine, gives Maman much pleasure. She has seen photographs of you and is certain she can see a resemblance in you to her grandmother. She is also an accomplished horsewoman and wishes to join me in riding the Common Ridings where I have missed your company. Luisa wishes to speak with Karl by telephone as soon as a call can be arranged. We will leave it to you to organise this.*

*Of the fate of your husband's children and that of his brothers and their families, she has learned nothing and is desperately worried. She is aware Prussia no longer exists and that the family lands are now part of Poland and under Soviet control.*

*With all our love to you and your family,*

*Papa*

She reads the letter to her husband on his return that night and they arrange a telephone call the following evening from Colonel Oakley's office at the British military headquarters to her parents' home in Berwickshire. Papa picks up the receiver and after a short conversation with her parents, she passes the telephone to her husband. She understands enough of the German language to appreciate the joy in the voices of Karl and his mother, but also their anxiety on behalf of the members of their family who are still lost to them. After a quarter of an hour the international operator interrupts the conversation to inform them their allocated time has been exceeded; there are others anxious to use the lines between Germany and Britain.

Once their son is settled for the night, they discuss how they could do more to locate her husband's family in what is now Soviet-held territory. All enquiries hitherto have been fruitless. The Red Cross is overwhelmed by the vast numbers of displaced people, the refugees of war, who are desperate to return to their homes and be reunited with their families. The newly created International Tracing Service uses concentration camp records as well as displaced person camps in its efforts to locate those listed as missing. The situation for those looking for family members in the Soviet-controlled zone is especially grim. Relations between the Western Allies and the Soviets have been deteriorating. Stalin shows no sign of relinquishing control over Eastern Germany and those countries adjacent to it.

The speech by former Prime Minister Winston Churchill on the 5th of March stressed the necessity for Britain and the United States to "act as guardians of peace and stability against the menace of Soviet communism which had lowered an iron curtain across Europe". These were dark words and highlighted the threat Stalin posed to world peace; Communism has replaced National Socialism as the new enemy. This disunity among the former allies will compromise efforts to locate missing children and other family members who had tried to escape the approaching Red Army.

'And Prussia has been punished twice over.'

'What do you mean?'

'Churchill believes our military traditions were responsible for both wars. He believes Hitler took strength from the knowledge that Prussians were loyal to the Fatherland and would fight for it, as we did, despite our distaste for Nazism. Now we have lost the war and with that our lands, culture, and worst of all, our children.'

She reaches out to hold him closer to her. She knows how much the loss of his family has meant to him. If they are alive, they might believe him to have "fallen" in battle or a prisoner of the Soviets in the *gulags* of Siberia.

There has been a distance between them recently. Karl was obliged to spend time in Hamburg in May and on his return had not been as impatient as usual to make love. He has looked tired and uneasy. She knows him so well and senses something significant is causing this and is fearful.

## 12

Despite her anxieties about her husband and the struggle to keep pace with the demands of her studies at the university, there are moments when Helen feels such hope for the future. True to their promise, neighbours drag a magnificent upright piano into the apartment. It is a 1930s Bösendorfer upright piano and apparently undamaged by the bombing. A piano expert is also brought to the apartment and he pronounces the piano to be in good condition but he will need to do some work on the hammer action and restore it to concert pitch. For this work he is promised supplies of good quality vodka, which Helen has learned can be bartered on the black market for gin bought at the NAAFI store.

Raisa and the Guadagnini cello arrive at the end of July, by which time Karl has returned to Hamburg. She is disappointed that they have not been able to meet. Karl never met her "guests" in the underground room of the old tower at Château des Tilleuls, but Raisa was aware of his discretion with regard to her activities.

They speak in French and her son sits on Raisa's knee. He is now walking and able to babble in three languages, none of which are instantly comprehensible. Helen tunes the cello to the piano in anticipation of Karl's return. When this will be, she has no idea. Raisa detects her mood of uncertainty but has her own concern, that of the fate of her mother Leah. She has visited the offices of the Red Cross in Caen and Paris. The International Tracing Service has no information other than Leah's arrival at Auschwitz on *Convoi 9* in July 1942. The Nazis had kept meticulous records of all those who arrived at the camps and their fate. Raisa's husband and father had been murdered on arrival at Auschwitz, but Leah's name is not on any list of the dead and this gives her hope. She has met with one *retournée* who believed Leah was transferred to another camp, possibly in Germany, but she could not be sure. Until Raisa has certainty regarding her mother's fate, she will not stop looking for her. Helen promises to do whatever she can to help but finds herself sobbing in Raisa's arms. She relates her anxieties regarding her husband's absences, and the feeling of a distance between them despite all they have suffered together. She does not want to believe that there could be anything other than total trust and love between them.

Raisa leaves the following morning but promises to return whenever she is able to do so. She takes letters to Helen's family in Normandy and has assured her that the horses, Batory and Doucette, are well; Ellana and Damian ride them regularly. This news brings more tears to her eyes as she remembers riding across the fields with her husband and making love by the stream in the woods on a summer's evening, now so long ago.

# PART FOUR

## Karl

## 13

The elation I felt following my conversation with my mother was soon replaced by the despondency that had been my shadow since my first meeting with Major Harrison. I had been tasked with hunting down a war criminal, a man who had never taken up arms for the Fatherland but used his authority to murder over 800,000 Jews in his time as Deputy *Kommandant* at Majdanek Concentration camp. He is the man who as Deputy *Kommandant* at Sachsenhausen murdered my cello teacher with his fists. That this man was a highly educated scientist and engineer made his crimes more heinous. He was not raised in poverty or brutal circumstances, but in an educated family; both his parents were professors at the University of Köln. He was an accomplished pianist and had joined me at the Canaris family villa to play at the many evenings of music which were held there. He was a practising Catholic, a family man who returned to his home outside the camp and said *"grace"* before the evening meal he took with his family. It was alleged his children complained about the dust that fell on them as they played in the garden. These particles of dust they found so unpleasant were the ashes of the Jews who had been burned in the ovens that day under the orders of their father.

If I refused or failed in this task, my beloved wife would

suffer the humiliation of receiving photographs of me in bed with a woman I had hoped I would never encounter again but with whom I had now been tasked with renewing acquaintance. I could only imagine how much more difficult Major Harrison could make our lives in Bonn.

The news that my mother's grandmother was a forebear of my wife did not surprise me. The instant feeling of recognition when I met the young French girl who greeted me on my arrival at the *château* was now credible. She was the one foretold to me long ago by my Scottish great-grandmother, who despite over sixty years in my country still held to her language and her ability to see the future.

I did not have to resort to bedding Adalie in order to protect my wife during our time in Normandy. The secret of our marriage was maintained by my loyal secretaries and cook, and moreover, Adalie had other fish to fry at that time. She had become the mistress of an ambitious young SS *Obersturmbannführer* while on a trip to Paris. There had been rumours that Hans would be replaced as *Oberfeldkommandur* by the young officer. The rumour was on account of Hans's unwillingness to implement a hostage round-up following the sabotage of the rail connection between Strasbourg and Caen. This destruction had forced me to fly from Strasbourg to Carpiquet and therefore arrive in time to save my beloved's life. According to Hans it was *Weihnachten* and not the time for hostage-taking, after all, no German lives had been lost. Adalie would have been delighted to be installed as "*châtelaine*" of the Château de Caen. But Hans was popular with the garrison in Caen and his cousin, Reinhard Heydrich, whom he much disliked, was by then Reich Protector of Bohemia and Moravia. The affair drifted on, and Adalie continued to flirt with me whenever she was in my company, but my cook advised me that she no longer posed a threat to Helen.

Military High Command eventually dispatched her lover to lead the *Waffen SS Karstjäger* unit in the mountains of Yugoslavia, where he met his death at the hands of Tito's partisans. Hans's duties were extended to my area of command when I returned to the Russian Front, and Helen had another to protect her.

# 14

May 1946
Hamburg, Germany

We arranged to meet at a small café close to the law faculty at the university, where I had been assigned to interview judges and lawyers who wished to practise law again. All had completed the *Fragebogen* and my task was to assist the British in verifying their university diplomas. She carried her cup of *ersatz* coffee to where I was seated. She was appropriately dressed in a well-worn coat and scuffed shoes; few German women were smartly or fashionably dressed at this time, unless they were the mistresses of high-ranking officers in the occupying forces. But she was still beautiful.

It was a bright spring morning in May and the ruins surrounding the café were bathed in warm sunshine: this fashioned a brutal beauty in them, in defiance of the devastation the bombing raids had wreaked on the city. The same precocious sunshine had encouraged a multitude of weeds to proliferate between the cracks in the pavements and among gaps in the walls of the derelict buildings. Nature could not be obliterated and was establishing itself before any human hand could restore the city to its former grandeur.

Hamburg had survived catastrophes throughout its history: Viking raids destroyed the early settlement, it suffered ruination during wars with Poland and Denmark, the Black Death killed sixty percent of the population, and the great fire of 1842 destroyed a quarter of the inner city. After each disaster, Hamburg had risen from the ashes, and it would do so again. The people of the city believed it was blessed by the mythical King Frederick the First, "Barbarossa", who granted the city Free Imperial City status. Together with Lübeck, it had become the core of the powerful Hanseatic League of trading cities.

It was she who spoke first; her blue eyes had a hypnotic quality and for a moment I felt like an animal in a trap.

'So, my dear General, we are to work together on a mission set by our former enemies, I to avoid the gallows and you to protect your wife and family from humiliation and poverty. I must say, you kept your marriage to the French serving girl a secret worthy of Hitler and Eva Braun; all the while she was waiting on us you were impatient to fuck her. You didn't have to marry her; a German girl would have been a better match for a man such as you. I always regarded her as a whey-faced mouse. Still, each to his taste and a man must learn from his errors.'

I wanted to defend my wife, but I realised that Adalie's low opinion of her could be to Helen's advantage. Adalie would never know of my wife's courage and determination, of what she is capable of.

I played along with her. 'If we are to work together and bring Altmann to the British, we need to establish our working relationship. I am here for three days. In this time, I expect you to apprise me of Altmann's whereabouts and his likely escape route.'

'Surely you do not expect me to do this without some form of payback from you. I know how to find Altmann and could find another to help me capture him.'

'You overestimate your abilities. I knew the man well, certainly better than any alive today could know him despite his many disguises. I will not share this knowledge with you. You need me more than I need you. While I am certain the British would not hang you from a meat hook with piano wire, as they did Canaris, who by the way could also have identified Altmann, I am sure you would not enjoy the feel of the rope around your neck, the hood over your head and the pain of your neck snapping, which would be your fate if you do not fulfil this mission.'

'The British would have other uses for me.'

'Not as many as you would like to believe.'

'However you feel about the situation, we have no choice other than to cooperate with our British masters. We have three days together. I know where you are staying, as I have also been reserved a room there, by Major Harrison, as the wife of "*Herr* Franz Wessels". Our *Gástgeber, Frau* Krantz, believes your beloved wife is joining you after many months of separation. She has been told to expect a joyous reunion.'

'What are you trying to tell me?'

'My instruction, our cover if you like, is that we are a married couple enjoying a tour of Europe to compensate for the tribulations and separation of war. We will be booked as such throughout our journey. "*Frau* Inge Wessels" has missed her beloved husband and is looking forward to a passionate reunion. We will have other identities on our journey. As you will discover, Germans are not welcomed in certain countries.'

'You make a mockery of what we are obliged to accomplish.'

'My dear Karl, it is what we spies have always done. We are the chameleons of the underworld. We cast off the skins of our real lives and embrace those which we need to survive. I have done this many times, as you may imagine.'

'I will not dishonour my wife in this way. The British are fools to trust you; you change your "skin" for your own selfish needs and ambitions.'

She laughs. 'Poor Karl, you really have no idea how it is for a woman such as I am. You are a soldier and of a noble family. You were born into privilege and life has treated you well. You fought bravely for your country and, until the defeat of Germany, you were rewarded for this with medals and promotion. For me, it has been a journey from poverty and abuse. I was raped by a drunken uncle at the age of eleven. My parents put me from my home when I became pregnant at the age of fourteen, by the same uncle. They blamed me, blamed my precocious sexuality. I was forced to go to a woman who removed the foetus from my womb but left me unable to bear children.

'My wits and beauty got me to where we first met. I have used these qualities, talents if you like, to my advantage from the age of fifteen. It was how I was recruited by my father's dear departed friend, Himmler. I was his mistress for a time, but he was a poor specimen for a lover, as I quickly discovered. But a girl must do what she needs to do. I intend to enjoy this "vacation" together. At each stage in our journey we will be under suspicion. Altmann has many who are helping him. If we arouse their suspicions we will fail. We must be convincing in our roles.'

'If what you tell me is true, I pity you. I can only imagine how hard life has been for you. But many have suffered such as you and have not turned to treachery.'

'You talk like a priest and not a convincing one. Come, we are expected by *Frau* Krantz at this time. She will serve us a delicious meal and then we will retire to our bedroom as lovers.'

# 15

It was not difficult. I knew what she enjoyed from our time in Paris. I felt a sense of humiliation, that I had been duped into this liaison by Harrison and forced to dishonour my wife. But there was some pleasure in our coupling; she reminded me of Svetlana.

Over the following three days she explained the many "ratlines" by which thousands of Nazis, many of them guilty of the worst atrocities of the war years, were able to escape to new lives. Some preferred to go to the Middle East, but many more chose the countries of South America. The fascist regime in Argentina was especially welcoming to fugitive Nazis, particularly those who brought with them a fortune in treasure looted from their victims. Also welcome were those with special skills in science or technology and those whose expertise lay in torture techniques.

She explained there was no single organised structure to these "ratlines", no single organisation had overall control of "*Die Spinne*". The escape from capture or imprisonment was usually the work of individuals, such as she herself, or on account of the fugitive's own ingenuity or that of their families. The first stage in the escape was to get the fugitive out of Germany either across the Tyrol into Austria or into Spain, where the fascist regime of General Franco was also a haven for Nazis on the run. The route Altmann would most likely follow was one devised and supported by an Austrian Catholic bishop by the name of Alois

Hudal, a fervent Nazi sympathiser. Altmann would travel over the Alps from a safe house in Innsbruck, possibly on foot, to avoid encountering Allied soldiers on the hunt for war criminals, or the Jewish Avengers, who were particularly determined to prevent those who had overseen the mass murder of their people escape justice.

Altmann would then be taken either to Merano in Italian South Tyrol to the monastery of the Teutonic Order, or to the Franciscan monastery near Bolzano, thirty-three kilometres south of Merano. He would be hidden in either monastery while money and false papers were arranged for him. When he had rested and been provided with clothing and food, the next stop would be Rome.

'Are you telling me that the Catholic Church is enabling these murderers to escape?'

'Of course, and there are many Nazi sympathisers within the highest ranks of the Catholic hierarchy, including Pope Pius the Twelfth himself. Hudal has described Eichmann and Mengele, for whom he secured new lives in Buenos Aires, as "persecuted and completely blameless". The Catholic Church believes communism to be evil and fascism the defender of the faith. Also, Catholics, along with all Christian religions, believe the Jews killed Christ and therefore deserve everything that was done to them under Hitler's rule and throughout history.'

'Do you believe the Jews deserved to be murdered, that generations of families deserved to be obliterated?'

'You will be surprised to know that I do not. I had many Jewish friends at school, but it was not my employment to assist those among them who begged me for protection. I obeyed my masters, and, as I said, a woman such as me has few choices. I do as I am commanded.'

'But you could have helped them. There were many ways in

which Jews were helped to survive.'

'Did you help them, while you were *Feldkommandur* in Normandy?'

'Not directly, but my wife did. I did not wish to know.'

'So the whey-faced serving wench was more than just a convenient fuck!'

'I will not have you describe my wife in such terms. If you continue to do so I will refuse to undertake this mission. I will tell Harrison to go to hell and take Altmann with him.'

'My dear Karl, you have no choice in this. Harrison will ensure that your wife not only receives the photographs of our time in Paris but also the ones taken during our recent "reunion". Do not forget that I am a spy by trade and secret photography is part of it. Furthermore, Harrison is in a position to make your family's life more difficult than you could ever imagine.'

I knew I was trapped and that there was no way I could withdraw from the mission Harrison had set me. I asked her to continue.

She went on to describe how Altmann, as with others before him, would be taken to Rome where the Vatican Refugee Organisation, *Pontificia Commissione di Assistenza,* would organise accommodation for him as well as Vatican papers. These papers would be used to obtain a displaced person passport from the Red Cross. The passport would be used to apply for a visa for entry into Argentina. The Red Cross officials were supposed to perform background checks on passport applicants, but, in practice, the word of a priest or bishop would be considered sufficient. Hudal was known to request Red Cross passports made to his specifications; such was the power he wielded. While in Rome, money would be found in the vast coffers held by the Catholic Church. Once all the documentation was in order, Altmann would be taken to Genoa where a first-class berth on a liner bound for Buenos Aires would be paid for by Hudal.

'How have you come by this information?'

'I have helped others in this way.'

'Do you know where Altmann is at this time?'

'I believe he is being concealed by his family somewhere in Bavaria. I have a contact who is watching a farm belonging to his cousin. As soon as I know he is on the move, I will contact you and you must be prepared to leave with me at once. Now, my dear Karl, *Frau* Krantz will be expecting more evidence of our pleasure in being together after so many months. Perhaps she too is part of *Die Spinne*. It would arouse her suspicions if she did not hear us enjoying ourselves.'

She opened a bottle of schnapps and toasted our mission. The alcohol dulled my senses. I had nothing to lose; the future of my family was in her hands, and in those of our "puppet master", Harrison.

# PART FIVE

## Helen

# 16

Karl has been given two weeks leave from his duties at the office of the judiciary and they are given the use of a small garden house, a *Dacha,* for one week. The air in the hills is much cooler and fresher. Their son grows strong and his body tans in the August sun. He no longer coughs and thrives in the care of both his parents. Her husband is as attentive and passionate as ever, and her doubts regarding a distancing of his affections have disappeared. As soon as their son is settled in his cot, they walk a short distance behind the cabin and he takes pleasure in slipping her dress off her shoulders where it pools onto the soft grass of the hillside. His fingers expertly release the fastening of her brassiere and he takes his time kissing her and fondling her breasts and touching that part of her that he has discovered gives her such pleasure, until she begs him to lie her down and enter her. When he is certain she has enjoyed his lovemaking many times, he takes her more roughly to his own, which he knows she enjoys equally. It is in their bed at night when he is naked and she can see again the scars of war that she is overcome by such a tenderness and weeps over his body.

They return to their apartment for the remaining days of her husband's leave and play music together. The years of separation slip further into the past as they revisit their favourite music. They finish each evening with "*Nacht und Träume*" which brings tears to her eyes. Their neighbours request a recital in the courtyard of the building which they have cleared of rubble for the occasion. The piano repairer assists in carrying the piano down the flights of stairs and retunes it. Makeshift benches of fallen masonry and wood are used for seating, and before long there is an audience of around fifty people. Their son sits on the lap of Helga, their neighbour's daughter. They begin with their own arrangement of Beethoven's *Ode to Joy* which elicits applause throughout. They then play the *Arpeggione Sonata*. As they play, she notices more people drifting into the courtyard. Their clothes are ragged, their bodies emaciated and their faces have the sunken cheeks and haunted eyes of people she has seen in photographs of the camps. The new arrivals are Jews, perhaps returning to their former home. One of the men still wears the tattered striped trousers and shirt of whichever camp he has survived, the inverted yellow triangles in an approximation of the Star of David visible on his jacket. They continue to play but the discomfiture of the audience is palpable. How many among them played a part in their "disappearances" and denounced their presence to the Gestapo?

She whispers *"Die Lorelei"* to her husband, and they immediately improvise the music of the song which had been forbidden by the Nazis on account of its Jewish association. As a child she had loved listening to this plaintive song and had attempted to teach her two pupils to play it on the piano, until their mother violently intervened. A ripple of surprise goes through the audience and all move along the benches to give seating space to the new arrivals. The audience request an encore and they reprise the *Ode to Joy*. Schiller's poem, *Ode to Joy,* is a vision of the human race as brothers, put to music by Beethoven who shared his dream.

The neighbours take charge of the arrivals while Karl and Helen pack up the music and cello. Once the piano has been reinstalled in their apartment, she goes to find the people who have returned. She finds them in Magda's apartment, where hot soup and bread have been prepared for them. One by one, neighbours arrive with gifts of food and clothing. Among the *Zurückgekommen* are two men: the only survivors of three Jewish families who had occupied apartments on the top floor of the building, which is now completely destroyed.

Helen knows there are two empty apartments on their floor but they are still in a state of dilapidation. There is no way these people could live there. She promises to visit the British Control Commission the following day to request that restoration work be started immediately, but meanwhile, they will stay as her guests. As Karl is leaving for Hamburg the following day, she will share the small bedroom of their son with the two women in the group. The three men will share the large bedroom. She makes this decision in the presence of the neighbours. Whatever happened here during the years of Nazi rule will need reconciliation and forgiveness, and this will take time. After the group has bathed and been given clean clothes, they sit and talk until late into the evening.

Two of the men, Isaak and Josef, are father and son. They had lived in their apartment with Josef's mother, Shoshanna, and Josef's three younger sisters. All had been taken from their home in June 1942. Many of their relatives had managed to flee Germany before Jewish emigration was forbidden in October 1941. The family had lived in dread of denunciation and never left the apartment for fear of arrest. A sympathetic neighbour had supplied them with food and hidden them during round ups in the building. They had seen families taken out of adjacent buildings late at night, with no warning, and with no time to pack even the barest of essentials. But for a while they had been hopeful, knowing the war was not going well for Hitler at that time. The end of the war would mean they would survive. It was not to be and they were betrayed by the young daughter of the neighbour, who, in return for the promise of chocolate, led the *Gestapo* to the apartment.

The family had been taken first to Theresienstadt, where they had been able to stay together, but weeks later they were loaded into the cattle car of a train and taken to Auschwitz-Birkenau. Shoshanna and the girls had been taken immediately to the gas chambers and crematoria. Isaak and Josef had been used as slave workers, first quarrying stone at Auschwitz, and then taken to the concentration camp at Mittelbau-Dora, in Thuringia in central Germany. This camp had been established in the late summer of 1943 as a sub-camp of Buchenwald to supply the slave labour of prisoners from many of the eastern countries occupied by Germany, as well as those who had survived Auschwitz. They were subjected to brutal and inhumane treatment, working 18-hour days on starvation rations and insanitary conditions. Men and women died as they worked and their bodies were thrown into pits. The work involved extending the tunnels for the manufacture of the V2 rocket and V1 flying bombs that had brought terror and death to London in 1944.

Their companion, Pavel, is Czech. He had watched his family taken to the gas chambers on arrival in Auschwitz-Birkenau. He had been a doctor in Prague before the occupation of his country and the rule of Reinhard Heydrich. He hopes to begin a new life in the British Zone where his qualifications as a specialist in infectious diseases will be recognised.

The two women in the group are French Jews of Polish origin. They were arrested in July 1942 in the *Vel d'Hiv Rafle* and interned in the velodrome, along with thousands of others, without water and sanitation, before being taken to a camp near Pithiviers. The guards at the camp were all French *gendarmes* and the treatment meted out to the Jews interned there had been brutal. Young women were subjected to humiliating internal examinations by male guards who sought out the most attractive to abuse. From there they were transported to Auschwitz, where they saw their children taken to be gassed and incinerated. Later, they and other survivors of Auschwitz-Birkenau were sent to Mittelbau-Dora, to work in the tunnels.

In 1945, most of the surviving inmates of Mittelbau-Dora were sent out of the camp on what are now called death marches, but they and the men had hidden in a secret compartment of the tunnel and on the 11th of April 1945 were freed by the US army. They decided to stay together for safety; they had heard accounts of Jews being murdered when they returned to their previous homes. Knowing that the Soviets now had control over Czechoslovakia, Pavel had no wish to return there and be a subject of Stalin. Isaak had suggested that they all return to his former home, which he knew to be in the British Zone. The French women, Celine and Simone, would travel to Paris from Bonn in the hope of finding surviving members of their families.

She decides to tell them her story, only part of it as all are tired, but the recent visit by Raisa and her relentless search for her mother needs to be addressed. She asks them if they had encountered a lady named Leah who had arrived at Auschwitz-Birkenau on *Convoi 9* 1942. She explains that the lady's husband and son-in-law had been murdered there, but that her daughter, Raisa, had survived and continued to search for her mother.

Simone knew of her.

'Leah was with us in Mittelbau. I do not know how she came to be there. She was strong despite her age. She was alive up to the time the SS evacuated the camp. I believe she was put to march with the others who survived. But many died on that march and she was not young.'

'Do you know where they were marching these people?'

'Away from the Soviets, to the west and the north: the SS guards would kill any who fell on the march. Leah was strong but not young, as I have said. She could not have survived.'

'But if she had survived, once she knew the war was over she would be travelling towards France, as you are, to the southwest and the French Zone?'

'It is possible and if so, she would be in one of the refugee camps, perhaps already in the French Zone. She would do as we did and follow the Rhine. She could be close to Bonn or beyond.'

Her heart begins to beat wildly. She knows there are camps for former prisoners close to Bonn and there is the possibility that she will find Leah in one of them. It is getting late and her "guests" are exhausted. She settles the women with mattresses and quilts beside their son and goes to find her husband.

He has taken the men into the courtyard to smoke. Neighbours have provided their rations of tobacco as well as food and she is pleased to see that the recently returned husbands of their neighbours have joined them. All address her husband as "General von Werstein", which she knows he finds unsettling in his present situation, but it is interesting that Isaak and the other two men do not appear to be offended. In their own way all the men in the courtyard this night are victims of Hitler's war. Perhaps this acknowledgement of collective suffering will be the path to the healing of this country and of Europe. Nobody would deny the atrocities of the Nazis, but few in Germany had been brave enough to reject the cult of Hitler. Those with the courage to resist paid a tragic price in the loss of their lives and the lives of their families. But watching her husband in the warmth of the late summer evening brings her comfort. She is certain there will be other wars. She is haunted in her dreams by visions of the fire storms in Hamburg and Dresden and the atomic holocaust of

Nagasaki and Hiroshima. But this memory she would cherish all her life, this time of *camaraderie* between men who have suffered so much.

Later, when the men have settled to sleep in their bed, Karl and Helen have time to talk. They return to the courtyard and sit under the remains of a sycamore tree that stood close to the archway to the building. A few rotted branches are all that remain on the main trunk of the tree. It will have to be demolished and their neighbours are already planning its demise and replacement.

He will leave for Hamburg early the next day, but he asks her to question their guests about their work in the tunnels and the commander-in-charge during their time there.

She jokes, '"Them that asks no questions isn't told a lie".'

He smiles and replies, 'At this time, *meine Liebchen*, I am not tasked with "watching the wall".'

It is then that she realises that her husband is not only an administrator but involved in something far more serious and dangerous. He kisses her and unbuttons her dress. In the darkness of the courtyard they make love, but already she can feel the shadows of fear and uncertainty threatening their lives.

## 17

September 1946
Bonn, Germany

Her husband leaves early the following morning to travel to Hamburg. She does not know when he will return. Following their conversation the previous evening, she feels she cannot question him regarding his time away from Bonn and their home. The insecurity she used to feel in the early days of their love has taken hold of her thoughts. She has no one to confide in now that Raisa has returned to France. Her neighbours, though kind and welcoming, have problems enough to deal with; the husband of one continues to awaken the building with his night terrors. Many are now resigned to the fact that their men will not be returning and widowhood is their future.

Her guests are still sleeping when she leaves to register for the new term at the university. She has six months of intensive lectures to complete before she will be allowed to join the doctors at the university hospital on ward rounds, assisting in admitting patients and ordering diagnostic tests. Their son was awake before daylight, in time to be kissed farewell by his father. By 8 a.m. they are both outside the building awaiting their transport; her son to spend the day with his friend at the barracks at Venusberg and she to the university medical school. As Iain drives them through the city, she tells him of her new guests and he relates how he, Morag and baby Jamie had been given leave to be with family in Scotland for the month of August. His enthusiasm for her country of birth suddenly breaks her and she starts to cry. Iain pulls the jeep over and puts his arms around her.

'*Dinnae* weep so, lass, *thae's daein'* a fine job here. *Mair mooths ta* feed *an'* that's for sure. But tell me, lass, what really *fashes ye?*'

She cannot tell him that she fears for her husband's life and feels his work is extinguishing the hope she'd had that their life together in Bonn would be free of uncertainty and dread, a fresh start in a new Europe. Neither can she tell him her husband is becoming a mystery to her again and that perhaps she does not know the man she loves.

She takes his offer of a handkerchief and blows her nose.

'I suppose I miss Scotland and the thought of living forever as an exile is hard to bear.'

Iain knows enough of her past to understand.

'*Lass,* it'll *tak* time. One *o'* these fine days *ye'll* be welcomed *hame* as a hero, and in France *tae.* Just *gae* it time.'

After he leaves her, she makes her way to the registration room at the medical school where she sees a ghost. It is the young soldier who had driven her to the church in Caen to make her confession to *Père* François and arrange her marriage. This now seems so long ago as to have been in another life. He had spoken to her in English that day, as he does now when he recognises her.

'*Mademoiselle* Gabrielle, or should I say Helen?'

She is overcome with emotion. She knows that many of her husband's division died on the Eastern Front, and in France and Belgium following the Allied invasion; it seems miraculous to find one alive. His name is Erik and he had been a student at the university in Bonn before conscription into the army. He knows of her husband's exoneration at Nuremberg but says he was not aware of his new role as an administrator in Hamburg.

'The British must hold him in high regard to have employed

him so readily. My mother and father are still struggling with the *Fragebogen* despite having refused to join the Nazi party. Perhaps it is helpful that he has a wife who is British.'

'My mother is French. I can claim citizenship in both countries and, of course, my husband is German.'

'And you wish to live in Germany?'

'At this time we have no choice. I am considered a collaborator in France by some, and as the wife of a former German general, my neighbours in Scotland would not be ready to accept me. It is the same for Germans in France at this time.'

'And you are happy in this situation, to be in Germany by default as there is nowhere else?'

'I do not consider it in this way. We have a son and we need to be together as a family. There is also the situation of my husband's children from his first marriage. They are still missing, and we can do more to help find them by being in Germany.'

'If they were in East Prussia when the Soviets arrived, they are either dead or living as wolves in the forests on the borders with Lithuania. Most of the adults died at the hands of the Soviets, or of exhaustion and hunger as they fled ahead of the Red Army. Many children are now orphans and have no memory of their families. Some, the strong ones, managed to hide on the trains to the West. It was a dangerous enterprise; if they were found, they were thrown off the train. Some died where they fell; others waited until the next train or returned to the forests. Some were taken in by Lithuanian families. If they are lucky, they are treated well, but many are used as slaves by these families and suffer much abuse from them.'

'How do you know of this?'

'I am a medical volunteer at one of the camps outside of Bonn. We have refugees from all over Europe: many are returning from the camps where we Germans tortured and murdered those we were taught to hate. With these people we have to gain their trust, help them back to health, and return them to their homes. Occasionally, a child from the East finds their way to us. Perhaps you would like to join me as a volunteer. I am there most evenings and at the weekends. It is the least I can do to atone for the wickedness done by my country.'

'I have to care for our son in the evenings, but perhaps I can make an arrangement with my neighbours for the weekends; they have been very kind. I have guests in my apartment who I also need to care for. They were in the camps, in Auschwitz-Birkenau and then in Thuringia, where they were used as slaves, digging underground tunnels for new weapons.'

'I have heard of these tunnels. They were used to assemble Hitler's Vengeance weapon as it was called, the V2 rockets. I also know that most of the scientists who allowed these slave workers to die in their thousands in the tunnels have been spirited away to the United States and are now working for the US government.'

'But surely they have committed crimes, war crimes, by killing these people.'

'The Americans have decided that their expertise outweighs their past misdeeds. The former Allies are still seeking some scientists. The Soviets are most aggrieved that a certain Wernher von Braun is now in Texas. There is a race to find the others and overlook their crimes, in order that they too can be useful. Where do you live? I understand the British are accommodated in the very best residences in Bonn.'

She laughs. 'Of course not. A former *Wehrmacht* general is not considered worthy of such a home. And I would not wish it either. I have met some of the wives of the victorious British army, the officers' wives, and I would not wish to be their neighbour. We share a building with German families and all of us work hard to make a home in the rubble.'

'So your life is much changed since the Château des Tilleuls.'

'It is the same for many. At least my husband is alive. Others in my building are widows or have husbands return having lost their minds as well as their limbs.'

She promises to make arrangements for the care of her son at the weekend. Erik will collect her from her apartment building on Saturday morning and take her to the camp.

As Ian drives them back to the apartment that evening, he tells her how well her son settled into the nursery at the barracks. She tells him of her meeting with Erik and the plan to work in the camp at the weekend. He immediately offers to help, but she assures him he is already doing enough; she will ask a neighbour to care for her son during the times she is working at the camp.

He bids her good night and promises that either he or another will be her driver tomorrow.

She returns to find the building the scene of a tragedy. Helga, the daughter of her nearest neighbour, the girl who has been so helpful with baby Karl, has hanged herself from the rails of the balcony of her apartment. Her mother, Magda, is prostrate on the floor outside the door to the apartment. She had returned from her day working as a *Trümmerfrau* to find her daughter's lifeless body hanging from the balcony. A doctor has been called and Pavel has been asked to confirm the girl's death.

Pavel and two of the women stay with Magda while Helen gives her son his supper and settles him in his cot.

Isaak explains what has happened. Magda is the kind neighbour who protected them before their arrest by the *Gestapo* and Helga is the girl who betrayed his family. Magda forgave her daughter and both held to the hope that the family had been "resettled in the East", which was propaganda at the time. Later they learned the truth: of the extermination of the Jews who were "resettled", but even then they had hoped the family would survive. They now knew that Isaak's wife and daughters had been murdered. Helga had left a note saying she could not forgive herself; her own death would atone for her crime.

Helen is appalled by the notion.

'But she was a child. She could not have known the implications of the betrayal.'

'She was ten years old at the time. We consider children of seven to be at the age of reason, to be able to distinguish between right and wrong. It is the same in your faith I believe.'

She has not considered her faith since the end of the war. It has not occurred to her to seek out a church to hear mass. She cannot believe in a God who allowed the horrors perpetrated in camps such as Auschwitz and Treblinka.

'It is not only a question of reason. The children of the Nazi era were indoctrinated from a young age to believe Jews were different, a sub-species, and that to exterminate them was honourable.'

'Her mother was not such a German. She did all she could to save us, at great risk to her own life. I do not mourn her daughter.'

She feels great sadness at Isaak's words. The companionship of the men in the courtyard the previous night has not altered the enormous sense of injustice and grief that will follow Isaak and others of the Jewish faith for the rest of their lives. Isaak goes on to tell her that he and Josef plan to leave for Palestine as soon as they can make the arrangements. Many Jews feel as he does, that Europe is now a cemetery for Jewish people; anti-Semitic incidents have continued despite the end of the war.

'Two months ago there was a massacre of Jews who tried to return to their homes in Kielce in Poland. We do not trust the people we lived among for so many years. There were a few such as Magda, but most were happy to deliver us to the camps. We want to start a new life and build a homeland in "*Eretz Yisrael*", the land given to us by our God, our "Promised Land".'

'Will you be able to travel to this place?'

'Not if your British government is part of it, nor the Arabs of Palestine; they restrict the numbers of Jews who are permitted to immigrate. But there is an underground movement we call "*Bericha*" which is helping families reach Palestine. It is still early days and there are many obstacles, but there is money coming from Jewish-American donors to help with transfers and living costs. Until we have an internationally recognised state, it is the best we survivors can do.'

'Is there any way in which I can help?'

'At the moment it is enough that we have your hospitality. When the time comes for us to leave, we will do so discreetly. If the British discover our plans, they will find a way to block our journey. We know we can trust you; you have told us some of your life during the war.'

Pavel returns to our apartment later that night. Magda has been given a tranquilizer and he has promised the doctor who administered it that he will undertake to care for her. The doctor was German and had recently been given his *Persilschein* certificate enabling him to practise again. He has invited Pavel to work with him in one of the refugee camps and will do his best to have Pavel's medical degrees recognised in Germany. A night that began so tragically now appears to offer hope, to some at least.

# 18

September 1946
Bonn, Germany

Erik meets her outside the apartment building the following Saturday morning. Her son is in the care of the young French women; it is a good arrangement as he can babble as easily in French as he can in English and German.

Pavel has been as good as his word and has cared for Magda through the days and nights that followed the death of her daughter. The family are Catholics and there had been opposition to Helga's burial in the family plot in the graveyard of Saint Remigius church. But it was argued that the girl had been out of her mind with grief and bore no responsibility for her actions. Her funeral took place on Friday and only the residents of the building were permitted to attend. Pavel supported Magda throughout the brief requiem mass and at the graveside. Helen feels confident he will continue to support her.

Helen is appalled by the situation in the camp, and more so when Erik explains that conditions are far worse in camps in the American Zone; survivors there see no difference in their circumstances than they experienced in the concentration camps, with insufficient food and armed guards patrolling the perimeter wire fencing. She sees overcrowded huts, insanitary latrines and malnourished people queuing to wash at standpipes. The camp is a place of disease and despair.

Helen is assigned to the women's medical hut where a young Jewish girl is in the late stages of labour. This is a time of celebration, a new life out of the "Night and Fog" Hitler had envisaged as the fate of the Jewish people. The girl has no family to support her, but other women survivors are with her and she is managing the contractions well. Helen asks permission to examine her and is proud to inform the assembled women that birth is imminent, the baby's head is in the correct position and its heartbeat is strong. She goes to wash her hands by the standpipe outside and notes the young father of the baby being supported by other men. She does a round of the beds; most of the occupants are elderly and frail and she does not want to imagine the suffering they have endured to reach this place. She organises fresh water to be available by each of the beds and instructs the nurses on how best to isolate cases of suspected cholera or typhoid. After a short time, she hears the first cries of a baby; a boy has been born to the young survivor. She rushes to wash her hands and then checks the baby; he has a strong heartbeat, his muscle tone is good and his mother immediately puts him to her breast where he latches on and feeds. She waits until the afterbirth is delivered and ensures the mother has enough food and water for her recovery. The mother encourages Helen to announce the birth to his father. Whoops of joy surround her. The father is permitted to enter the hut and hold his son in his arms while he recites the *Hatov Vehametiv* blessing.

It is late in the evening when Erik comes to take her home. As he leaves her at the entrance to the building, he invites her to a meal at his parents' home the following day. She accepts without hesitation.

# 19

Erik and his family live in an apartment block not far from where she lives. As they walk he explains that the family owned a large villa close to the Rhine but this has been requisitioned by the British; a colonel and his wife now live there.

'I believe I have been to this villa. Karl and I were invited there by the colonel. I did not enjoy the experience; I am happy where we live.'

'Among the *Trümmerfrauen?*' He smiles as he says this.

'Yes, it is what we wish, for now at least.'

She tells him about her neighbours and guests but not of Isaak and Josef's plans to escape. She questions him again about the possibility of finding her husband's family and tells him of the survival of Karl's mother and the surprising connection between their two families.

He uses a common German expletive when he hears this story.

'Perhaps you believe fate determined that you and the general should find each other? But surely "It is not in the stars to hold our destiny but in ourselves".'

She laughs. '"What will be will be". I know how popular Shakespeare is in Germany. Certainly, there were times when I felt we were "star-crossed lovers".'

Erik is silent for a while as they walk. He offers to carry her son. He is no longer a baby and has long outgrown the baby carriage, but she has no alternative for him. He enjoys taking short walks holding tightly to her hand, but now he is faltering and the September sun is warm. Erik effortlessly swings "Karlchen" onto his shoulders and holds him securely by his feet. Her son gleefully clasps fistfuls of Erik's blond hair and both take off along the dusty road at a fast jog. It is in this mood of gaiety that they arrive at Erik's apartment. The building is in better repair than her own, and the apartment is more spacious. It is clear to Helen that the family had been able to salvage many of their treasured belongings before they were evicted by the colonel and his wife, which pleases her.

Erik's parents are both doctors. They are aggrieved that the British have not yet authorised them to practise despite the fact they had not been members of the Nazi party. It crosses Helen's mind that no German she has met so far admits to having been a Nazi. She remembers the film reels of cheering crowds, with thousands raising their right arms to salute their *Führer*. Where are they now?

Erik is the eldest of five; his younger brothers and sisters are already seated at the table awaiting their arrival. All stand up to greet Helen and her son is taken onto the knee of Erik's mother. As Erik's siblings do not speak English well, they speak in German. Helen apologises for her stumbling attempts at conversation but is secretly pleased by her progress in the language; her son appears to understand everything that is said. All exclaim over Helen's hair and comment on her beauty. Erik's father goes as far as to say it was a pity the general got her before his son had a chance. While all laugh at this, Helen remembers how her father was wont to say "Many a true word is said in jest" and feels uncomfortable. But all raise their glasses to her health and future in Germany.

The food is delicious despite the constraints of rationing. Helen is aware of the black market that exists in the shadows of the derelict buildings. Neither of Erik's parents smoke and their tobacco allowance would be used to barter for meat, which has come from the countryside where farmers are allowed to slaughter their cows, pigs or chickens, albeit to supply the occupying army. There is always a "surplus" to bring into the city to be exchanged for tobacco, vitamin pills or cloth to make clothes for the family on the farm. Where there is a need, there will be a supply. Helen also knows that many young women are forced to sell themselves for sex in exchange for food for their families; one of the lectures at the university focused on the diagnosis and treatment of venereal diseases.

After the meal, the family invite Helen to join them on a walk to a park close to their home. Most of the trees in the park have been destroyed by the bombing raids, but the leaves of those that have survived are already tinted with the golds and reds of autumn. There is a small lake and Erik's mother takes "Karlchen" to see the ducks that have returned to make their home there. Erik and Helen take a path through the remains of an archway, which he explains was once covered with scented roses; only a few withered and burnt stumps remain of what had been a beautiful place to walk on a summer evening.

'Did my father embarrass you when he said what he did...?'

She feels his discomfiture and wishes to reassure him.

'Of course not, it was said in good humour.'

But that is not how she feels. She senses Erik's attraction to her, and with that comes the familiar feeling of loss and uncertainty with regard to her husband. Nearly a week has passed since he left the apartment and she has received no letter from him. The British Control Commission has promised that a telephone will be installed in their apartment, but she knows there are many who have priority over her for this privilege.

'We all admired you, wanted you. I am sure you understand

how it was for us in France. There were many young women available to us, but among all in the garrison at Caen, and those of us installed at the *château*, you were the one we most desired. But as soon as we realised that our General had you for his own, we looked elsewhere.'

'I did not see myself in that way at all.'

'We realised that, and so our attraction increased; such a beautiful young girl but one without vanity or artifice, well perhaps not so the latter.'

She does not feel comfortable with the direction their conversation is taking but decides to use it to her advantage.

'It seems you all had high regard for my husband.'

'Yes, and those of us who survived would follow him again. He has courage and is an honourable soldier. As with all men, he has his faults and made errors of judgement, but that is how it is in war.'

'I know of Svetlana. I found that hard to forgive. He broke the bond of trust I felt was between us, but that is now in the past.'

'And did he speak with you of Poland?'

'No, I often wished to ask him, but then I could not. But if there is anything you feel I should know, now is the time to tell it.'

*

### September 1939
### Poland

*We were defending our homeland against foreign aggression. Throughout August the* Führer *had delivered ultimatums to Poland following reports of border violations by the Poles and the persecution of ethnic Germans. We were told such acts of aggression could not go unanswered, and nor could the pleas for liberation by* the German minority in the port of Danzig. We had been trained for this since childhood and when the call to arms came, we were ready to fight for our homeland and the future of our people.

It was not an easy choice for me, to leave my place at the university in Bonn, where I hoped to follow my parents' choice of career and become a doctor. But as their eldest son and of military age, it was made clear to me that I must take the honourable path and fight for my country. As a student of medicine, I could have claimed exemption from immediate military service, but my parents encouraged me and assured me my training would resume as soon as a glorious victory had been won.

As part of Army Group South commanded by General Gerd von Rundstedt, our division was among the first to cross the border into Polish territory. We progressed rapidly north-eastwards, over the flat plains towards the city of Łódź, which we took in one day. Our Kommandant was Karl von Werstein and we knew him to be a fearless leader who led from the front; many of his rank stayed behind the lines to issue the orders to advance.

On the 3rd of September, we passed through the village of Czatków, where we came under machine gun fire from a house on the road. Our Kommandant halted the advance; he and two others would enter the building. I was one of those tasked with accompanying him. As we entered the house, bullets flew towards us and my comrade was killed. We pressed forward under fire and found a woman reloading a mounted machine gun. I sensed my Kommandant's reticence in taking arms against a woman, but he aimed at her right leg and she dropped to the ground immediately. We disabled the gun and made to leave the house, but at that moment a unit of infantry arrived. Misunderstanding the situation, they believed the gunner to be active and set fire to the house with flamethrowers. The woman shouted for her children and they came running down from the upstairs of the house, but *all were trapped by the flames. Our* Kommandant *tried to go back for the woman and her children, but the flames and the infantry soldiers held him back. Their screams were terrible to hear. We later heard the fire burned so fiercely that the following infantry were forced to walk to the other side of the road to avoid the heat.*

*We moved further into Poland and came across the strafed bodies of women and children, victims of our* Luftwaffe's *indiscriminate murder of civilians. In every town and village we passed through as we approached Warsaw we found burnt-out homes and the charred remains of their occupants. We found the bodies of men, women and children hanging on gallows in town squares. This had been done by our German army to instil terror into the population. Many times I heard my* Kommandant *utter the words that this was not war but murder. As we got closer to Warsaw, we came under heavy counter-attack by the Polish forces and suffered many casualties, but this was war and soldiers have to fight. But my* Kommandant *was never the same; he became detached from us as a man and became a fighting machine, one who gave orders but took no pleasure from victory.*

*After the surrender of Warsaw on the 28th of September, he did not join the other officers in celebration, drinking champagne with beautiful women of the type who are always available to the victors; Von Werstein requested leave to care for his wife, who was by now very ill in a clinic near Berlin.*

*The death of the woman and her children in Czatków was later recorded as a war crime.*

\*

Helen watches Erik's face as he relates the horror of that day in Poland and afterwards. It continues to haunt him as much as it has her husband for all the years she has known him. It explains much of his strategy during his time as *Feldkommandur* in Normandy; his tolerance of her activities and his deliberate inaction over implementing the race laws and round-ups in his area of command. Wars should be fought on the battlefield and not waged on innocent civilians.

'But these deaths, of the woman and her children, were not mentioned at Nuremberg, at the trial. My husband was accused of many atrocities but this was not one of them.'

'There would be some who witnessed his attempts to save the woman and her children. But it is possible that the prosecutors are playing a waiting game, how do you say it...?'

'Biding their time is what we say. Do you think he could be put on trial again?'

'It is well known that many of the perpetrators of the murders and tortures in the camps, and innocent civilians throughout Europe, are either safely in Argentina or sought by the Allies to be "turned" into useful agents against the Soviets. There are others at large, living in disguise and in fear of arrest; they may eventually be brought to justice, but for the moment only the most useful are being pursued.'

'You did not answer my question. Could my husband be arrested again?'

'In short, yes. The Allies want the world to believe justice is being done. The fact that so many murderers have escaped justice has meant they are seeking to prosecute more of the military to compensate for this. Surely you know of the Malmedy trial, that of Jochen Peiper.'

'I know nothing of this man.'

'I never met him, but a member of *SS Leibstandarte Adolf Hitler* joined our division on the Russian Front, at Kursk. He and others had become separated from their unit. He told us of the courage of Peiper, who was their commanding officer, and how he always led from the front and put his own life at risk to save his men. He is a man such as your husband, but of course, as SS he would be a Nazi and a fanatical one at that.'

'And what of this Jochen Peiper?'

'He has recently been sentenced to death by hanging at the Dachau war trials. He took the blame for the massacre of eighty-four American soldiers near a town called Malmedy in Belgium.'

'I have heard of this massacre, but I did not know of those involved in it.'

'There are many who believe him to be innocent, including witnesses of the massacre and members of the American government. It would appear the killing was done by some recently drafted Hitler Youth SS. They were teenagers, without doubt fanatics, and taking amphetamines, a lethal cocktail in such a situation. Peiper, by all accounts, had moved on to take a bridge vital for German supply lines and was not near the scene of the massacre. Now he, and many of his unit, face the hangman's noose, while the likes of Eichmann and Mengele are still free men. Not long after the massacre at Malmedy, eighty German prisoners of war were massacred by their American captors at a place called Chenogne, also in Belgium. As history belongs to the victors, I do not expect you to know of this. Some are now saying that Churchill and Shawcross want to halt the war trials, fearing atrocities by the Allies may be revealed.'

Helen has no answer. She shivers at the sudden drop in temperature. The days are getting shorter; she briefly wonders how it will be for those still crossing Europe in search of their homes and families, and for those in the refugee camps. Erik looks at her with concern.

'I have upset you. I am sorry, but I feel it is important the truth is known. There were atrocities on both sides. The Allies were not saints, as your British officers would have you believe, and now many of them, and their subordinates, strut around ensuring that Germans beg for forgiveness and have barely enough food to keep us alive.'

'Not all are as you say, and my family is surviving on the same rations. It would not be in the interests of the Allies for this situation to continue. Montgomery said we must win the peace and that will mean rebuilding Germany and bringing our peoples together. Perhaps one day there will be a united Germany, but I fear it will not be in Stalin's time.'

Erik does not reply but gently takes her arm to direct her towards the lake, where she hears the sound of her son imitating the ducks; "quacks" and Erik's mother's laughter drift towards them. Helen does not move her arm and it is still resting on Erik's as they reach the lakeside. Her son runs towards her, and only then does she move her arm to swing him onto her hip.

# 20

That evening, Celine and Simone announce they will make their way to the French Zone the following day. They are confident they will find others to accompany them on their journey. Isaak and Josef have been invited to Magda's apartment where she and Pavel have prepared a meal for them. Both young women promise to look out for Leah on their journey. Helen wraps a loaf of bread and the remains of her cheese ration for them; she will have to wait until the middle of the next week for more rations. At least her son is well-fed at the nursery and is more often than not sent away with a "*wee piece*" from Morag's pantry.

Erik meets her at the entrance to the university medical school and she thanks him again for the hospitality of his family. In reply he admits that she would be invited more often were it not for the limitations of rationing. She is comfortable with this explanation, but the memory of her arm on his and the feeling she should have discouraged this intimacy has made her feel disloyal to her husband. Erik would not have taken such a liberty if he had been present. But it had not been unpleasant, the gentle guiding of her towards her son; she realises how lonely she is without her husband.

The following Saturday, Magda and Pavel take charge of her son while she is working at the camp. Pavel will start work at the same camp on Monday. His medical qualifications have been accepted without question by the British Control Commission and his expertise in infectious diseases is much valued.

Erik is accompanied by the older of his two sisters, both on bicycles. His sister dismounts and passes the bicycle to Helen, in this way they will travel to the camp; his sister will return to the family apartment on foot.

Helen is again assigned to the women's medical hut where she finds that the young mother who gave birth the previous week has been permitted to remain. She will receive extra rations of food here and better access to sanitation. The baby, named Noah, had been circumcised at daybreak, according to tradition. A rabbi had been in attendance when the *Mohel* performed the circumcision, and the proud father is now celebrating the event in the community hut. The baby is sleeping peacefully. Helen explains to the young mother that as a medical worker she must check the baby's penis for bleeding as well as his general health. The young woman, Salome, is Italian but speaks some English. She expresses her gratitude to Helen and asks her if she has children of her own. Helen tells Salome of her son but does not speak of his father; there is no language in which she can explain her circumstances.

Another week passes and there has been no contact from her husband. Helen and Erik travel together to the refugee camp. They cycle in companionable silence, each to their own thoughts. Helen has decided to visit Colonel Oakley that evening to enquire about her husband. So be it if she arrives uninvited, she does not care for protocol, she just wants to know how she can contact her husband.

Late in the afternoon her work is interrupted. Erik comes to the women's medical hut to tell her of a new arrival, a boy from the East of Germany who has been travelling for months and is weak with malnutrition but able to speak. He is twelve years old and his name is Leon.

She goes immediately to the boy and takes his hand. She asks him if he remembers who his father is.

'My father was a general in the *Wehrmacht*; his name is Karl von Werstein. My mother is dead. The brother of my father and his wife were killed by the "Ivans". My brother, sister and my cousin have been taken by the Ivans, to the East, perhaps even to Russia.'

Erik leaves them together. Helen quietly explains that his father is alive, and she is his wife. She tells him his grandmother, Luisa, is in Scotland and will be coming to Bonn later in the year. She will contact his grandmother as soon as she is able, to tell her the good news of his arrival at the camp.

Leon will stay in the medical hut until he is strong enough for other arrangements to be made for him. His identity will be verified by the International Tracing Service. Any information he can give regarding his siblings and cousins will be followed up.

She asks Erik to accompany her to the house of Colonel Oakley. As it was his former home, he would know the easiest route to it. They are admitted by a uniformed maid, who ushers them into the comfortable salon Helen and her husband had been seated on the occasion of their visit months ago. Sybil appears and diffidently offers both tea, which they politely refuse. She explains that the colonel is taking a telephone call but will be with them very shortly.

Helen introduces Erik as a fellow medical student and a friend from her time during the occupation of France. She takes pleasure imagining Sybil relaying this "titbit", this bit of gossip, to the other officers' wives. While she and Erik wait, Helen imagines the conversation:

*"She turned up at our door with a young man. Both of them were covered in dust and they left their rusty bicycles on the front lawn. Elke admitted them to the salon, as she recognised* Frau... *Helen. I*

had to talk to Elke about this in the strongest terms later and the covers of the chairs had to be thoroughly cleaned after they left. She should have kept them waiting in the hall. As it was, Elke and the young man appeared to know each other, and I had to interrupt their conversation and send her back to the kitchen."

Gasps of indignation at this and sympathetic smiles all round. Sybil would be at a "charity meeting", the ladies wreathed in smoke, and red lipstick would adorn the stubs in the many ashtrays around the room. There would be a bottle of gin, or two, on the table and a uniformed maid would be tasked with replenishing the glasses.

"Do go on Sybil, tell more."

"She introduced the young man as a fellow medical student but... wait for this, he was a German soldier in France during the occupation, which is where she met and married the former general, her husband."

More gasps, but this time of disgust.

"She put herself about didn't she?" says one.

"Or went straight to the top and nabbed a general, and he was a bit on the side."

All are rolling about in laughter and Sybil is enjoying the limelight; there is little else other than gossip to entertain them.

Helen is so absorbed in this imaginary theatre that she fails to notice the colonel enter the room. Erik nudges her and she stands up to shake his hand. She informs the colonel that she wishes to know the whereabouts of her husband; he has not been in contact with her since he left over two weeks ago. Furthermore, she has important information to impart to her mother-in-law in Scotland. One of her husband's sons has arrived at the refugee camp and the grandmother should be told of this and other family news as soon as possible. The colonel is more welcoming than his wife and takes Helen into his study, where he arranges a telephone call to her parents' home in Scotland. Papa picks up the receiver and Helen struggles to control her emotion as she explains to Papa that she is well and her son is thriving, but she needs to speak to Luisa von Werstein, her mother-in-law.

Luisa comes to the telephone and Helen informs her in German that at least one of her grandsons is alive and is in Bonn. They speak in both French and German and are in tears by the end of the call. When Luisa is told that her son, Frederic, is dead along with his wife, she breaks down in tears. There was no easy way to break this dreadful news to her, but the fact of Leon's survival is some consolation. It is Helen who starts to cry when Luisa asks after her husband. Helen cannot tell her he is rarely at home, that she is desperate for news of him, and she fears for his safety and their marriage. She tells her mother-in-law that he is very busy but will write as soon as he is able. Helen has time to speak briefly to *Maman* and Papa before the call is terminated by the international operator.

Helen takes a moment to wipe the tears from her eyes before asking the colonel about her husband.

'He has been away from our home for over two weeks. I do not know when he will return. When he is at home he is withdrawn and seems anxious. I fear he is involved in more than administration and his life may be in danger. Also, he needs to be informed of the survival of his son, Leon.'

'My dear Helen, you will have to be patient. I am not in a position to reveal any more to you than the fact that your husband is on British Government business and this requires frequent absences from his home. Now, please leave and take care of your family, which now includes a stepson.'

Helen feels her anger rising. How dare he patronise her in this way and make her feel as though she is an irrational woman who needs to be told how to behave. But she does not reply and turns to leave the room. She makes her way to the hallway where she finds Erik waiting; it is clear that Sybil has evicted him from the comfort of the salon as swiftly as she could.

'Please take me back to Leon. I need to speak with him.'

It is dark by the time they arrive back at the camp. Erik will go to her home and ask Magda and Pavel to care for her son while she stays with Leon. She also requests that he then return to the camp. Leon does not speak English well enough to explain what has happened to his family, and her German is equally inadequate. Erik agrees and promises to return as soon as he can.

# PART SIX

## Leon

# 21

## 1938-1946
### East Prussia

My earliest memories are beautiful ones. My mother's family owned a villa in Königsberg. It was a splendid house which stood out amongst its neighbours on account of its three stories, each with wide balconies overlooking the Pregel River where it forks in the middle of the city to make the Kniephof, or city island. If I looked one way from the balcony of my grandmother's salon, I could watch the ships and boats passing to and fro, as far as where the two forks of the river meet and flow into the Baltic Sea. If I looked the other way, I could watch the trains being unloaded onto the docks and the great wheels of Tilsiter cheese being taken to the waiting boats.

We had a large garden that ran down to the banks of the Pregel and here my grandfather had fashioned a swing on the lower branches of a magnificent Baltic Oak. Lilac trees grew close by, and I remember delighting in their pungent scent as my grandfather gently swung me back and forth. Another memory I have of this time, and I can only have been three years old, is of my mother nursing my baby sister in the shade of the lilac trees. My mother rarely had the strength to hold Maria-Sophia and our nursery maid was always nearby, to take my sister from her arms and my mother would return to her bedroom, where she spent most of her days sleeping or weeping. But on this early summer's day, she had ventured out to a reclining chair to enjoy the scented air of the first warm winds of summer. My older brother, Alexander, was engaged in fashioning a sword from a branch. Alexi, as we called him, was enthused by the stories our grandfather had told him of the Teutonic Knights of the Baltic Crusades and he wanted to be a soldier, as our father.

Later in the same year, I remember we travelled to the beach at Kranz where my father's mother had a large villa that looked out across the Baltic Sea. I never met my paternal grandfather as he had "fallen" in the Great War, but it was a source of pride between my father and his mother that he had died fighting as a loyal Prussian for the Fatherland; there could be no greater glory in death. Alexi wanted to follow in the military tradition of our grandfather, as our father now did.

Alexi and I learned to swim in the shallows of the Baltic. Papa joined us at Kranz, and we spent every day on the beach with him, building fortresses of sand and watching him swim far out to where the sea met the horizon, or so it seemed to us. Our grandmother preferred to swim in the Ladies Pool but would join us on the beach as the sun was setting. We would picnic on salmon, potato salad laced with dill, and fresh breads. Our favourite bread was one she called a "scone", which was round and slightly sweet and melted in our mouths as we ate it. My grandmother told us that the recipe for these small breads came from her own grandmother who had been born in Scotland. My grandmother had travelled there as a young woman, and we marvelled at this; to young children, this country seemed so very far away.

In the evenings our father would take his cello into the orangery and play to us. If Mother was feeling well enough, she would accompany him on the piano, but she soon tired. My memories of our mother at this time are of a frail and insubstantial creature who seemed to fade from life, despite the loving care she received from my father and our grandparents. When I look back this must have been one of the last summers of peace; after this time my father was always in military uniform. We children spent more time on our estate to the west of Königsberg where we were often joined by our Uncle Frederic and Aunt Alicia, and their children, Felix and Johanna. Also by this time, our mother was in a clinic in Berlin and there was talk of another war in Europe. My cousin Felix told us that Germany was under attack from Poland, and Britain and France would join against Germany. He and Alexi spent their time playing as soldiers, with shoot-outs among the trees in the woods. But we also played other games; we built tree houses and pretended to be lost in the forest as in the story of Hansel and Gretel. One of us would go ahead and drop a trail of breadcrumbs and we had to follow the trail, all the time pretending to be lost. We could never have foreseen that forests would become our home, and we would have to risk our lives for crumbs of bread.

We were war children and avid for news of German success on the battlefield. Our father returned to our estate for *Weihnachten* in 1939 and we were joined by our grandparents, Uncle Frederic and his family, as well as cousins of my father and their children. The latter were much older than me and my siblings and cousins, but they joined us in decorating the huge fir tree cut from our woods, which our servants placed in the great hall of our home. Our mother was too ill to be with us, but Isolde, the daughter of my father's cousin, Beatrix, became as a mother to us that year. On *Heiligabend* she held us in her arms to reach the top of the tree to place ginger biscuits and fruits on the highest branches. She also ensured that none of the presents under the tree were opened until the correct time for the exchange of gifts. Isolde had hair of a rich red-gold. As a young child, I remember being struck by this because we were all either blond or dark-haired. To me, she seemed to be a fairytale princess, with her long, fantastical hair which fell below her waist whenever she let it loose. My father's mother told us her grandmother had possessed such hair.

My memory of my father at that time was his silence and how he withdrew from the family for much of what should have been a time of celebration. We understood he had been given leave following Germany's victorious campaign in Poland and had spent much of this time with our mother in the clinic in Berlin. He went for solitary walks in the woods or took one of the horses and disappeared across our lands for the whole day.

The next time we saw our father was following the death of our mother. He returned from France in time for her interment on her family estate. Our uncle had taken her from the clinic in Berlin to our estate, and we were with her when she died. She asked to see all of us together during her final moments, which were peaceful and without suffering.

The war years passed, with Germany conquering the world, or so it seemed to us as children. We now had a governess and tutor, and lessons took up much of our days. Our grandparents remained in Königsberg and our grandmother at her estate, which adjoined ours. Alexi, Maria-Sophia and I were taken to live with Uncle Frederic and his family, but there were no more holidays in Kranz and there was talk of shortages of meat and bread.

There came news of the Soviets bombing Königsberg and that our mother's parents had died in the fires that followed the bombing. Nothing would remain of the wonderful villa. I imagined my swing in the charred branches of the oak tree, and the ghost of my former self using my legs to move it back and forth in the desolate garden.

Our father's mother came to visit and told us that our father had married a woman in France who would be a mother to us in time. She expressed hope that we would be happy for him, as she was. This news meant little to us as we had not known how it was to have a mother for so many years. We knew our father was fighting on the Eastern Front and we overheard the adults in the household whispering of the losses of whole battalions. We feared for our father.

The war in Russia was lost and our uncle and aunt began to listen to the BBC News Service on the wireless, which had been forbidden since the war began. Our uncle was called up to fight in the East; he had been exempted up to this time on account of a heart condition. He returned after only two weeks with the loss of his right leg. We learned that the Allies had landed in Normandy and Italy, and in August of that year, the RAF reduced our beautiful city of Königsberg to ruins in bombing raids. Then there came the news that the Soviets were defeating our armies westwards, deep into our Prussian lands. Panic took hold of our servants. They had heard of the brutality of the Ivans, that thousands were fleeing the advancing Red Army and they urged us to escape while we could. Our uncle said we must stay and defend our land, and our aunt agreed with him. There was still talk of a secret weapon that would change the war to Germany's advantage. Furthermore, it would be too dangerous to leave in the cold and snow of winter.

Most of the workers of our estate had left, loading up carts with clothing and food supplies. It was the middle of winter and the land was deep in snow. We watched convoys of bedraggled soldiers passing through our land, and with them, carts laden with crying children and the household goods the adults had salvaged from their homes. We found the frozen bodies of children, some crushed by tanks, close to our home. No one stopped to ask for shelter as all were desperate to move west, as far from the Russian army as possible. As the weeks passed, we found women lying in the snow, their lower bodies covered in blood. When we told our aunt she became very agitated and told our uncle that we too should prepare to leave. But it was too late.

The Red Army soldiers arrived on our land in March. Our stable hand, Fritz, had stayed to take care of the horses and he chased us into the woods, telling us to hide there and make no sound. My sister and her cousin Johanna had clung crying and sobbing to Aunt Alicia's skirts, but my aunt pushed them off and told them to follow us. After a while, we heard gunshots and screaming from the house. My aunt ran out pursued by the Ivans. They tore the clothes off her and we watched in horror as each one took his turn entering her naked body. Her screaming stopped after what must have been hours, and then the soldiers returned to our home. We heard singing, shouting and occasional gunfire, and then all was silent. We stayed in the woods all night and late into the following day, until we were certain the soldiers had left; but all the time we were afraid that others would come.

We found our uncle in the entrance to the house; at least his death must have come quickly as there was only a wound to his head. Our aunt had died of the wounds inflicted by the soldiers to her lower body. We had no time to mourn them as Fritz appeared with a cart laden with clothing and food. There were two horses harnessed to the cart. He had been preparing for this for some time he said; the cart, provisions and horses had been hidden deep in the woods. He told us we would be travelling to the north-east, towards Lithuania, where he said the people of that country would help us. To go further west would mean encountering the Ivans and being caught in the battles between the *Wehrmacht* and the Red Army.

After two months on the road, we reached the forests that border East Prussia and Lithuania. In this time, we saw the corpses of women and children rotting in the fields, burned-out villages and abandoned *Wehrmacht* vehicles of every kind. We did not want to look at the corpses of German soldiers for fear it was our father among them; we needed the hope he had survived.

Fritz knew how to avoid the mass of people struggling to move west and north. When we asked him how he knew which direction to take and which roads to follow, he laughed and told us his mind was a compass and his eyes followed the stars. We marvelled at this and asked him to teach us at least some of it, which he did. We were deep in the forest when we were attacked by a group of our own people. Fritz did his best to defend us, but they shot him. They took our cart, horses and the provisions we had. We were now on our own, real children of the forest.

We did not know where we were, whether we were in East Prussia or Lithuania. We walked as Fritz had taught us, but after days of walking, we were still deep in the forest. We had managed to keep some bread hidden in our clothing and we shared this between us, just a few crumbs at a time. For water, we drank the snow melt. Hunger and exhaustion made us weak and slowed our progress. To ease our hunger pains, we chewed on small plants or sucked on pebbles. Our shoes and clothes were now in tatters from the rain and rough undergrowth. We made a shelter in the trees and Alexi and Felix set off on foot to find food. They hoped there would be a village close by, that perhaps we were already in Lithuania and would be made welcome. They returned two days later with news that there was a village a few kilometres from our shelter. The village was in Lithuania, but we would have to learn to beg. The Lithuanians had been ordered not to give refuge to "Nazi brats"; the punishments for doing so were severe. Alexi explained that there were many children such as us, orphaned by the war and desperately looking for food and shelter. They had met a group of these children close to the village and had been invited to join them, but we would have to share in the begging and stealing, and the beatings that would be meted out by the villagers if we were caught.

The children ranged in age between four and fifteen years. All had witnessed the deaths of parents and siblings from hunger and disease, as well as brutal trauma. They understood that although the war was over, their suffering would continue. It was essential to avoid the Ivans who would beat and imprison them if they were caught. The girls, though young, were at risk of the same treatment they had witnessed suffered by their mothers. There were rumours that trainloads of orphans were being sent far into Soviet territory, on journeys taking up to seven days with no food or toilet facilities. The important thing was to survive and find a way to the West, where the British and Americans would care for them. Two of the youngest girls from their group had been taken in by families in the village, who hoped to adopt them covertly, passing them off as their own children to Soviet officials. There were frequent gun battles in the forest between the "Forest Brothers" and the Russian soldiers. The Forest Brothers were partisans from Latvia, Estonia and Lithuania who were determined to fight against the Soviet occupation of their countries. They shared what food they had with the children and, in turn, the children became adept at informing them of the location of Ivans in the forest.

In this way, we learned how to beg and steal. We crept into henhouses and lifted the eggs from under the hens, taking care to leave at least one to avoid suspicion. We fought like wild animals over a loaf of bread that Alexi stole from a cottage; it was still fresh from the oven and the woman of the house had left it to cool on a window ledge. But the people of the village were also starving; many were kind enough to offer us a bowl of soup in their kitchen, sharing the little they had with us.

Then one day we were warned that the "Ivans" were rounding up more children to be sent east. We were determined not to be captured and ran deeper into the forest. Johanna and two of the very youngest children fell back and were taken into the arms of the Forest Brothers, who promised to find homes for them, but that we should run. We became separated and I found myself alone by a train track. I waited there for days, but one day I heard a train approaching. I waited until most of the train had passed and jumped in between two freight cars. I clung onto a rail between the wagons and in this way travelled for three nights and days. My hands were numb when the train came to rest late at night in a freight yard. In the darkness, I crept out of the yard where only a sleeping porter was guarding the entrance. To my astonishment, I found that the street signs were in German and Russian. I did not know this, but I had arrived in the Soviet sector of Berlin.

I had never been to Berlin and had no way of knowing how to find help. I lay down exhausted in an alleyway that smelled of vomit and stale urine, and fell into a deep sleep. When I woke up, I was lying on a mattress in the ruins of a church. The gables of the roof were fractured but still held, of the main structure only rubble remained. A priest stood over me with a cup of hot soup. As I drank it, he explained that I was in Soviet-occupied Berlin and that I was one of many children who had arrived in the way I had. One of his clergy patrolled the freight yards of the trains arriving from the north and east looking for children. They were brought to this church to be identified and reunited with their families. I explained that my siblings and cousins were either in Lithuania or being transported east by the Soviets, that my mother was dead, and I'd had no news of my father for two years. I gave him my name and that of my father.

I was given clean clothing and was able to wash under an outdoor shower. After two days the priest returned. He told me I should make my way to Bonn where an address for my father had been found, but I had to leave that night and be guided through the checkpoints by someone who knew how to cross between the sectors. The fact that my father had been a general in the *Wehrmacht* would be a reason for the Soviets to detain me. I would not be allowed to cross to the British or American sectors of Berlin but could be arrested and transported to the *gulags*.

At close to midnight my guide arrived. She was a young woman, very beautiful, with long blonde hair which escaped from her Soviet Army cap; her name was Svetlana. She walked me past the Soviet guards, who stood to attention when they saw her, and led me to a checkpoint manned by British army soldiers, where she handed me over. As she left me, she whispered that I had to make my own way to Bonn, but to remember her to my father.

I waited for days by a train track for trains going west, hopping from one to the other over the following weeks. Many times I was caught and thrown off, but finally I arrived at this camp.

# PART SEVEN

## Helen

## 22

September 1946
Bonn, Germany

Helen stays all night and into the following day with Leon. Once he begins to speak it seems he cannot stop. At times he weeps when he speaks of his brother, sister and cousins. She wonders how many thousands of children are wandering in the forests of the East, searching for food and shelter. These are children who had enjoyed happy lives in loving families, but who are now orphans, with memories of the rape and murder of their mothers and the deaths of their families from hunger and disease.

Erik leaves in the early morning, but returns in the evening with soup and fresh bread rolls which he explains he bartered against the promise of a bicycle. She wonders how he obtained the two bicycles they both use and realises how resourceful he is. After a while, they leave Leon to sleep and Erik accompanies her to her apartment building. He takes over the care of her son while she sleeps beside the *Kachelöfen*. Isaak and Josef have been invited to Magda and Pavel for supper. While Helen sleeps, Erik prepares a meal for her. It is nearly midnight when she wakes. Her son is asleep in his cot and Josef and Isaak have settled in the bedroom. Erik encourages her to eat and she is grateful for the care he is giving her. This does not stop the familiar wave of loneliness and fear returning to overwhelm her. She is certain the woman who took Leon over the checkpoint is the same Svetlana she had hoped to banish to the shadows of her life, the woman with whom her husband had betrayed her and enjoyed in his command centre at the Russian Front; the woman who now knows where he lives.

She begins to weep. Erik takes her in his arms and soothes her. He kisses her, first her eyes and then her mouth. She returns his kisses, and he starts to undress her slowly, and then, sensing her desire is equal to his, with greater urgency. His touch is tender as he strokes her breasts, his tongue brushes her nipples and he lowers her to the floor. She lifts his shirt to feel the warmth of his skin and the firmness of his muscles and is comforted by his body against hers. She is exhausted by the events of the past days and gives herself up to him. He is a good lover, intuitive and patient as well as passionate; it is not the same as with her husband, but there is pleasure and release for her in his lovemaking and this is what she needs.

Erik leaves before dawn; they will meet at the university later in the day.

# 23

The following morning Helen vomits in the bathroom. At first, she attributes this to exhaustion following the weekend at the camp, and then she remembers that she has not bled since August. She feels her breasts; they are tender from Erik's lovemaking, but her nipples are swollen and a deeper shade of pink. She thinks back to the time she and her husband made love, the time in the courtyard following their recital. They had not taken their usual precautions and she would have been at her most fertile time.

She is pregnant with their child.

At the midday break in lectures, she and Erik walk in the gardens that surround the university. She tells him she is pregnant by her husband and that she cannot permit their relationship as lovers to continue.

Erik is clearly disappointed by her words, but nevertheless takes her hand in his and kisses it.

'I do not let you go easily. But I will continue to support you and love you; I owe it to my former *Kommandant* to be honourable, he saved my life on many occasions. But "all is fair in love and war" as I learned from my English tutor.'

'I know that quotation. It is not from Shakespeare but from the book by John Lyly, Euphues: "*The Anatomy of Wit*". But I cannot agree with it, that the rules of fair play do not apply in love and war.'

'So you continue to believe that your Allies did not adhere to this sentiment; that honour prevailed on the battlefields, but only on their side of course.'

'From what you have told me the rules of The Hague Convention were broken by both sides. I have learned that the people of Denmark deliberately allowed German refugees from the East to die of starvation and disease, even after Germany capitulated and the refugees became prisoners of war. The young and the old, including babies and children, died in this way. Danes who took pity on them were ostracised, and after the war ended were beaten and exiled as collaborators. Many of these refugees remain in prison camps in Denmark. But Germans do not appear to accept that they are paying for the acts of barbarism which were committed in a war they started and supported. I am not alone in believing that your country has forfeited its former reputation as the nation of Goethe and Schiller and that Beethoven has been eclipsed by Wagner, whose music was much beloved by Hitler and the Nazis.'

'You know I agree with you with respect to my county's guilt. But I am also talking about love. I am a patient man and "Love is not love. Which alters when it alteration finds". I will bide my time.'

She smiles. 'You Germans and your Shakespeare. The Bard must be better known here than in his own country.'

'You are correct in this. As a way of bringing our peoples together, the British government thought it a good idea to bring your National Theatre Company to Berlin to perform *The Merchant of Venice*. Naturally, the depiction of the character Shylock was not one that rested lightly with the Jewish members of the audience.'

She knows she should be shocked by this and cannot help but laugh, as he does; the bitter irony and crassness of this must have shocked all Berliners. Not for the first time is she ashamed to be thought British.

They return to lectures; she feels very tender towards him and values his companionship all the more for what has passed between them.

# 24

She returns to her apartment to find that Isaak and Josef have left. There is a note with one word on it: "*Bericha*". She burns the note on the stove; Isaak and Josef are on their way to Palestine.

There are more surprises later that week. A soldier arrives at the university with a message for her from Colonel Oakley. She is invited to his home that evening to take a telephone call from Scotland. Once again, Erik accompanies her to the villa, and again they leave their rusty bicycles lying on the lawn. Erik is in a wicked mood and ensures that his bicycle lies on the flower beds Sybil has ordered to be dug: fussy arrangements of dahlia and cyclamen now adorn what had been a pleasant place to sit and watch the boats passing on the river. Elke admits them but on this occasion they are both instructed to wait on a hard bench in the hallway. They hear Sybil's voice from somewhere in the house, but she does not deign to greet them. The colonel comes to the hallway and shakes both by the hand. He at least is doing his best to be kind; perhaps he regrets his dismissive words of their previous meeting. He takes Helen into his study and invites her to take the chair next to the telephone.

'I happen to know the reason for this telephone call, but I will wait for your mother-in-law to give the news. I must say, it does rather alter your situation here.'

After a short time the telephone rings, she picks up the

receiver and after a few clicks Luisa's voice comes through. It appears Luisa has been busy since their last conversation. She informs Helen that she is making travel arrangements to come to Germany to take possession of her inheritance: a large country house, the Schloss Mariendistel, near the city of Lübeck in Schleswig-Holstein. The city of Lübeck is in the British zone of occupation but was formerly a Prussian Province. Lübeck had been an important Hanseatic port; for centuries trade between Scotland and Germany had flowed through there. The 4$^{th}$ Earl of Gordon, Luisa's great-grandfather, had business connections with the port and it was through these that the Von Blumenthal and Gordon families first met. As a condition of the marriage between his youngest and favourite daughter, Lady Isobel Agnes Gordon, and Count Otto von Blumenthal, for which a substantial dowry had been paid, the Earl had demanded that part of this be used to buy a house and land close to Lübeck. This would be purchased under Scottish property law and registered on the Sasine Register, as a security for his daughter's future in a country which was constantly at war with itself and its neighbours. Luisa has documents from the Recorder General of Scotland attesting to this and has obtained the title deeds from the National Records Office. She will bring these with her to Bonn and looks forward to being with Karl and Helen and her two grandsons.

After the call has been terminated by the operator, Helen takes a moment to absorb the implications of Luisa's news. Her bewilderment must be evident to the colonel as he takes her hand.

'It is all perfectly in order. Your mother-in-law wrote to us about this property, and of course we checked with all the relevant authorities. It is most fortuitous that the property is in the British Zone; things would have been more complicated if it were in the American Zone, and impossible if under Soviet occupation. But what we have here is a piece of Scotland in Germany. At the very least it will provide a good home for your son, and the son who has returned from the East.'

'It does not alter the fact that I have not seen or heard from my husband for weeks now and he knows nothing of his son's return.'

'My dear, you know perfectly well that I am unable to discuss this... absence with you.'

Again she feels her temper rising, but then there is a roaring in her ears and everything goes dark; she has fainted on the floor of the colonel's study.

When she regains consciousness she is lying on a sofa in the same room but Erik is there holding her hand. Her legs have been raised over the curved arms of the sofa. Elke is beside Erik with a glass of water and the colonel is standing by his desk, with a look of consternation on his face.

Helen makes to sit up, but Erik advises her to stay where she is until he is satisfied she is fully recovered. After a while, she feels well enough to sit up and drink the water. She is deeply ashamed this has occurred, and the inconvenience it has caused the colonel. When she tries to express this the colonel is kind.

'My dear, my concern is for your health. Do you get enough to eat? All this study and work at the camp cannot be good for your health.'

'I am used to hard work and the food is enough. It is the same for my neighbours and all Germans at this time. Thank you for your concern, but we have troubled you enough today.'

As she makes to stand up, a gripping pain crosses her lower abdomen and she falls back onto the sofa. Erik goes to her aid. He feels her abdomen and informs the colonel she should be taken immediately to a hospital; Helen is in early pregnancy and needs urgent medical care.

Helen is taken to the British Military Hospital and, after a week, is allowed to return to her home. The pains have stopped and the loss of blood was minimal. The baby has survived, as far as it is possible to confirm. She is advised to rest and is given extra ration coupons. Erik has visited every day and assures the nurses and doctors that he is not the father of the baby, merely a concerned friend. She is not sure this is believed, but she does not care; they can think what they like of her. This will give the *bavards* at their charity meetings something to *blether* about.

The colonel and his wife send flowers, but Helen consigns them immediately to the dustbin; she would rather receive news of her husband. Iain and Morag now come every morning to take her son to the nursery.

'*Noo, lassie, yae've* got *ta* rest more and let that *bairn* grow. *Yae've* a good friend in Erik, he will *mak sure ye* keep up with *yer* lecture notes and stuff. And when *al* has settled *doon*, we'll get *ye* back *oot* and *aboot.*'

Helen is grateful for their kindness but wonders how they would be if they knew Erik has been more than just a "good friend".

Magda and Pavel are now very much a couple, and there is talk of marriage between them. She wonders at the compromises Pavel has to make in this relationship, in his own conscience; Magda's people are responsible for the deaths of his wife and children. But Helen herself has long been reconciled to this ethical dilemma. If Magda is guilty, her own husband, and her lover, or whatever Erik is to her, are equally implicated in the mass murder of innocent people.

She thinks back to what Erik told her, that Churchill and Shawcross are considering closing down the hunt for war criminals; so much for the promises of the Moscow Agreement in 1943, "To pursue them to the uttermost ends of the earth and deliver them to their accusers in order that justice be done".

But Churchill had also said he was against "the cold-blooded execution of soldiers who fought for their country". Stalin and Roosevelt had been in accord with the idea of killing the whole German command structure. This at least is reassuring; her husband is safe in the British zone.

Churchill has stressed that in order to revive the post-war British economy and restore Britain to its pre-war world status, a more moderate attitude towards Germany is required. Britain's economic recovery is tied to the restoration of European trade and the opening of market agreements; a prosperous and stable German economy is essential to this. Furthermore, Britain fears the spread of communism in post-war Europe; Germany would act as a bulwark against the "Russian Bear".

# 25

A letter arrives in her mailbox from France. Simone and Celine are now in Paris and searching for their missing family members. Helen wishes she had given them the address of the Erharts; they would be pleased to help them, as they themselves had narrowly escaped arrest during the *Vel d'Hiv rafle* They have news of Leah: she is in the French zone, in Koblenz, but she is in a hospital and her situation is grim. She has become aphasic due to trauma and malnutrition on the forced march from Mittelbau. She has no identification, and the French authorities would not accept their testimony as to her name and nationality. They could do no more for her and left to continue their journey to Paris.

Helen asks Iain to drive her to Colonel Oakley's home. On this occasion, Sybil cannot be inhospitable as Iain is a member of the British army, albeit of lowly rank compared to her husband.

Ian does not stand on ceremony with military wives and presents Helen as a hero of the occupation of France. Sybil is more courteous towards Helen and acknowledges her "condition" by inviting her to take a seat in the salon. When the colonel arrives, Iain takes his leave and goes to wait in the jeep outside. Helen explains the situation. Her friend Leah, who was in her care up to the time she was deported to Auschwitz, has been found in Koblenz and is seriously ill. She wishes to travel to Koblenz to be with Leah but requires the necessary papers to do so. She will also need a document enabling her to authenticate Leah's identity and thereby ensure that Leah is permitted to travel to her family in Normandy if she recovers.

'Can you assure me that you are well enough to travel at this time?'

'I am well enough, but I need your help in this.'

'I will arrange for Lance Corporal Robertson to take you tomorrow. Koblenz is within a two-hour drive of Bonn. You will have the letters and documents you require but your papers will be in the name of *Mademoiselle* Helen Douglas. The French will not be eager to help a woman with a German name. It will be up to you to persuade the French to allow your friend to be repatriated. Robertson will return to base after delivering you to Koblenz, and I will request that a French officer return you to Bonn.'

Helen is grateful for the colonel's immediate approval of her request, but wonders whether this is to compensate for his lack of assistance in the other matter, the disclosure of her husband's whereabouts.

They set off early the following day. Morag has taken her son to stay at their accommodation at the barracks; he will be well cared for and among friends.

The French accept her papers and letter of affirmation. She wears her wedding ring on a ribbon around her neck. She is pleased to be speaking French again, and is welcomed with much gallantry despite a moment of apprehension that she could be identified as a collaborator. Iain leaves her at the hospital and she is taken to Leah's bedside.

She is shocked at the sight of the dishevelled emaciated woman in the bed. There is no drinking cup beside her and the bedclothes are dirty, soiled with faeces and urine. Helen is outraged and goes in search of an *infirmière*. She finds three of them in a nearby office, where they are relaxing and flirting with two army medical officers. Helen tells them they are all a disgrace to their profession and demands that clean bed linen and drinking water be brought to Leah's bed immediately. She also demands that the nurses help her put Leah into a bathtub where she can be thoroughly cleaned. As they do her bidding, she asks why Leah has been so neglected, and they have the grace to look thoroughly ashamed. One of them, the youngest of the three, admits that in cases such as Leah's, there is an attitude of "*laissez mourir*"; her life is ending and they can do no more for her.

Helen bites her tongue and together they carry Leah into the bathtub where antiseptic soap has been added to the warm water. Helen bathes her friend and tries to hide her revulsion at the sores that cover her emaciated body. Not all of these sores have been caused by the SS guards on the march, many of them are due to neglect by the nurses. When Leah is thoroughly washed and in clean bedclothes, Helen sits with her and encourages her to take water. Leah opens her eyes and Helen senses some recognition from her friend, but no words come from her lips, and soon her eyes close again and she sleeps.

Helen speaks to the doctors, and they agree to start a liquid diet to replace the minerals and vitamins Leah has lacked for so many years. This regime was successful at the Bergen-Belsen camp, where inmates had died when given food by well-meaning liberators; starvation had altered their bodies' metabolism, and although they seemed to recover and put on weight, many suddenly died. It had been named Refeeding Syndrome; their bodies had gone into shock as a result of the introduction of calories. Doctors discovered that introducing an intravenous solution containing mineral supplements, particularly phosphorus, was the key to survival. This is available at the hospital and the doctors, chastened by Helen's criticism, agree to start the treatment immediately.

Helen asks if she can telephone her uncle in Normandy.

Damian picks up the receiver and is delighted to hear her voice. She explains she is at the hospital in Koblenz with Leah and asks him to help Raisa and her daughters travel here. Leah is gravely ill and may not survive; her daughter and granddaughters should be with her at this time. She tells him she is well and that baby Karl is thriving. She does not tell him of her new pregnancy, or the disappearance of her husband.

Three days later, Raisa, Ruth and Ellana arrive at the hospital. In this time, Leah has begun to show signs of recovery; she opens her eyes and tries to speak, although no words are forthcoming. The doctors explain that this type of aphasia, the inability to communicate by voice, despite understanding what is said, is rare. Leah has not had a "stroke" but has been subjected to severe mental and physical trauma; recovery, should she survive, will take months. She is now strong enough to move her legs and arms and has taken a short walk around the bed. She will stay in the hospital until she has reached 56 kilograms in weight, which they have estimated is the critical weight for her height. Currently she weighs only 36 kilograms.

Helen meets Raisa and her daughters at the train station in Koblenz. The journey has been a difficult one; train services are irregular due to the damage to tracks and bridges during the final months of the war. She warns them that they will be shocked by Leah's condition, but that she is responding well to the treatment she is receiving. Raisa will stay with her mother until she is well enough to return to Normandy.

When she is certain Leah's treatment and care will continue, Helen asks to be taken back to Bonn. Raisa and the girls embrace Helen, and she takes her leave of them. They inform the medical staff that Helen was responsible for their survival during the occupation, and she should be honoured for the risks she took during that time. The French officer who drives her back to Bonn has evidently been given this information.

'So you were a *Résistante, Mademoiselle*. You must have been very brave. How is it that you speak French and come to live in Germany?'

'My mother is French but married to a Scotsman. They met in France during the Great War. I was born in Scotland but was a *gouvernante* in Normandy when the Germans came. It was not a question of courage; it was my duty to protect those who were persecuted by the *gendarmes* and Germans. As for why I am in Germany, I am not permitted to say.'

He accepts her explanation. Perhaps the beautiful *Mademoiselle* is now working for British Intelligence. He knows that former *Résistants* in France are aggrieved that General De Gaulle has suppressed the fact of their special courage and role in helping the Allies win the battle for France. De Gaulle's message has been that all French people resisted the occupation, and there had been no collaboration with the occupying army. It has suited the general's narrative of the special place France now has in a free Europe. His resentment that France was not immediately given a zone of occupation in Germany still rankles him.

Erik is at her apartment when she returns late in the evening. He has made supper for her son, and a simple dish of fried potatoes and ham is ready for her. She wishes to bathe before she eats and finds that Erik has cleaned the bathroom and there are fresh towels on the door hooks. She rocks her son and sings his favourite songs until he is sleeping, and then places him in his cot bed. After they have eaten, Erik makes up a bed for himself by the *Kachelöfen* and she goes to the bed she once shared with her husband. She had hoped to return to a letter from him, but the mailbox is empty.

She is awakened by the return of the night terrors that have afflicted her since her torture by the *Gestapo*. She struggles against the sensation of being dragged down to a pit from which there is no return. Her husband knew of these terrors and understood he must awaken her from them, but he is not with her. Instead, it is Erik who gently rouses her from the terror, and having made sure she is fully woken and calm, lies on the bed beside her, holding her in his arms.

# 26

Luisa arrives at the end of the following week and with her is *Maman*. Helen is overjoyed to be with her mother after so many months. Both grandmothers are enchanted by young Karl as he babbles in three languages and shows them his favourite toy: the spinning top he received at the NAAFI shop. Luisa comments on the resemblance of Helen to portraits of her Scottish grandmother, and also to her niece Isolde.

But neither is happy with the condition of the building in which the family are living; much of it is in ruins and they fear that falling masonry and water leakage will be a problem in the storms of the approaching winter. Luisa wishes to know when her son will be home, and Helen breaks down in tears. She admits that she has not seen her husband since the end of August and that she is pregnant with their second child. *Maman* is concerned and Luisa is outraged.

'What manner of son have I raised that he abandons his pregnant wife and his son?'

'He does not know of the pregnancy.'

'Has he not written to you, or you to him?'

'I am not permitted to know where he is. The British authorities tell me nothing. I fear for his life and our family, the more so since the return of Leon.'

'And why is that? What has this to do with Leon?'

'He was helped to the West by a woman I would not wish to meet, nor for my husband to meet again.'

So she tells them about Svetlana. She feels she is betraying her husband by divulging his relationship with the woman, but there is no easy way to explain the sense of foreboding she now has; the fact that the woman has made herself part of their lives again.

It is *Maman*'s turn to be outraged.

'Your husband was unfaithful to you? That should never happen in a marriage. Your Papa would never have done such a thing; it is dishonouring the sacred vows of the church.'

Luisa is dismissive of *Maman*'s indignation.

'*Unsinn*! That is what soldiers do in wartime. My husband did the same, I am sure. It would be a comfort to me to know that he died on the battlefield following a night with an available woman.'

*Maman* is visibly shocked that such behaviour would be tolerated by a wife. Both are now glaring at each other, and Helen feels she should make an effort to reconcile the two of them. *Maman*'s opinion of her husband and his family has clearly plummeted, and she feels she should attempt to defend her husband. And she too has a secret, one she does not feel guilty about. Perhaps she has more affinity with Luisa's view of the situation than *Maman* could ever have. But this does not lift the sense of foreboding she feels with regard to Svetlana.

It is Luisa who breaks the hostile mood which has caused young Karl to look apprehensively at his grandmothers.

'I will go to Colonel Oakley and demand you are given the means to contact my son, your husband. The colonel has been most helpful in organising the travel for me and your mother, and I need to make arrangements to travel to my home. I hope to bring my family to live with me while this situation is resolved.'

It is no use attempting to explain to Luisa that she needs to continue her studies at the university as far into her pregnancy as possible. She feels a whirlwind has entered her home. And then Erik arrives at the apartment. He lets himself in with the key she gave him before she left for Koblenz.

Luisa and *Maman* look first to Erik and then to Helen, and at each is raised an eyebrow. They are united in this moment of conjecture at least.

# 27

Colonel Oakley has arranged accommodation for *Maman* and Luisa in a renovated apartment close to his villa. Luisa has been reunited with Leon and he will be well enough to travel with her to Lübeck within a few days.

They are invited to dine with the colonel and his wife. Helen and Erik are included in the invitation, as well as young Karl. Both grandmothers remark on their grandson's attachment to Erik.

'Since my husband left us, Erik has been like a father to my son. Sometimes I fear that he will not know his own father when he returns.'

She also explains the help she has received from Iain and his family and the circumstances of their first meeting. She has never told her mother the full details of her life at the *château*; *Maman* would be horrified. There can be too much truth.

Sybil is more welcoming, at least to Luisa and *Maman*. She is a woman who is impressed by titles and Luisa and *Maman*'s connections to the aristocracy of Scotland and Germany make her well-disposed to both. Not so with regard to Helen and Erik. Helen supposes there would have been a fair amount of negotiation between the colonel and his wife for the invitation to be extended to them. Luisa had insisted they were included. Her daughter-in-law owes her life and that of her unborn baby to Erik; without his intervention, both could have been lost.

Helen has little appetite for the food; she has been far more nauseous in this pregnancy than with her son. After the meal, the colonel invites *Maman* and Helen to give a recital on the Bechstein piano in the library of the villa. Erik whispers to her, 'My father's Bechstein piano!'

After conferring together, *Maman* and Helen entertain them with Schubert's *Fantasie* in *F minor*. Helen cannot play without fighting back her tears; the emotions it stirs in her are too much to bear. *Maman* notices and takes her hand; she understands how it is for her daughter.

Erik reminds them that Beethoven was born in Bonn and lived close to this villa. He relates how as a child he used to imagine a young Beethoven walking along the path by the river.

'Did you live close to here?' asks Sybil.

'This house belonged to my family. I was born here, as were my sisters and brothers.'

There is an embarrassed silence. Erik attempts to rescue the situation by telling of the recitals Helen and her husband, General Karl von Werstein, had given during their time at the *château* in Normandy. This only serves to cause further embarrassment, especially as Erik has used the military title of his former commander.

It is time to leave. The colonel arranges transport for all except Erik. He offers to walk to his home, but Helen insists he accompany them; he can walk to his home from her apartment.

She whispers to Erik, 'No doubt Sybil will find that most convenient for you. She will be the star attraction at her charity meetings.'

He whispers back, 'I wanted to say "we gave you Beethoven, you gave us bombs".'

She suppresses a giggle.

'I don't suppose we will be invited back.'

Erik spends another night beside the *Kachelöfen* and Helen falls into a deep sleep in which images of her husband in the arms of Svetlana return to haunt her.

## 28

*Maman* returns to Scotland a few days later, and Luisa reluctantly leaves Helen and young Karl in Bonn, but only after Helen promises to seek her help if necessary. Luisa has been no more successful than Helen in extracting information regarding her son's whereabouts from the colonel.

*Maman* faced a long and arduous journey to Scotland, but Colonel Oakley arranges for her to be taken by plane to London, from where she can take the train to Berwick-upon-Tweed. *Maman* has never flown before and is nervous at the prospect, but Helen assures her that she will be in safe hands.

'You met George, just think of the number of flights he had to make.'

'That is how you met, his airplane crashed.'

They both laugh. There is time for another embrace before *Maman* is taken to the airfield by Iain.

Helen attends lectures in spite of her nausea, but Erik will not permit her to join him at the camp; she cannot risk another threatened miscarriage of the baby. Erik hopes to specialise in Obstetrics and Gynaecology when he graduates, as his father did. Neither of his parents has been granted permission to practise and this is worrying him. He left for Poland in 1939 and, excepting two short periods of leave, he did not return to his home until 1945. He was captured at Bastogne, along with General von Werstein, and spent months as a prisoner of the Americans. He was well treated by them and feels his war ended well. He survived the Russian Front, which he attributes to luck and the courage and ingenuity of his *Kommandant*. Due to being a prisoner of war, he did not have to face further action in the East.

He tells Helen he owes his life to her husband as they sit together by the *Kachelöfen*. He now stays at her apartment three or four nights a week, but this is conditional on him sleeping apart from her, which he honours. She is grateful for his company and has assured him she values his friendship and very much enjoyed him as a lover. She blushes as she makes this admission; she knows it to be true.

# PART EIGHT


## Erik

## 30

Normandy, 1940 – Bonn, 1946

I had been captivated by her long before the day I was ordered to drive her to the church in Caen. On that day, she was still recovering from the infection that had brought her to the point of death by the time we arrived in the deep snow of late December 1941. I understood she and the general were to marry.

It was no secret among our division that the general had become enamoured of the *schöne fräulein*, and we watched how their love flourished through the music they played together. On the one hand, we had been pleased for him; we knew his wife to be dying in a clinic in Berlin and also knew him to be an honourable man. After the Polish campaign, he returned to care for his wife, while other officers and soldiers enjoyed the fruits of victory, which included beautiful women eager to satisfy their sexual desires. While we were not surprised by his restraint at the beginning of our time at the *château*, we were astonished by *her* lack of awareness of the effect she had on men. It was not only her beauty and her hair, which was revealed to be a rare shade of red-gold, but that she was kind to all and worked hard to make our occupation comfortable.

We were forced to look elsewhere in the town to satisfy our needs for female company, and there were plenty of young women eager to bed with us. We were young and healthy, and their men, if not dead on the battlefield, were either captive or bitter and half-famished. Despite what is said, we did not have to bribe the girls of the town with luxuries. They were not drawn to us as the victors or considered by us as the spoils of war. In many cases, true affection developed between us and these women. My sadness is for the treatment meted out to them when the Allies took control of France. The women were abused by their own countrymen, who shaved their hair and stripped them naked to be spat on and exiled from their towns and villages. They were young women who looked for love. They did not betray their country, and they did not deliver up their neighbours to the *gendarmes* to be deported to the camps. I will remain angry for all my life when I remember those joyful young women, who wanted to keep company with us and were made to suffer for it, while the *gendarmes* and collaborators, who delivered the Jews and *Résistants* to the *Gestapo*, escaped punishment.

I realised that *Fräulein Gabrielle* was no ordinary French girl with a talent for music when I overheard the general call her by the name I now know to be her true name, Helen. They spoke in English together as they walked in the woods; she was still weak from the infection and he had put his army coat around her to keep her warm. She leaned into him, as though his body close to hers gave her the strength she required to live.

She did not appear to be surprised when I spoke to her in English that day at the church. She had begun to weep, and it was as I helped her into the staff car that we spoke. So it was a great pleasure to meet her in Bonn on the day of registration at the university. It was not only her beauty which struck me that day but her vulnerability. I had never doubted her courage; I had suspected that *Fräulein Gabrielle* had other roles besides that of housekeeper, and later as mistress of the general at the *château*. I had noted her frequent disappearances at night and watched her come and go from the woods. But I respected my general's acquiescence in her activities; I too would protect her if necessary. But on that glittering early autumn day, when the trees of Venusberg were already touched by the gold and red tints which would deepen during the coming months, I felt not only desire but also the urge to defend and protect.

The time we made love was unlike any other of my many sexual experiences. She was a married woman, and knowing of my general's previous lovers, she would have learned much from him: how to enjoy a man and give pleasure accordingly. She was gentle and compliant with my every desire, allowing me to take my pleasure until her passion equalled my own. Later, she slept in my arms. I watched over her until daybreak and knew I could never let her go.

When she informed me she was again pregnant by her husband and that we could not repeat what had been between us the previous night, I cannot deny my disappointment and sadness; but my determination to protect her remained as strong as ever.

My parents were a concern for me. As their eldest son, I had always felt a responsibility to honour and obey them and set an example for my younger siblings. I came home after many years of absence from the family while I fought for the Fatherland, and felt they were strangers to me. They were angry and bitter at the loss of our beautiful home by the Rhine. Many Germans had to endure this, and many had lost their sons and other family members in the war. They were angered by the British authority's refusal to permit them to resume their profession. They had been interviewed twice and subjected to the *Fragebogen* but had been told further investigation was necessary.

It was my youngest sister, twelve-year-old Hildegarde, who betrayed them. My parents were in a park close to our apartment with my brothers. I had stayed at home to study my lecture notes and care for my sister who was unwell. She came into the bedroom I shared with my brothers wearing the brown jacket and navy-blue necktie of the *Bund Deutscher Mädel*, the swastika emblem clearly visible on the sleeve. She explained that the jacket had belonged to our sister Hannelore and she had wished to try it on. She herself had never owned one, but her sister had worn it to school and at rallies. I asked where she had found the jacket, and she took me to a cupboard in our parents' bedroom. There was a wooden chest with a key in its lock. Hildegarde explained that this chest was normally locked and the key hidden. Father had been looking for something in the chest but had been called by *Mutti* to join her on the walk, and in his haste had left the chest unlocked. I looked inside and saw the Hitler Youth uniforms my two brothers had worn and under these a folder of papers: my parents' Nazi Party membership documents, as well as copies of their applications to join. Each application, dated March 1939, included an extensive genealogy of my parents' antecedents to prove the purity of their Aryan heritage.

I took out the papers, arranged them on the dining table, and awaited their return.

## 31

November 1946
Bonn, Germany

I asked my parents to close the door on my younger siblings while I confronted them with the evidence of their deceit.

*Mutti* started to cry but I had no patience with her.

'You and Father took me from my medical studies to fight in a war that set a world against itself at the cost of millions of lives. I would have preferred to have remained a student and become qualified to save some of those lives. You lied to me, you lied to the *Fragebogen*, and the British have doubtless uncovered your lies. You do not deserve to be doctors, you belong with those of *AktionT4*, delivering your patients up to be murdered because they were not useful to your society.'

By now I felt such anger that I could have killed my parents. They had lied to me, and by their deceit made me part of what they are, Nazis who deny ever having been Nazis, who had cheered and saluted the absurd figure responsible for the loss of millions of innocent lives and the destruction of our world. My parents are the same Nazis who are part of the collective German victim narrative; they were under Hitler's spell and cannot be blamed for what happened. They believe they can distance themselves from those who forcibly removed their Jewish neighbours from their homes, while they looked on. They never questioned where their neighbours were taken or why they did not return. Perhaps they were among those who looted the vacated apartments of Jews or took part in the auctioning of their belongings. They encouraged me to fight for my country when I would have preferred to remain a student. The fact they bemoaned the loss of our lovely home made me even angrier; they deserved everything that had befallen them.

My father tried to explain but it was my mother who found the words.

'We had no choice. By 1939, both of us were threatened with removal from our positions at the university hospital unless we joined the party. Hitler was riding high on his successes in duping the British about his intentions, despite the annexation of Austria and Sudetenland, and then all of Czechoslovakia. We had five children to consider, their futures. Yes, we sacrificed you, as our eldest son and of fighting age, but we did so praying that you would survive, as you did, while others with the same hopes never saw their sons again. We thank God for your survival.'

'Do not bring God into this. Where was your God in Poland, at Stalingrad and Kursk, in the camps, in the cells of the *Gestapo*, the *Ustashe*, and wherever else Hitler's poison spread? You do not know this, but Helen was tortured by monsters such as those you supported.'

'We did no more than apply for the papers to join and we were accepted. Your brothers and older sister were made to wear the uniforms at a few parades, nothing more; Hildegarde was too young. Please tell us how we can make this right between us.'

'You can take the Nazi party papers to the British tomorrow and burn the uniforms in the *Kachelöfen* tonight.'

It was past midnight when I let myself into Helen's apartment. She was sleeping with her son beside her in the bed. I did not disturb them.

# PART NINE


## Helen

## 32

November 1946
Bonn, Germany

The mailbox contains a large brown envelope. There is no postmark on the envelope and her name has been written in bold capitals, doubtless to conceal the identity of the sender. She shakes the contents of the envelope, six photographs, onto the small table in the kitchen. All of them reveal her husband on a bed with a woman; both are naked and in a variety of coital positions. She looks more closely at the photographs and recognises the woman as one of the women from Alsace who regularly came to lunch at the *château;* the one who had been particularly arrogant and peremptory. Helen had never been introduced to either woman, so they remain nameless.

She immediately vomits into the sink and then collapses in despair onto her bed. She has received no news of her husband and now it seems he betrayed her with this woman. She is certain the photographs were taken during their time in Normandy.

After a while, she ceases sobbing and miraculously, or so it seems to her, the baby makes its first fluttering movements inside her; Papa would have described these as "bubbles in the porridge", and this causes a shift in her thoughts. Whoever sent these photographs had a particular motive; it is not by chance they have arrived at this time. It is over two years since Karl left the Château des Tilleuls; sufficient time for the person who held

155

the photographs to send them to her.

She decides to go immediately to Allied High Command and confront Major Harrison, her husband's interrogator; there is no point in going to Colonel Oakley. She asks Magda to care for her son and fetches her bicycle from the rack in the hallway. It is bitterly cold, and frost and fog grip the late afternoon air.

The darkness is thickening as she reaches the austere building, and she remembers that she has no lamp on her bicycle for the return journey. The building is guarded by "Tommies" and she has difficulty gaining entry as a special pass is required. She is not deterred and informs them that Helen Douglas von Werstein demands to speak to Major Harrison and she is prepared to die of cold outside the building if she is not admitted. As she says this, she opens her coat to reveal the swell of her pregnancy. She hazards a guess they will think she is a hysterical woman who has come to claim her rights from the father of her child. Two of the guards are sniggering while another does her bidding; this is too much of an opportunity for some barrack bar-room ribaldry at Major Harrison's expense. Before long, the guard reappears.

'You are to follow me, miss.'

The air inside is fuggy with cigarette smoke and sweat; the building must be the warmest in all of Bonn.

The major dismisses the young soldier, and before Helen has a chance to speak, informs her, 'If you have come to ask about your husband you can leave immediately. It has been made abundantly clear to you by Colonel Oakley that we cannot inform you of his whereabouts.'

'I am here to ask you about these.'

She leans forward and tips the photographs onto his desk. He drops back into his chair and indicates that she should sit down on the one opposite. He is clearly bewildered, more than bewildered, infuriated, by what she has brought to him.

'How and when did you obtain these?'

'They were in my mailbox this afternoon.'

'You were not meant to receive these photographs, certainly not at the present time.'

'I will not leave your office and I will cause an embarrassing scene of the like you have never witnessed in a woman unless you tell me what is going on. Do not forget, Major Harrison, that I too have signed the Official Secrets Act; you and Colonel Oakley need to respect this more than you have so far in our acquaintance.'

Her temper is rising and she is struggling to maintain her cool, inwardly at least. The major offers her a cigarette, which she refuses with a look of disdain. He picks up his telephone and asks his secretary to bring him the Von Werstein file.

By the time she takes her leave of the major, who has organised a military vehicle to convey Helen and the bicycle to her apartment, she has been apprised of her husband's mission, but also of the fact that none in British Intelligence are aware of his location at the present time. She understands that the photographs and her husband's affair with Adalie Franck, the woman in the photographs, pre-date his arrival at the Château des Tilleuls. She knows that Franck was captured in Italy in January 1946 and handed to the British who gave her the choice of the hangman's noose, on account of her activities in the SD, or to work for British Intelligence. She does not believe that her husband and Franck will be returning Otto Altmann, a former SS concentration camp commander, to the justice he deserves. She knows from Erik that former war criminals such as Altmann are only actively hunted down when they are useful to the Allies. If her husband has been blackmailed into assisting Adalie Franck, he could well be falling into a trap, compromising his life as well as his integrity.

She detests the network of deceit that has evolved since the end of the war. She is surprised Major Harrison does not, or so it seems, suspect that a person within his own organisation could have sent the photographs to her.

Later, as she soothes her son to sleep, she wonders if his life, as well as her own and that of her unborn child, could be at risk. Her husband is a soldier, courageous and resourceful. For the moment she can only hope he survives whatever he encounters in the pursuit of Altmann. She will need to speak again to Harrison.

Erik does not return to the apartment. She misses his company more than she cares to admit to herself. Her anxiety for her son deepens and she brings him into the bed with her. She will ask Harrison for a gun.

# 33

Helen awakes to the smell of *Arme Ritter*. Her son is not beside her in the bed but at the kitchen table where Erik is making "soldiers" of the fried egg and milk-soaked bread for him. She has regained her appetite and is happy to be served two thick slices. She teases him that German men are better cooks than Scotsmen and remembers the meal her husband prepared for her at the *château*; the diffidence and insecurity she felt then are in contrast to the easy confidence and happiness she has with Erik. She realises she is in love with him.

Erik leaves before Iain arrives to take her to the university and young Karl to the nursery, but they have time to talk about the events of the previous day. Erik informs her that his parents will be visiting the *Fragebogen* office today. He tells her of his discovery and confrontation with his parents. They may now face a military tribunal. He hopes this does not alter her trust in him or their friendship in any way. She knows no other way of demonstrating that their friendship is unchanged than by putting her arms around him and kissing him tenderly on the lips with a restraint that she finds difficult; all the while considering if she can influence Major Harrison to ensure his parents have their medical degrees validated.

Helen leaves the university during the midday break. She has arranged for Iain to collect her and drive her to Allied Command.

With Iain's help, she circumvents the security detail outside the building and makes her way to Major Harrison's office. She does not wait to be invited to be seated but draws up the chair opposite him and demands his attention.

'Surely you have considered the possibility that the photographs were sent at this time to compromise the mission my husband is engaged in. It is two years since he left our home in Normandy. There have been other opportunities for the owner of those photographs to embarrass and humiliate my husband and cause me distress. Have you considered that someone in your organisation sent the photographs? Someone who is not content to have Altmann in British hands, and able to reveal his secrets, whatever they may be.'

'Altmann is a war criminal and will be tried in a court of law for his crimes.'

She smiles at this.

'You have not answered my question. Do you believe you have a "mole" in your organisation? As for the other, Altmann will not face justice. I know of "Operation Paperclip". The Americans spirited away those useful to their government and they now live as free men in Texas, irrespective of their crimes. I know there are those who are quickly forgiven and those who will not be forgiven, depending on their usefulness, of course.'

'It has crossed my mind that the timing of the delivery of the photographs was unfortunate... and inopportune.'

'Please do not talk in riddles. You know perfectly well, or you should, that my husband's mission is now compromised by others who are equally anxious to get Altmann, and to forgive his crimes as quickly.'

This has clearly resonated with the major and angered him.

'I can have you removed from this office at any time, young woman.'

'And if you do, I shall no longer feel obligated by the Official Secrets Act.'

'I could have you branded a traitor for what you are threatening.'

Helen feels a sudden calm descend on her. She has the major exactly where she wants him.

'You forget that I also hold French citizenship, as Gabrielle Doucet, born in Lisieux in 1920. I still have my identity papers to prove it. Furthermore, there exists the marriage certificate, proof of my marriage to a German citizen by the name of General Karl von Werstein, which happily for me has finally been located in the archives of Caen *Mairie*. A copy of this marriage certificate rests with my uncle and aunt in Normandy. It could be argued that I hold citizenship for both France and Germany. You would find yourself in quite a dilemma, a pickle as you would say, if you tried to have me arrested for treason. It could provoke a great deal of bad publicity for the British Occupation, not to mention a deterioration in your relations with the French and the Germans, your much-needed future military and trading partners.'

The major's face has gone from puce to the shade of an unripe Camembert cheese. He has smoked at least three cigarettes since she entered his office. It is clear to Helen that he has never been spoken to in this way, certainly not by a woman.

'You have been talking too much to your friend Erik, or whatever he is to you.'

'While we are on the subject of Erik, our relationship is no business of yours, or indeed of the gossips among the military wives. His parents will have visited the *Fragebogen* office this morning and admitted to having joined the Nazi party in 1939, to safeguard their family which included young children. Their involvement in the party was negligible. I expect them to be fully reinstated as doctors, and most certainly not face a military tribunal. Please make a note of this.'

She waits while the major writes down their names and lights another cigarette, then she continues.

'I believe you have at least one Soviet agent in your intelligence organisation. This person wants to halt the British pursuit of Altmann and thought that by sending the photographs to me, you would no longer have leverage on my husband. This person knew the address to send the photographs. I could suggest that the person who sent the photographs is someone who also knows that my husband is more capable of achieving the capture of Altmann than your own agents.'

'If you have any information that could jeopardise British Intelligence, you are bound to reveal it.'

'As a French citizen married to a German, I am not bound to reveal anything to you. Please stop threatening me; I am tired of threats and lies.'

'Tell me what you want.'

'For the moment, a gun. I fear for my life and that of my children, born and unborn.' She takes a moment to draw attention to the swelling of her pregnancy. 'I fear they may be in danger, and in the absence of my husband it is up to me to protect them.'

'Do you know how to use a gun? Have you ever used one?'

She resists the opportunity to laugh.

'My dear major, regardless of what you and the good women of the British Women's Association may wish to believe, I did not spend the war years opening my legs to any passing German soldier, the higher the rank the better. You may or may not have read my war record, but the facts are that I killed three men in cold blood, two of them with a gun. I also killed a female enemy agent with a knife and shot two *Gestapo* officers as they attempted to arrest those I was protecting.'

She can read his mind; he does not wish to speculate on the death of the third man.

'If you do not provide me with a gun, I will either have to steal one or find other ways to protect my family. Living as I do among the *Trümmerfrauen*, I know that everything can be bartered for, that everything has its price.'

## 34

Helen now has a gun, an Enfield No. 2 revolver and a supply of cartridges. The gun is lightweight and perfect for rapid action at short range. She keeps it under the mattress of her bed at night and concealed in her "peggybag" by day. She does not reveal it to Erik.

Erik informs her that his parents have now been cleared by the *Fragebogen* and have positions at the hospital in Bonn, with pay and seniority reinstated. She congratulates him on his honesty with his parents and says nothing of her part in this.

It is now December, and she is in the second trimester of her pregnancy. She has an appointment at the British Military Hospital and has been introduced to the midwife who will assist in the delivery of her baby. Helen has requested a home delivery as she wants the baby to be truly born in Germany, not in a British hospital, under a British flag. According to the doctor, the baby will be born in May and Luisa has tried to persuade her to come to Schloss Mariendistel for the birth. Much as Helen loves Luisa, she does not wish to spend the final weeks of her pregnancy with her if her husband cannot also be there. If Karl is lost to her, she would prefer to be with Erik; she would be in safe hands as Erik has now delivered nine babies at the camp and all are thriving.

Major Harrison has assured her that the search has begun for the mole within Allied command. The mole would be part of the

Soviet espionage network, the NKGB, which is responsible for countering British and American efforts to acquire useful Nazis. The Soviets have already secured the talents of a group of four nuclear physicists, whose expertise would give them superiority in the weapons that wreaked such destruction on the cities of Nagasaki and Hiroshima in 1945.

She understands that Altmann's use to the Soviets and the British lies in his knowledge of rocket technology; he had worked with Wernher von Braun at Mittelbau, the same Von Braun who is now working for the Americans. Altmann had been in command of the Mittelbau-Dora Concentration Camp where her friend, Leah, and the group who had stayed in her apartment had been beaten, starved and worked as slaves. Altmann had also been deputy commander at Sachsenhausen Concentration camp from 1940 to 1943 and had been notorious for his brutality. Altmann will probably hope to escape to Argentina, where the fascist government of Juan Perón is welcoming Nazis escaping justice. The point of exit for these Nazi fugitives is through the port of Genoa. Altmann would be accompanied by others of no interest to the Allies and unaware that a trap was being set for him. British Intelligence is now certain that NKGB agents, alerted to her husband's mission by the mole, will be at the port waiting to intercept her husband and Franck and to snatch Altmann. Karl and Franck would be delivering him into their hands and would then doubtless be killed. She knows that the Catholic Church plays a significant role in aiding the escape of Nazi war criminals; various safe houses are provided on a route through Austria and over the Alps into Italy. The Vatican views Communism as a greater threat to religion than National Socialism; money will change hands and tickets to Argentina will be provided.

Helen considers all of this as she waits in the examination room at the hospital, and it seems possible that Svetlana has a role in this. Svetlana knew Leon would reveal her words. The mole would have informed Svetlana that her former lover was on a mission for the British which could cost him his life. She would know of the photographs which were being held to ensure his compliance. She would not want to stop the operation, thereby betraying her NKGB colleagues and her country, but she would know where to have the photographs sent. It was a warning; perhaps she expects Helen to find a way to protect her husband while ensuring that Altmann is transferred into Soviet hands. Nevertheless, her husband is falling into a trap and Svetlana's warning will not be enough unless he can be alerted.

Helen does not understand why Altmann would wish to escape to Argentina. By now he would be aware that his former colleagues are safely in the USA and all has to do is surrender to the British or the Americans; his war crimes would be overlooked in exchange for his expertise, as other Nazis before him. She ignores the calls and rebukes from the nurses, puts on her clothing and leaves the examination room and the hospital. She walks to Allied Command and Major Harrison. She will find a way to get a warning to her husband, to save his life and deliver Altmann into British hands.

She explains her suspicions to Major Harrison and asks him to arrange a telephone call to Caen, to the church of Église Saint-Pierre.

'And why this particular church?'

'The priest there is a former prisoner in Sachsenhausen. He was also a *Résistant* and has been a good friend to me. He suffered Altmann's brutality, and while I am sure he would not wish Altmann to escape justice, he would not wish my husband to be harmed. Karl knew who I was sheltering at the *château*.'

'I have read your file.'

'And *Père* François will be able to identify Altmann I am sure.

I am anxious we may be out of time. Perhaps Altmann is already at Genoa and the trap has been set.'

'We have dispatched agents to the route Franck and your husband may be taking and there has been no sighting of either of them. We believe Altmann is still on the run and that they are following him.'

'Could your agents not warn my husband?'

'That would compromise their identities; even I am not a party to that information.'

'Please make the call.'

They speak in French, and it is a pleasure to speak to her old friend. Despite his age and suffering at Sachsenhausen, he is well. The church is still to be restored but enough of it exists for mass to be said at least once a day. She explains that she is bound by secrecy and cannot fully reveal the reason for her request.

She asks him if he has any contacts in the port of Genoa, perhaps a priest he knows who could help in a certain situation. He admits that for the moment he does not but will think about it and would need more information. She places her hand over the receiver and asks Harrison if she can give him more details; she will have to tell him about Altmann and Harrison has to trust him.

Harrison nods in assent and she continues.

'Do you remember a commander at Sachsenhausen by the name of Altmann?'

'I remember him. He had moved to a camp elsewhere by the time I was imprisoned there, but he came from time to time to Sachsenhausen to select prisoners to be transferred to another camp, those prisoners who looked fit enough to work.'

'Would you be able to identify him?'

'Yes, despite his brutality, he still professed to be a Catholic. When he was told I was a Catholic priest, he asked if I would say mass with him. I refused; he was not in a state of grace, and I would not make such a mockery of my vocation. I remember his left hand. He took off his gloves to slap me across the face with his bare hands and I saw he had the stump of a sixth finger on his left hand. I am sure he tries to keep this hidden, but I would know him again, whatever his disguise.'

'Altmann is attempting to escape justice and it is believed he is travelling to Genoa. My husband is following him to get him into British custody, but it is a trap and my husband needs to be warned, otherwise he could be killed... by others who also seek to catch Altmann.'

'I understand this situation. You do not need to explain more. Just tell me what I should warn your husband.'

'If it is possible, he should be told that he must beware of...'

She thinks quickly, 'The bears, the Russian bears.'

He understands.

'Leave it with me and I will do what I can.'

## 35

December 1946
Genoa, Italy

The *Locanda La Rondine* is close to the port. When the big ships arrive and leave, guests can hear the waves lapping furiously against the harbour wall. The small family hotel is not taking bookings at this time; the rooms will be taken by family members arriving to celebrate *Natale*. Maria-Costanza, the proprietor, has tasked her eldest son, Alessio, with decorating the windows with festive lights while she plucks a goose and boils onions for the sauce which will accompany it. She is interrupted by the ring of the telephone. The caller asks for Alessio and the voice is not Italian. Maria is never happy when *stranieri* call; it reminds her of the days when her son was on the run from the *Gestapo* and she feared every knock on the door and ring of the telephone. Those days are over, and her son has returned from the camps. He suffers from tuberculosis and his body bears the scars of beatings and torture, but he is alive. She wishes for a peaceful life. She no longer attends her local *chièsa*, not since she discovered the priest of the church is helping fugitive Nazis escape on the ships that leave the port to travel to Buenos Aires. She now goes up to the hills above the port, to the church at Marisi. The priest there had been sympathetic to the partisans and never assisted the Nazi thugs who killed her youngest son and tortured and imprisoned her eldest.

She is tempted to cut the caller off, but the voice is kindly and very polite. He speaks Italian well, but not as an Italian, and most certainly not as a German. So she calls Alessio to the phone.

The call does not take long and soon Alessio has returned to the decorations. The only words she heard him utter were "*Va bene, saremo pronti per loro*". She will not ask who her son will be waiting for.

Far away in the ruins of a once magnificent church in Caen, an elderly priest prays at the altar that what he asked to be done will be achieved. Alessio and his friends will be watching the port. All he can do is to pray for Helen. She has suffered enough, and Altmann should answer for his crimes. He and Alessio are witnesses to them.

## 36

27<sup>th</sup> of December 1946
Bonn, Germany

Helen's peggybag no longer holds the gun. She has rifled through the lecture notes in her satchel, and in a panic tips them onto the snow-covered flower beds. It is early evening and now dark; another bitterly cold winter has Europe in its grip. Apart from Christmas Eve and Christmas Day, there has been no break in the university semester; so much study time was lost to the war years, and the country needs doctors.

She shivers despite her warm coat, and her feet are numb as the cold seeps through the soles of her boots. Erik has already left for the camp, and she is awaiting collection by Iain, who is now over an hour late. She felt sure someone had been following her as she walked from the university building to the place where Iain would pull over and collect her, with her son on the seat behind him. She wants the gun in her hands, to be able to protect herself and her family, and it is not here.

She is certain she took the gun from under the mattress that morning and placed it as usual among papers and a ball of wool in her peggybag. Perhaps pregnancy is making her forgetful, but no, she remembers how careful she was to remove the gun from its night place without her son or Erik observing. She considers if at any time her bag was not with her, either across her shoulder or on her chair in the lecture theatre. Erik had been seated next to her, as always. He did not know of the gun or did he? If so, he could have taken it from under her mattress, if he knew about it. It does not make sense. Then she remembers: she and Erik had been called to assist the lecturer, one she had not seen before, in demonstrating percussion and auscultation in a patient with pneumonia. Another student had moved into Erik's seat.

She realises she has been betrayed. Cold fear grips her heart and her hands are shaking as she gathers up her papers and folders. She is in mortal danger and needs to escape. But someone emerges from the bushes behind her and places a cloth over her face.

She is at the hospital in Berwick where *Maman* has agreed for her to have her tonsils removed. She is sitting on a bench with other children from the village school in Foulden; all are anxious about the procedure. *Maman* has assured her she will have no more of the painful sore throats that have afflicted her since she was a very young child; all the children have been told the procedure will be painless because they will be asleep.

It is the sweet, antiseptic smell of the chloroform she remembers when she wakes up on the hard floor of a prison cell. She is cold and hungry and has no way of telling what time of day it is. She worries about her son, but she knows that whatever happens to her, Iain and Morag will take care of him. She then considers her unborn child, whether the chloroform could have damaged her. She has decided the baby is a girl; this pregnancy has been so different from that of her first. She feels around her lower abdomen, the baby is moving gently inside her. She needs to urinate and notices there is a bucket in the corner of the cell. She relieves herself there, and as she does so the door opens and Harrison enters. She is certain he has timed this visit to cause her maximum embarrassment. She rearranges her clothing and stands up to face him.

'Where am I and why have I been brought here?'

'You are at the Combined Services Detailed Interrogation Centre, at Bad Nenndorf, a department of the British War Office. As to why you are here, it is for you to tell us what you know of the killing of one of our agents in Genoa and the escape of Altmann. You are accused of spying on the Allies for an enemy power, the Soviet Union.'

'That is ridiculous. I have been assisting you in your hunt for Altmann. It was me who first suggested you had a Soviet spy in your organisation. I claim my rights as a citizen of France and of Britain to be released at once.'

'My dear Miss Douglas or whatever you call yourself, you have no rights here. We can do as we wish to get the information we require. We wanted Altmann and we are certain you assisted in his disappearance, we believe, into the hands of the Soviets.'

'You are no better than the *Gestapo*.'

'Then you will know our methods. As I told you, I have read your file.'

'And what of my husband?'

'He has disappeared along with Altmann and a known Soviet agent. At this time, as you have been made aware by your friend Erik, we are not interested in capturing Nazis to punish them, but to use their knowledge and expertise. We believe war with the Soviets is only months away and we need information on Soviet military intentions. Those who we feel can give us this intelligence are brought here, and that includes your... friend Erik.'

'So you have Erik. Does he know I am here?'

'Of course, and he is all the more likely to talk when he knows of your torture and is made to witness it.'

'You will also be harming my unborn child.'

'We do not concern ourselves with the brats of a whore and a spy.'

'I am neither and well you know it. And what of my child?

Where is my son?'

'He is with a foster family and will be put up for adoption if necessary.'

She knows that he means in the event of her death. She wants to beg and plead with him, if only for the sake of her son, but she knows it will not help her situation. There will be no Rommel to come to her rescue or husband to care for her if she survives. She is utterly defenceless and without hope.

They come for her during the night. She has been given nothing to eat. An enamel jug, chipped and stained, was passed to her through the wicket hours after her incarceration; the water in it had a musty metallic taste and she had to force herself to drink it.

The interrogation room is in the basement of the building. Harrison is seated at a desk and beside him sits a doctor; she assumes him to be a doctor by his white coat. Two guards, one of them female, stand on either side of the desk and they move to place her on the chair opposite Harrison when she enters the room. There is a bath in the corner of the room. She knows its purpose. She has suffered this before; these people really are no better than the *Gestapo*.

She is asked for her name and when she gives it as *Frau* Helen von Werstein she receives the first blow to her face, from the woman.

'You were the whore of Werstein. The marriage certificate you boasted about is in the name of a French woman.'

'I was never a whore. My file acknowledges my marriage and you know it.'

She receives another blow to her face, this time from the male soldier. As he administers the blow the woman drags her by her hair over the back of the chair.

'Now what is your name?'

She repeats her married name and further blows are directed at the side of her face. She feels her teeth loosening and blood is gushing from the side of her mouth. The chair is suddenly pulled from beneath her and she collapses onto the floor. She rolls onto her side to protect her abdomen and the fragile life inside her, and receives a blow to her back as she does so. Then there is blackness.

When she regains consciousness, she is in her cell and lying on the cold floor. A filthy blanket has been placed over her and blood is oozing from her mouth. She tentatively feels her abdomen; the baby is moving within her. She feels around her jaw, her teeth are still there but her face is excruciatingly painful to touch.

It is dark when they come for her again. She has received no food since they returned her to the cell, but she would have found it difficult to eat as her jaw aches and her tongue is swollen and numb. This time Erik is brought into the room. His face is badly bruised and one arm hangs loosely by his side. They tear the clothes from her body and take her to the bath. Her hands are pulled tightly behind her back while they force her head under the water. Erik protests and she can hear the blows he receives for doing so. On this occasion the question has changed. They ask her about the whereabouts of a Russian woman, Svetlana Zharovskaya. Through gasps of breath, she informs them that she has no idea, the woman was in Berlin, in the Soviet sector, at some time last year, but she has never met her. The woman helped her stepson pass into the British sector. That is all she knows of her.

Again her arms are dragged behind her back and she is under water. She knows she is drowning because the old memory of the sea pool at Berwick returns, with *Maman* and Papa encouraging her efforts to keep afloat and to swim like a fish. She is falling asleep, just as her friend Robby described when he was drowning. She is deeply asleep, or so it seems until she hears a voice exclaim "this has gone too far. We are not here to murder her and the child within her".

She awakens on a mattress in a room with two other women. One of them comes to her when she opens her eyes.

'They will leave you to recover here until they start on you again. We have suffered the same.'

The woman speaks to her in German and explains she is from Poland. Her name is Ilona and she was arrested at a refugee camp three weeks ago. Her family died at Auschwitz-Birkenau, where she was taken along with other Jews from Łódź in 1940. She had survived the forced march from the camp, the beatings by the SS guards and starvation, and had joined others to go west, where they were told they would be well treated by the Americans and the British. Instead, she and others were accused of being communists and spies for the Soviets.

'Our German tormentors live as free men and women while we who have suffered so much are made to suffer again.'

Helen tells her some of her own story, but it is difficult as her mouth is swollen and her tongue is split. Her whole body aches. She feels her abdomen, there is no movement; she fears they have killed her baby.

She makes to stand up, to check if she has any bleeding. As she does so, she notices there is a window above the bed. Through the window she can see men shuffling around a yard; they are emaciated as in the photographs she has seen of the inmates of Bergen-Belsen, and as Leah was when she found her in the hospital at Koblenz.

Ilona explains, 'They are suffering as in the camps, but it is British soldiers and not the SS in command of them. Only the name is different but the tortures are the same. After a few weeks here you will be as I am.'

Ilona's clothes hang in rags around her wasted body, the bones of her hips and sternum clearly visible through her thin tunic. Helen has been dressed in a similar garment and she has been given underwear. There is no bleeding, and as she moves she feels a gentle flutter deep inside her. She falls back on the bed, exhausted but relieved.

Later a bowl of food is brought to her by an orderly; the woman cannot be a nurse as she wears a soiled tunic over her everyday clothes. She places the bowl on the end of the mattress out of Helen's reach, and Helen gently requests that it be brought closer to her as she cannot move easily. She has spoken politely but the woman turns on her.

'*Yeh* never learned no manners, did *yeh?* What about a "please" or did *yeh* traitor parents not teach *yeh* how *teh* speak.'

Helen feels her anger rising.

'I asked as nicely as possible. It was not necessary to add the word "please". And my parents are not traitors. They are good people and well-educated. At least they can speak their own language correctly, as you do not.'

The woman responds by pouring Helen's food, a thin porridge, over the mattress and struts out of the room.

Ilona comes to Helen and shares some of her meal with her.

'It does no good to get on the wrong side of that one. She knows her power. She can make our lives even more difficult if we cross her.'

Helen does not sleep that night. It is cold, and every footstep she hears she believes to be the approach of guards to take her for further torture. The bedclothes are thin and are now wet and sticky from the porridge. At least there is water. Ilona helped her to a small lavatory at the end of the room where there is a basin and a cold water tap. The water tasted fresh and she drank all she could. She has large areas of bruising over every part of her body except her abdomen. Her baby must be protected.

The woman on the other mattress has not moved since Helen

arrived. She asks Ilona about her and is told that she is from East Germany and arrived at the refugee camp at the same time as she did. She was arrested with her as both had been overheard speaking a language that sounded Russian.

'The Germans in the east can speak a form of Polish and we were discussing the Soviets, but only that they had taken over our land and we did not wish to live under their rule. The British are useless at languages; they believe everyone in the world should speak English.'

'And many can't even do that correctly.' She explains the exchange of words she'd had with the orderly.

Early the following morning, they come for her again. On this occasion, Harrison pushes a paper towards her and orders her to sign it.

Through her painful mouth, Helen asks what she is signing.

'It is an admission of your participation in an act of sabotage, namely, permitting an enemy agent to obtain access to classified information and enabling the escape of a war criminal.'

'What enemy agent and what classified information? And as for the war criminal, you planned to use him to your own advantage. He would have enjoyed all the privileges of a top scientist and never answered for his crimes. I will not sign it.'

'Your friend, Erik, has already done so and has been freed.'

'You are a liar. Erik would not do such a thing.'

Harrison nods to the guards behind her and she is again taken to the bathtub; the water is streaked with blood, this could be her own or Erik's. She assumes he has been subjected to the same treatment.

She refuses to sign the paper and is left choking on the floor beside the bath as she tries to cough the water from her lungs. On this occasion, there is no doctor present. The female guard approaches her, and Helen instinctively rolls onto her side and curls into a ball. The woman's shoe hits her lumbar spine and Helen cries out with the shock of it.

While she is lying on the floor, a soldier enters the room and hands Harrison a piece of paper. He looks at it and then at Helen.

'Get her out of here.'

# PART TEN

## Erik

## 37

29<sup>th</sup>of December 1946
Bad Nenndorf, Germany


They took me as I was leaving my evening session at the camp. I was pushed into the backseat of a military vehicle and my hands were shackled to a soldier on either side. It was a journey of some hours and late in the night when we arrived at the town of Bad Nenndorf.

I knew the town well from my childhood. My grandmother suffered from arthritis and my parents took her there every year to bathe in the sulphur springs which gave her so much relief from her pains. We used to rent a villa close to the town and swim in the many bathing installations there. We avoided those supplied by the sulphur springs as we did not enjoy their pungent odour. Before the springs had become known for their healing power, people referred to the smell as "devil's excrement".

When I demanded to know the reason for my arrest they did not reply. I was taken to a cell where a man sat in chains. The cell was freezing and the only sanitation was a bucket in the corner of the room. I was not chained and immediately responded to the man's request to bring the bucket to him to relieve himself. He told me his name was Werner Mentel. He had been captured by the British at Rees at the end of March 1945 and was well treated as a prisoner of war. He was released from captivity in October of that year and returned to his home in Hannover, to discover that his wife and children had died in bombing raids. He moved in with an older brother who had returned from the Eastern Front after his release from imprisonment by the Soviets.

'That was why they took us. We were considered to have Soviet sympathies; why else would my brother have been released by them? The same twisted logic was applied to Russian soldiers returning from captivity; they were considered to be tainted by interaction with those of the "capitalist fascist West". Of course we were not communist sympathisers! After the war, we just wanted to mourn our families and make another life for ourselves. We had done our duty, obeyed the *Führer*, fought for the Fatherland and paid for the loss of his war in our grief and humiliation. But the British took us both. They said neighbours had reported seeing us in the company of known communists. It was as in the years of Hitler; neighbours spying on each other and reporting to the police. We rarely frequented bars; we had no money to do so and most of our friends and comrades were either dead or missing. Nevertheless, we were both arrested. We understand now that the Allies are no longer seeking Nazi war criminals but Soviet sympathisers.'

He went on to tell me his hands had been chained behind his back for up to sixteen days at a time, while his interrogators repeatedly punched him in the face. He had been imprisoned in this freezing cell throughout. It was common practice for his captors to douse him in cold water every 30 minutes, from 4.30 a.m. until midnight. His brother was now held in another cell; the British had discovered that comfort and solidarity were not conducive to extracting "confessions". He was occasionally able to communicate with his brother during exercise sessions in the yard. His brother had scars on his shins which he whispered were the result of torture with shin screws the British had retrieved from a *Gestapo* prison in Hamburg. Other men had been starved or beaten to death, died of illnesses or had lost toes and fingers due to frostbite. There were women here and they suffered the same.

None of this surprised me. It seemed not only was "All fair in love and war", but in victory too.

He asked me why I had been arrested. I could not admit it was due to my own folly in falling in love with a woman who might never be mine and whose life was now in danger through my own fault. I could not forgive myself.

I was recruited by the Americans at Bastogne, as were many of us who had been captured. We were treated well, but when the news of the Malmedy massacre reached our guards we sensed a change in their attitude towards us. Soon after, we heard of another massacre at a town called Chenogne, also in Belgium, in which around eighty captive German infantrymen had been machine-gunned by an American combat unit. We felt we had no choice; we could be next. The war was lost and the future could not be bleaker.

The Yanks were not interested in SS or fanatical Nazi supporters. They wanted educated Germans, who spoke English well; those who could be useful to them in peacetime.

The trial of my *Kommandant*, General von Werstein, was of interest to the Americans. He had been highly regarded by his captors as a courageous and honourable soldier. Before his tragic death, General Patton had written in my *Kommandant*'s defence for the trial in Nuremberg.

It was my *Kommandant*'s connection to the daughter of a high-ranking Russian general that interested them, the woman we had captured as she fought beside her comrades at Stalingrad. The *Kommandant* had taken her for his own and we did not begrudge him the pleasure. He had fought alongside us, taking the same risks as we did. He was a master of tactics, saving as many of his unit as possible in the bloodbath of Stalingrad while inflicting death and destruction on the Reds. She was beautiful and fought like a wild cat when we took her prisoner. Von Werstein saved her from the depravities many of my fellow soldiers would have inflicted on her. He kept her for over two weeks before negotiating a prisoner exchange with the Reds. They were well matched. He took her roughly as we often witnessed; there is little privacy at a battlefield command centre, even for a general, but she was equal to him. When she left, I knew it would not be the end for either of them.

On my release and return to Bonn, I was informed by my American "handler" that my former *Kommandant* and his wife, Helen, who was the same Gabrielle Doucet I had so admired at the Château des Tilleuls, would be living in the city and I should make their acquaintance as soon as possible. I was informed that she would be registering at the medical school in Bonn.

It was on a bright autumn day in 1946 that I saw her. I have always loved the season of autumn, the reds and golds of the trees, the sharper mornings and the mellowness of the afternoons. There are no false promises to autumn; not as in spring, when a spell of warm weather in February can deceive us into believing winter to be over, only for a cold wind from the east to bring the blue-grey snow fog which can linger until April. I was entranced by her again, and my only desire was to protect her.

Soon after that day, I was approached by another. The Soviets also had an interest in my *Kommandant*. The Allies were no longer concerned with hunting high-ranking Nazis, those responsible for the worst atrocities; now it was a race to capture those Nazis most useful to weapons research, in particular rocket technology and nuclear fission. For the Americans and the British, it was now the Soviets who were the enemy; Nazis could be useful allies.

The agent who approached me had buried deep into the Allies' intelligence structure from the early days of the war. He informed me of the mission my former *Kommandant* had been tasked with by the British; the capture of the former deputy commander of Mittelbau-Dora labour camp, Otto Altmann.

Altmann was guilty of war crimes at Mittelbau-Dora and other camps. He was also a renowned scientist, who had collaborated with Werhner von Braun in rocket technology research and nuclear fission with Manfred von Ardenne. He would be a useful Nazi to the British, who ostensibly sought to bring him to justice for his "crimes against humanity". The Soviets had secured Von Ardenne but wanted Altmann for his work with Von Braun.

Altmann was on the run, and with the help of Nazi sympathisers was making his way to the port of Genoa where he would take a ship to Buenos Aires. My *Kommandant* was travelling with a young female agent who knew the routes Altmann would take to the port. The woman, Adalie Franck, was a double agent, working for the British as an alternative to death by hanging, but who had also been "turned" to work for the Soviets. She knew the route Altmann would take, and my *Kommandant* would recognise and deal with Altmann. There were photographs held by the British which had been used to blackmail the *Kommandant* into undertaking the mission. If he refused or failed they would be sent to his wife. It would be useful if these photographs could be located and delivered to the wife as soon as possible. If my *Kommandant* were to be informed his wife had already received the photographs, he may not be so happy to cooperate with his British handlers and Adalie would ensure that Altmann was turned over to Soviet agents.

'And if I refuse to cooperate?'

'I will ensure your parents will never be permitted to practise as doctors and your *Kommandant's* interest in the daughter of a Soviet general will be made much of by the British and Americans. He will be treated as an enemy agent. I feel his wife will suffer more than he will.'

It was not difficult to locate the photographs; the official in British Command was careless with his keys and his secretary easily seduced. Of course, I knew where to send the photographs.

# PART ELEVEN


## Helen

## 38

January 1947
Bonn, Germany

Helen has been returned to her home and Erik is with her. Pavel is attending to their injuries and Helen is confident her baby has survived. Magda brings food for both; she is shocked by the bruising to Helen's face and more so when she is shown the bruising to her lower back. Helen assures her she will recover, that it is not the first time she has suffered in this way. At her request, Pavel has taken photographs of her injuries and of those inflicted on Erik; they will be useful evidence in her plans to avenge their mistreatment. Erik's arm had been broken in two places, but Pavel and a colleague have set it in plaster; he is more upset that it will be some time before he is able to resume his duties at the camp. Both will return to lectures immediately and attribute their injuries to a fall from their bicycles.

Iain is not convinced by this explanation.

'*Morag* was beside *hersel'* when they came to *tak wee* Karl *awa'*. She *wouldna'* hand him *ower ta* begin with but they threatened her with the Military *Polis*. We were right *feart* for *yer*, lass. I *cannae* believe a word *o'* this bicycle crash. *Ye've* been *dun* over *by thae sleekit* bastards at intelligence.'

Her silence is answer enough for Iain; he and Morag will continue to do their best to support her.

There is a difficult conversation with Erik. He has confessed

191

his role in sending the photographs, but she understands his motives, which she regards as honourable, and he has suffered for them. She has no love for the British, certainly not the military hierarchy and Intelligence. She understands the shadowy world of treachery that defines post-war Europe; she thought to have left deception and betrayal behind her on D-Day. The knowledge that Erik can identify the mole, the Soviet agent in Allied High Command, could be very useful. If necessary and when the time is right, she will use it to her advantage, to protect her family.

The reason given for their release has provided little comfort for Helen. The note Harrison received while she lay on the floor choking from the foul water of the bath revealed that Altmann had been handed over to the British in Switzerland, but not before his captor, the former General Karl von Werstein, had beaten him so badly that his face was almost unrecognisable. Altmann will cooperate with the British on condition that he is protected from Von Werstein. His desire to seek refuge in Argentina was self-preservation. He feared the retribution of those inmates of Sachsenhausen, Majdanek and Mittelbau-Dora who had survived. The body of a former guard at Majdanek had been found hanging from a tree in a London park, his eyes gouged out. He did not trust the Allies to protect him, however useful he could be to them. His wife and children had been waiting for the arrival of the "Santa Fé" at the dockside in Buenos Aires. A comfortable villa in the suburbs and a senior position at the university would have been his, organised and paid for by the Perón government. Now he would be forever looking over his shoulder for a potential assassin.

The British agents in Genoa had witnessed an Italian man "dispatch" two of the Soviet agents and seen her husband take Altmann as his prisoner, accompanied by the third Soviet agent. This had led the British to believe that Altmann had been handed to the Soviets. Her husband has not returned, and it appears the British do not know of his whereabouts, if she can believe them. The return of her gun, placed in discreet brown paper packaging in her mailbox, provides some comfort; the British have honoured that promise at least.

But she has scores to settle with Major Harrison, and there will be relief from suffering for those at Bad Nenndorf.

## 39

February 1947
Bonn, Germany

Erik has asked if he can stay with her in the apartment and she has agreed. She is grateful for his company and her son worships him. They attend lectures together and note that the lecturer who requested they leave their seats to demonstrate percussion and auscultation is not on the teaching staff. Nor do they see the student who had taken Erik's seat when he left it. She is more alert than ever to the dangers she faces. At least in Normandy she knew who her enemies were. Here the situation is more opaque; allegiances can shift according to expediency. Proof of this comes a week later when to her surprise and delight she meets Hans Schultz, the former *Oberfeldkommandur* of Caen.

He is waiting in a car outside the NAAFI where Helen is exchanging coupons for extra milk and orange juice. Her son is with her and she needs to get warm clothing for him. It has been another bitterly cold winter and he is growing fast. His second birthday had been celebrated at the barracks nursery. Morag baked a cake and there had been more than enough to share among the children and to bring some home for Pavel and Magda. Helen's sadness that her husband was not there to celebrate his son's birthday had weighed heavily on her. Erik had been invited to the party and had helped to organise the games for the children, explaining he had done the same for his younger brothers and sisters. The women at the party were smitten by his good looks and easy-going charm.

He saw her before she him. She hears a voice calling her name and a rotund figure emerges from the driving seat of a new Volkswagen sedan car.

'Helen! Is it really you, after all this time?'

She struggles to remember his name; she had always addressed him by his rank and this would not be popular with the British soldiers and their families who throng the entrance to the building. She goes to the car and is embraced warmly by him. He looks at her son and remarks how he resembles his father, but when he poses the inevitable question of her husband's whereabouts, she dissembles. Hans would not know of Karl's covert activities, perhaps not even his ostensible one. So she tells him her husband is very busy with an assignment in Hamburg but returns to Bonn regularly.

'And I see another Von Werstein will soon be born.'

She does her best to look the embodiment of contented motherhood, but Hans knows her too well.

'I sense all is not well between you. This is not for the first time as I remember. Do you wish to speak of it? Uncle Hans is a good listener as you know.'

She smiles at this, remembering the conversation in the kitchen of the *château*.

'No, I cannot, and especially with our son here. But tell me about yourself and how you are here? I did not know you were alive, that you had survived the Battle of Normandy.'

'As for being alive, I was lucky. I was captured by the British during the battle for Caen. Naturally, I had to answer charges regarding my time in Caen. I spent some months in a very unpleasant prisoner-of-war camp in Belgium and then, with other officers, taken to England, to a magnificent house in

County Durham for further interrogation. I was considered more an ineffective administrator than a war criminal. A file was produced attesting to my refusal to take hostages as a reprisal for the blowing up the rail track between Strasbourg and Caen. It was Christmas after all.'

'And your family in Köln? Are they well?'

'They all died in the bombing raids.'

She expresses her condolences but is surprised by the cheerful response she receives.

'I have a new wife, a British woman. I met her in England. She was a nurse at the prisoner-of-war camp. I am now the manager of the new Volkswagen dealership outside of Bonn. The British are rebuilding the factories and see a great future for German cars. Life moves on and we must make the best of what we have. Here is my wife now. I will present her to you.'

She notes how much his English has improved since the last time they spoke.

Jennifer is an attractive lady in her mid-forties. She is from Newcastle and is very interested to learn that Helen went to school there. She is friendly and expresses the hope that Helen will come to their home in the suburbs of Bonn. Jennifer has adult children from her marriage to a seaman in the British Merchant Navy. He was on the crew of the icebreaker Krasin, part of the Arctic Convoys to Murmansk and Arkhangelsk carrying supplies and munitions for the Soviets. She is proud that ship had been built in the shipyards of Newcastle. Her husband died of hypothermia and frostbite during one of the convoys.

'We would not be so ready to supply the Soviets now,' says Hans.

She has no answer to that; whenever she thinks of Russians, she thinks of Svetlana.

They part, and Helen resumes her mission to find clothing for her son and exchange her food coupons.

Erik is home and preparing a celebratory meal. Both have completed the lecture stage of their medical training, with honours in the examination, and will commence work as trainee doctors at the hospital on Venusberg. Her son has been tasked with placing small glass candle holders at each place. He prefers to stack them one above the other, but Erik patiently shows him how they should be placed. Pavel and Magda will be joining them. They have bartered their tobacco allowance for a bottle of champagne, not the best champagne, but certainly a rare treat for Germans.

Pavel has interesting news: the interrogation centre at Bad Nenndorf has been closed down and there is an investigation underway into the practices there. The doctor at her interrogation has been summoned to London to face criminal charges and will be struck off the medical register by the General Medical Council. Pavel has sent copies of the photographs he took of Erik and Helen's injuries to the GMC as evidence. The internees are now in the British Military Hospital. Some are not expected to survive, given their emaciation and injuries. Helen hopes the two women who were in the room with her are among the survivors. Pavel has also learned that Major Harrison has been relieved of his post.

She is pleased she managed to get the letter to Montgomery. It took a great deal of ingenuity on Iain's part to get it past the censors and directly into Montgomery's personal mailbag. She had detailed the torture she suffered on Harrison's orders, reminding Montgomery of her war-time activities. She described the barbaric treatment of those imprisoned at the interrogation centre and the cruelty of the female orderly. She recommended that the latter be given a custodial sentence for abuse of prisoners. The Hague Convention does not exclude such as her from punishment.

Helen knows the rules of engagement with the enemy.

The celebration lasts late into the evening. Erik puts her son to bed while Helen serves the dessert, an apple apiece, but each pretends it is their favourite dessert, vying to describe the most extravagant. Helen has drunk a glass of champagne and admits that she is known among her French family as *La Poire Belle Helene*. She does not discourage Erik when he places his arm around her and says the name is most appropriate.

It is after midnight when their guests leave and Erik makes to clear the table. Helen puts her arm around him and leads him to the bedroom she has slept in alone for far too long. Hans was right; life moves on and we have to make the best of it.

## 40

April 1947
Bonn, Germany

Helen is at work on the medical ward of the newly built hospital on Venusberg when her labour pains begin. She has persuaded Professor Steudel that she is capable of continuing into the summer semester, despite the early spring heat and the workload. She ignores the pains, dismissing them as Braxton-Hicks contractions; the midwife has assured her the baby will be born mid-May and *Maman* will arrive in time for the birth. Luisa has won her over; the baby will be born at Schloss Mariendistel, with or without her husband, and under Scottish and German flags. Erik will bring young Karl to join them as soon as Luisa thinks Helen is able to receive them. Luisa has strict ideas surrounding the etiquette of birth, in contrast to the laxity of her approach to marital indiscretions; she and Luisa share common ground in that respect.

Erik is gentle in his love-making and assures her it can do no harm after the early weeks. She does not compare him to her husband; for too long has he been absent from her life. She has hidden the cello in a cupboard and no longer plays the piano. The memories the cello evoked, the melancholy reminiscences for a past that can never be retrieved, have made music too painful to contemplate.

She understands that Erik hopes to be a father to the new baby, as he has been to her son. She also knows that in time he would wish to father a child with her. She is comfortable with this.

It is late in the same afternoon and she is at home with Erik and her son when she feels a strong pain gripping her back. At the same time, she feels a flow from her vagina. She goes into the lavatory and there is the mucous plug in her underwear and more fluid is leaking as she sits. She calls for Erik who helps her to the bedroom. The pains are coming faster and increasing in intensity and there is no time to get her to a hospital. She remembers *Maman*'s relief when she told her the baby would be born in May. *Maman* would worry about an April birth, remembering the death of her own baby son born during that same month and who died so soon after his birth. This causes Helen to become distressed, and in her pain and fear it is not Erik she calls for, nor *Maman* and Papa, but her husband. She wants him with her holding her in his arms as he encourages her to drink the tisanes as he did when he brought her back to life and played the *Arpeggione Sonata* by her bedside. She is aware that Pavel has been called to assist and Magda is holding her hand. A neighbour has been called to take care of her son. She understands there is concern about her baby. Both Erik and Pavel are discussing seeking help from the military hospital; the baby's heart rate is giving cause for alarm as its shoulder is trapped in the birth canal. She knows this is a serious complication and without expert care her baby will die. There is more pain, then the sweet smell of chloroform; and soon all is dark and she is floating above the world.

She can see the *château* and the walls of the rose garden, which shield the old tower from view. For a while the fragrance of the roses mingles with the sound of snow falling softly around the *château*. She looks down and sees that the snow is now in drifts around the *château* and the roses are no more. She hears the voice that came to her in the darkness of that time, and it calls her

"*Liebchen*" and asks why such things happen to her when he is absent. The voice puts his strong arms around her and tells her they have a beautiful baby girl, that she is healthy and has red hair and green eyes, and the same small birthmark his daughter, Maria-Sophia, has on her left arm. She opens her eyes and her husband is there holding a tiny bundle in his arms. The baby is waving her arms frantically and he is laughing.

'She has her mother's temper, of that I am certain.'

He places the baby in her arms. and Helen puts her to her breast. The baby pulls hard on the nipple and then feeds contentedly, and after a while she sleeps. Erik and Pavel come to check that Helen's uterus has contracted and that she is no longer bleeding. There will be time enough to ask of what happened during the night. For now there is only the fact that she has a healthy baby and her husband is with her.

She has not thought of a name but her husband has already decided. She will be called Rosalin, "Little Rose" after the roses that he remembers were his first impression of the *château*. She agrees this is a good name but tells him it is pronounced and spelt as *Róisín* in the Gaelic language, and she believes that is how Papa would prefer it to be.

'Very well, but to satisfy all of our family, she will need more names.'

Finally they agree on Róisín Marie-Luisa von Werstein. She will be baptised at the church of Saint Remigius, the church where Beethoven was baptised.

# 41

Luisa is impatient for them to travel to Lübeck, to Schloss Mariendistel, where *Maman* and Papa will join them. Helen needs time to convalesce from the trauma of Róisín's birth and their son will benefit from time away from the dust and dirt of Bonn.

Helen acquiesces in this; her husband needs to be reunited with his mother and with his son from his first marriage. She knows how anxious he has been about the fate of his family and that he hopes Leon can provide some clues to their whereabouts. They will leave for Lübeck after the baptism of Róisín. Erik offered to be godfather to her daughter, but this has been overruled by Luisa and *Maman,* who insist both godparents should be of the Roman Catholic faith. Magda will be godmother and Iain will be godfather. All are happy with this arrangement.

Helen has been told of the events of the night of Róisín's birth. The shoulder of her daughter had descended into the birth canal and obstructed normal delivery of her head and body. Róisín's heart rate had slowed and she was passing meconium. These were signs of severe foetal distress. She herself had been exhausted and losing blood. Erik and Pavel had discussed the terrible decision they would have to make: which life to save, that of Helen or of the baby. In the absence of the father they had realised that they alone must make this decision. Helen and her husband are of the

Roman Catholic faith and Pavel was aware of the creed of the Catholic Church: the baby's life must take precedence over that of the mother; the baby is unbaptised and, therefore, unable to enter Heaven. Erik had vehemently disputed this; Helen's life was precious and her death would have a lasting impact on her son. They agreed to do their best to save both. It was too late to get her to the British Military Hospital, and both knew Helen would not have wished her baby to be born under the British flag.

Pavel had witnessed a birth with this complication as a medical student in Prague and remembered the technique used to resolve it. He was also aware that it could go badly wrong without experience and both lives could be lost. After administering chloroform, Pavel instructed Erik to push Helen's legs up against her abdomen while he applied pressure above her pelvis. This would prevent the baby's head from retracting from the birth canal and release the shoulder. Magda took over from Erik once he had shown her the technique, and it was Erik who gently eased the baby's head and body through the birth canal and into his arms. Magda took the baby girl, and after cleaning the mucous from her mouth and wrapping her in clean linen, pronounced her healthy. Helen had started to bleed heavily and had not regained consciousness. Erik applied pressure to her uterus while Pavel took ergotamine from his medical bag. All knew the baby's suckling would help to stem the bleeding, but Helen showed no sign of awakening. It was at this moment the door of the apartment opened and Karl von Werstein entered the room.

# PART TWELVE


## Karl

# 42

April 1947
Bonn, Germany

It was Hans who found me and informed me of my beloved wife's condition.

On his release from captivity and return to Germany, Hans had joined one of the many covert veterans groups that had proliferated in the wake of the defeat of Germany and occupation by the Allies. For many in these groups, the 8th of May 1945 had not proved to be *Stunde Null*, Zero Hour, and the irreversible departure from their lives before the defeat of Nazi Germany. On the contrary, they had quickly gained positions of influence within the occupied zones. Hans had no interest in politics and was content with his life as a sales manager for Volkswagen, but he knew who to go to for information.

After handing Altmann over to the British, I was then responsible for ensuring the safety of the daughter of a high-ranking Russian general. The general had apparently fallen into disfavour with Stalin, had been stripped of his honours, and dispatched to the *gulags*. His daughter had fought bravely at Stalingrad under the command of General Zhukov. Following her capture by the *Wehrmacht,* she had been part of a negotiated prisoner exchange, which included Zhukov's son. She was now on the run from her former comrades.

She had been part of a team of NKGB agents assigned to

ensure the capture of Otto Altmann. In the skirmish between the former Italian partisans and the NKGB, she had evaded the bullets and sought my protection. We escaped from the harbour and from the British agents, who I knew would have given Altmann a comfortable return to Germany. The partisans organised a safe house for the agent for the night, while I kept Altmann drugged and shackled in the crypt of a church in the hills above Genoa.

She told me it had been no coincidence that she had volunteered to participate in the Soviet's scheme: to snatch Altmann as he made to board the ship to Buenos Aires. She knew the identity of the two British agents who were on Altmann's trail; this would be the means to her survival. She told me of the fate which would await her on her return to Moscow; even if the mission were successful she would, nevertheless, be sent to join her family in the gulags of Siberia.

We drove from the hills above Genoa to Rome, stopping overnight at an address given to me by the Italians. From there we drove to the Swiss border where the British military police, alerted by the Italians, were waiting at the village of Gandria on Lake Lugano. I made no apologies for the condition of my prisoner and requested that a telephone be made available to me. I informed the office of Major Harrison that Altmann was now in British custody, and that I had a Soviet agent with me who wished to defect. I would not be returning to Bonn until her safety was guaranteed.

We crossed into Austria where I knew I would find refuge near Graz, in the area of Austria known as Styria. The family of my first wife had a *Schloss* in the hills above the city. We would find sanctuary there while waiting for the British to decide the fate of my companion. It was fortunate that this part of Austria had been given to British occupation in 1945.

Despite the unusual circumstances of our arrival, we were

made welcome. My companion spoke excellent German and we all exchanged stories of our wartime experiences. When the subject of my family in Prussia was raised, my companion revealed that one of my sons was already safely in the British Zone and the others were alive in Soviet East Germany. This news added to the sense of discomfiture I now felt in the presence of the woman I was obliged to protect; she was withholding information about my family in order to wield more power over me.

The winter passed into spring and I had received no communication from British Intelligence regarding my companion. A dead letter box in Graz assured me that my wife and child were well and that they believed I was soon to return to them. I had to trust the British in this.

I was taking a stroll around the gardens when I heard a car on the steep winding road from the town to the *Schloss*. A Volkswagen sedan drew up and to my great astonishment out of it stepped my former *Oberfeldkommandur,* Hans Schulz. We embraced. I'd had no news of him since the battle for Caen in July 1944. He did not waste time in reminiscences but ordered me to accompany him to Bonn without delay as the birth of my second child was imminent. I smiled at his "order".

The journey took two days, during which time he described the predicament of my wife: she was in an advanced stage of pregnancy and did not know my whereabouts. She had been forbidden to enquire after me and had been arrested and tortured by the British. When it seemed Altmann had disappeared with me and a Soviet agent, they had accused her of being a spy for the Soviets.

We stopped to rest close to Nuremberg, where I telephoned my in-laws in Styria. I instructed them to place my Soviet *protégée* under house arrest and to regard her as an enemy agent until I informed them otherwise.

It was soon after midnight on the 29th of April when I arrived at the apartment in Bonn. I found my wife close to death, despite the efforts of the two doctors attending to her. From a small crib close to the bed came the cries of an infant. I asked Magda, our neighbour, to take care of the baby while I took my wife in my arms. I told her of my love for her and my sadness this should happen without my support. She opened her eyes and I knew she would live.

## 43

July 1947
Schloss Mariendistel

There comes a time for truth.

I was required to remain in Bonn for several weeks after my return. During this time I was interrogated by British Intelligence on my pursuit and capture of Altmann and of the Soviet agent who wished to defect. Thus, it was July before I joined my wife and family at Schloss Mariendistel.

I soon realised that my former guard, Erik, had become more to my family than merely a fellow medical student and companion of my wife. It was Erik who delivered my daughter, whose arms first held her, and it was on account of his care, and that of Pavel, that I owed the lives of my wife and Róisín. When my son stumbled on the stairs to our apartment he turned from me to take Erik's hand for support; he went to Erik for comfort when he was stung by a wasp, and my wife's eyes met those of Erik and avoided mine.

We walked together in the gardens of the *Schloss* with Róisín in my arms and our son running ahead of us in pursuit of the young collie dog, Meg. Helen's parents had brought the dog with them from Scotland and my son Leon was much attached to her. Helen's parents had explained that Gordon Setters were more favoured in the family, but Angus, her father's cousin, had been given a collie puppy when he was a child, and he preferred the breed to the traditional setters which bore his family name.

My wife told me of her arrest and torture and how she had avenged her suffering. Once again I was in awe of my wife's courage and resourcefulness. She had repeatedly sought to discover my whereabouts and had believed I was lost to her. I knew then that I could not endure peace under the terms of the British Occupation. Harrison, Oakley and all at Allied Command knew of my wife's war record, but had lied to her and permitted her to be despised, ostracised and tortured. Nevertheless, she made little of it.

'It is over now and the perpetrators have been punished. But there is much to talk about, and it will not be easy for either of us.'

She went on to admit that she and Erik had become lovers.

'We grew close during the months of your absence. When Leon returned and told me of Svetlana's role in his safe passage to the British sector of Berlin, it changed between us. Svetlana knew of your address in Bonn and asked Leon to remind you of her. I had hoped this woman would never again be part of our lives and was distraught to realise she had every intention of being just that, part of your life anyway. Erik made love to me the night of Leon's return. It was not as with you, but he gave me pleasure as well as comfort. When I realised I was expecting your child, he respected my decision that he could not be my lover during this time. As the months passed and you did not return, I invited him into my bed and we lived as man and wife until the birth of Róisín. I have been very happy to have him with me; he too has suffered torture by the British. But there is more to this than I wish to tell you at this time.'

'And why is that? Are there to be secrets between us even now?'

'You have told me nothing of your time away from me. I believed you had abandoned me or worse, perhaps murdered by the Soviets during the capture of Altmann, or by the British because you knew too much and were no longer useful to them. I also know you were accompanied by the woman from Alsace, the one who used to take pleasure in humiliating me when she was a guest at the *château* and with whom you enjoyed your time in Paris.'

'Who told you of the time in Paris?'

'I received photographs of you both, you and the Alsace woman, Adalie Franck. But do not upset yourself on account of the photographs. I knew they were taken before we met, before I loved you and thought you loved me.'

'And I still love you, *Liebchen*. I know of these photographs. Harrison promised you would not receive them. He would keep them from you to ensure I fulfilled the mission he set me, to bring Altmann to the British, which I did, and that our lives in Bonn would be very unpleasant if I did not succeed.'

'But the British thought you had betrayed them; you disappeared with Altmann and a Soviet agent. That is why they arrested and tortured me.'

'I see now how you have suffered on my account. For that I cannot forgive myself. But I too was betrayed by the British. They sent the photographs to cause you distress.'

'As I have said, the photographs did not distress me. I would have been distressed had they been revealed to me while we were in Normandy. I would not have found it easy to serve Franck, as I was obliged to on many occasions. The photographs were sent in the hope I would somehow contact you and persuade you that you owed Harrison nothing. The British believed I had warned you, and that you handed Altmann to the Soviets, and disappeared with one of their agents.'

'But this does not explain who sent the photographs to you. Harrison promised they would not be sent to you.'

'He did not send them. I took them to his office and he was most surprised and displeased when I tipped them onto his desk. He explained your mission and informed me who was accompanying you on the trail of Altmann. He permitted me to telephone someone who could warn you that a trap had been set for you in Genoa. I was certain a Soviet agent was working in Allied Command, and this agent, or mole as such a person is known, was attempting to prevent you passing Altmann to the British.

'The Soviets knew you could identify Altmann and capture him. I suspected that Svetlana was involved. She knew the address to send the photographs. Leon had given your name to a priest in Berlin and your address was located. I assumed she also wanted to save your life, for her own reasons of course, and this was a torment for me. But she did not send the photographs.'

'But you know who did?'

'As I told you, I do not wish to tell you at this time.'

'You were correct. A trap had been set for me, in more ways than you could have known. Adalie... Franck was a double agent, working for the Soviets. I suspected this to be so, but I needed to be certain.'

'And when you were certain?'

'I killed her.'

'And of the Soviet agent? The one who you took with you from Genoa?'

'It was Svetlana.'

*

*Helen does not wish to continue this conversation with her husband, and Róisín is hungry and struggling in her father's arms. Helen believes the baby has detected conflict, and the voice of the one holding her is not familiar. Helen feels they both need Erik at this moment.*

*Her husband calls their son to his side, and they sit together on the ancient verdigris-encrusted bench that overlooks the Elbe-Lübeck Kanal.*

*Her husband sits their son on his knee, and both stroke the dog while talking about the scene before them. Their son is excited by the ships making their way to the port at Lübeck, and onwards to the Baltic. Her husband tells him of Königsberg and his memories of the port and seaside where he would swim so far out that his children would fear he would fall off the end of the world.*

*Their son has met Leon, his stepbrother, but neither has warmed to the other. Leon is too traumatised by his life in the forests of Lithuania and his memories of the fate of his uncle and aunt. His coldness extends to both Helen and his father; the latter for losing the war, for which he perceives his father holds responsibility, and to Helen as the enemy of his people. Only Luisa is able to break through the shell of bitterness and grief which engulfs her grandson. She has reminded him that his father fought courageously for the Fatherland, and that Helen is brave and honourable and also kin by blood and marriage to his father. This has not alleviated the sorrow and anger Leon exhibits in their presence.*

*While Luisa feels the situation will improve with time, Helen is of the opinion her presence, and that of her children, will always be an obstacle to peace within her husband's family.*

*It was never going to be easy. It was never going to be the way it was. She feels such a wave of nostalgia and a longing for the past, when her love for her husband was all she needed to give her courage and purpose. Now this love has gone, or at least it is no longer enough to face the future.*

## 44

July 1947
Schloss Mariendistel

I watched my wife with our daughter at her breast. I knew at this time she could not understand how much I loved her, how I wished to have back the life we had enjoyed during our time together. War and peace had driven us apart, and I could see no way of redeeming this. Her trust in me had been destroyed, and it was my fault. On my account, she had suffered torture and humiliation, and now she was enduring rejection by my son, Leon.

I could forgive her time with Erik. I hated him at that moment but understood how easily she would have fallen for his handsome looks and charm. He had been brave and loyal under my command, but I had known he was not at heart a soldier, that he had been withdrawn from his medical studies and coerced into taking up arms. I also knew how much he had desired my wife. But he had not been alone in this; all under my command at the *château* had wanted her.

I waited until our daughter was fed and asked my wife if she would like to return to the *Schloss* or walk further. I offered her my hand but she ignored it and went to take hold of our son.

'I am tired and our son needs to eat. We will talk later, but before we return, I wish to tell you that I have invited Erik to stay with us at the *Schloss*. He has a week of holiday from the university

216

and our son has missed him. It will give us all time to consider our situation and for more honesty between us.'

Later in the evening we sat together in the gardens. My mother, sensing we needed time alone, took our children to her bedroom, but before we went out, she gave me a letter that had just arrived by courier.

My wife informed me that Erik was a double agent, working for both the Americans and the Soviets. Under the threat of reprisals against his family, Erik had been ordered by his Soviet handler to send the photographs to her. This was in the expectation that I would no longer cooperate with the British if I knew she had them. The Americans had recruited Erik to spy on me in Bonn on account of my connection to Svetlana, the daughter of a high-ranking general and confidant of Stalin. The Americans believed my association with her could provide useful intelligence, and they would use this association to compromise me into working with them.

'He also told me of the woman and her children in Czatków.'

'So you know what happened there?'

'Erik told me everything of that day and all you encountered in Poland. I know you are innocent, but in these times it is those such as you who suffer, while the guilty escape justice. Now you understand how afraid I am for our future. We are living among people who have no scruples. We thought the war was over, but now a more insidious and treacherous conflict is underway: between the former Allies, between the West and the Soviet Union; each trying to gain military and political superiority. They do not care about those who are sacrificed in this, they do not care that there are murderers among us, and they do not care about us. We are only valued for our usefulness to them. They seek the most creative ways to tell lies, and there is no one to hold them to account.'

But she also told me that the Italians who had fought off my Soviet killers had been there on account of her request for help. I wondered again at my wife's resourcefulness, but I could not tell her that this was but a small part of the drama now unfolding. The letter I had just received informed me that Svetlana had disappeared from her hideout in Graz.

It was now time to explain my time on the trail of Altmann, and my renewed acquaintance with Svetlana Zharovskaya.

# 45

## 24<sup>th</sup> December 1946
## Genoa, Italy

After concealing our car inside one of the bombed-out warehouses that line the harbour at Genoa, we took a room in a small *pensióne* in the *carruggi,* the myriad of narrow passages linking the old town to the port. The car was one of many we had bought and sold during our journey through Austria and Italy, on the trail of Altmann and his guides. We knew how alert his escort would be to the risk of being followed. There would be a reward for his safety at each stage of the journey.

Adalie suggested we go separately to observe around the port, and to watch for the berthing of the 'Santa Fé', the ship which would transport Altmann to Argentina. This ship was one in a fleet owned by Alberto Dodero, a close friend of General Juan Perón, the fascist sympathiser and now president of Argentina, and his wife Evita. Since 1945, Dodero's ships had been transporting hundreds of Nazi war criminals to safety in Argentina and, once there, the same war criminals used the proceeds of wartime looting to bankroll Perón's presidential campaign. Now ensconced in the presidential palace, Perón and his wife were coordinating the escape of Nazis, particularly those with scientific skills, such as Altmann. As well as their political sympathies for the Nazi regime, the Perónist government profited from the expertise of German scientists in Argentine factories and armament plants.

Also welcome were those Nazis whose skills lay in interrogation and torture techniques, who were soon employed by the region's militaries to instruct in death squad operations.

I waited for her return before I set off to the church of San Giovanni, where we had watched Altmann furtively enter the side chapel earlier in the evening. I needed to know whether the church was guarded. Adalie had informed me that the priest of the church had been a known Nazi sympathiser during the war and responsible for the deaths of many partisans. As a former SD agent, she would have this information, but not for the first time during our travels together did I wonder how far I could trust the woman. She had enjoyed having me in her bed and I had done my best to pleasure her. Harrison had made it clear this would be necessary to retain her usefulness and loyalty.

I was not convinced a woman such as Adalie could be bought in this way, but if it meant my family was assured of a secure life in Germany, it was worth the price of my guilty conscience. I remembered from my history lessons the words of Henry the Fourth of France, the Protestant King of Navarre, forced to convert to Catholicism to marry Princess Margot de Valois and thereby accede to the French throne. "*Paris vaut bien une messe*", or "Paris is worth a mass" he had said to his courtiers. I wondered whether he had felt the same repugnance with Margot that I felt with Adalie. I was fulfilling my promise in this "Faustian pact"; Major Harrison's "deal with the devil".

While I watched the church, which stood close to the harbour, I noticed the massive ocean liner approaching. I waited until its moorings were secured and went back to report its arrival to Adalie. She was not in the room. We had arranged two hourly surveillance missions and I had been away for less than one hour. I immediately suspected her of treachery. I returned to the harbour and saw the figure of Adalie with three companions in the shadows of a yacht moored close to where the 'Santa Fé' had berthed. I noticed a small guesthouse close to the harbour. The sign on the door announced it was *chiuso per Natale* but I saw there was a gate to the side of the building. I tried it and found it to be unlocked. From behind the gate, I watched the priest, Hudal, leave the church and board the ship. He carried a satchel which I knew would contain a substantial amount of gold and Swiss Francs, payment in full for Altmann's escape from justice. I was too far from Adalie and her companions to overhear their conversation. I noted one of the three was a woman. They too watched the priest as he made his furtive boarding of the ship and his equally furtive departure from it. I had seen enough and made to return to the *pensióne* and await the return of Adalie.

She made no attempt to dissemble; she knew the game was up and her strategy was to win me over with a bribe. A considerable amount of gold would be mine if I assisted her Soviet "friends" in ensuring Altmann was passed into their hands. She reasoned that the British were inept in the new order of espionage and, furthermore, would not honour their promises with regard to my family. One of the agents had news of my children's whereabouts and would ensure their safe passage to any country of my choosing.

'And what of my wife and child in Bonn?'

'They will soon forget about you. You have been absent enough in their lives. My intelligence is that your wife has already found a substitute.'

'If that is so, it is for me to resolve and no bribe from you will encourage me to do otherwise.'

She drew the pistol I knew she kept hidden in the pocket of her coat. Unfortunately for her, I had taken the precaution of unloading it before she left on her earlier reconnaissance excursion. I took up my pistol and fired two shots into her chest and she fell to the ground. I left her body in the room and made for the harbour. As one against many I did not reckon my chances of capturing Altmann, but I would have to try, for the sake of my family.

I watched the ship as a red dawn broke over the port. A strong wind was already causing the seas to lash against the harbour walls. The 'Santa Fé' was due to sail at 7 a.m. It was possible this would be delayed by the approaching storm. I returned to my hideout behind the gate and watched as the three Soviet agents took up positions around the harbour; all three carried suitcases. Their occasional checking of their wristwatches gave every impression they were passengers impatient to board the ship. I watched as two young men left the front door of the guesthouse, one was carrying a bagpipe-like instrument which I later learned was called the *zampogna,* traditionally played at Christmas time to "pipe" the ships that set sail from the port on the 25th of December. This distracted me, and so I failed at that moment to notice the opening of the church doors, and the emergence of Altmann and two others, one of whom was the priest, Hudal.

The agents sprang into action. They drew their guns and made to grab at Altmann but the "musician" was too fast for them. From under the bag of his pipes, he drew a machine gun. Two of the Soviets fell to the ground and the third jumped into the sea, disappearing under the breakwater. I ran towards Altmann, who by then was attempting to break free from the scene and return to the church, along with Hudal and his accomplice. I gave chase and wrestled the priest and the other to the ground. My Italian "saviours" went after Altmann. They returned with him after a few minutes and, together, we bound and gagged him and loaded him into the trunk of a car parked close to the harbour. One of the men, "Alessio", explained in French that he had been a prisoner in Sachsenhausen. He had welcomed the opportunity to avenge the suffering he had endured there, and the death of his younger brother at the hands of the *Gestapo*.

They provided me with syringes of a strong sedative, which they explained would keep Altmann quiet for some time. I thanked them as I made to leave in the car they had given me. I then noticed a car outside the *pensióne* where Adalie and I had been staying. Two men stepped out of the building and aimed a gun at my car. At the same moment, a woman threw herself onto the rear seat of the car. It was Svetlana.

## 46

I had no choice; she was shivering and streaming from her dive into the sea, and desperate to escape the bullets now being fired at my car. I threw my coat over her. The men continued to shoot at the car, but I accelerated out of the port and into the hills above the city. We stopped at the church Alessio said would give me refuge, the one attended by his mother. Fearing the two men who had shot at the car would follow us, I asked for the car to be hidden in the nearby forest. Svetlana was taken to the home of a woman whose communist partisan son had died in the war. Altmann was chained in the crypt of the church and I stayed to guard him.

The following morning, my hosts gave me breakfast and clean clothing. I took food and water to Altmann and gave him a partial dose of the sedative; I wanted him awake and in full strength for what I planned for him later that day.

Svetlana was brought to the church, radiant in warm clothing, with her long blonde hair coiled around her neck and singing the *Bella Ciao* partisan song in chorus with the family who had given her hospitality. Communists were welcome in the village and Svetlana had evidently persuaded her hosts of her credentials in that respect. All wished the *"bellissima signorina"* good luck and my good fortune with her. As I had spent the night guarding Altmann, I was in no mood to respond to the festive atmosphere

Svetlana had conjured to her advantage.

We drove to Rome, stopping at an address given to me by the Italians, and then onwards towards the Swiss Border.

In Rome, we gave Altmann food and a comfortable room, albeit one locked and guarded, and a night of sleep without sedation. In the morning I challenged him to a fight to account for his crimes. It was a fair fight and it did not take long. As with all bullies and cowards, he could not fight as an equal. After he had begged me to stop, and by which time his jaw was broken, his face swollen and the fingers of both hands dislocated, I reminded him of the treatment he had so frequently administered to his victims at Sachsenhausen, including my professor of cello: he had greatly enjoyed crushing the testicles of his victims. It was now his turn to experience what he had so frequently meted out. He passed out with the pain; there was no need to sedate him again before we reached Gandria on Lake Lugano, where I handed him over to the British.

I felt an extreme sense of exhaustion as well as elation. I had fulfilled my side of the bargain with the British and my only responsibility was to guard Svetlana, until such time as the British agreed to the terms of her defection.

I decided to drive her to my first wife's family *Schloss* above Graz, where she was when I departed with Hans Schulz on the 27th of April 1947.

# PART THIRTEEN

## Helen

## 47

July 1947
Schloss Mariendistel

Helen sits quietly as the shadows of the trees around them lengthen, and shivers in the damp chill that rises in the swathes of mist from the canal far below them. But she is more numbed by the cold dread and despair she feels as her husband reveals the details of his renewed association with Svetlana.

Svetlana had sought his protection at Genoa and wishes him to prevail upon the Allies to give her protection. Her husband expects that in return she will provide information on the whereabouts of his missing children. Helen asks why the Allies should do this for a known communist agent, one with connections within the highest echelons of what is now called the "court of the Red Tsar". He replies that she would provide useful intelligence regarding the operations of the NKGB, and of those Nazis whose expertise has been acquired by the Soviets.

'How can you trust her? And how can I trust that you will not sacrifice what is between us to satisfy her demands.'

'I do not understand what you are saying.'

'You are taking me for a fool. This woman has you in her thrall. You want to believe her lies, that she will give you back your children, and thus you will forever be grateful to her, be controlled by her.'

'The British will want her for what she knows about Stalin's plans, and I want my children back with me.'

'At the cost to our marriage, and the children we have between us? Your son Leon loathes me. I am sure he would welcome Svetlana, his saviour, as your new wife and as his mother.'

'That is not what I want. I love you; what was between Svetlana and me, and with Adalie, was not love.'

'What is love? I often wonder. You disappeared from my life for months. I was not permitted to ask where you were, or when you would return. I assumed you to be dead. I then discovered that you were crossing Europe with a woman who you bedded with great pleasure during your time in Paris. And now you expect me to believe that the woman your men watched you enjoy on the Eastern Front has been with you for months, without you touching her. I know from Erik how it was between you and Svetlana. Forgive my disbelief but you ask too much.'

'And what of you and Erik? How do you imagine it is for me, knowing how he enjoyed you, and has become more of a father to our son than I now am? That it was his arms that first held our daughter and he knows your body better than I do.'

'That is nonsense. It is the same for Pavel. They are doctors. It is the work they do. But as for Erik, if what is between us is love, then yes, it is so. I enjoyed his love-making, and the care he gave our son. Without him, and Ian and his wife, I could not have lived as I did in your absence.'

'You know I had no choice. It was not only the photographs; I knew you would understand they were from the time before we met. It was my fear for our lives, or how our lives could be made so much more difficult if I did not bring Altmann to the British. I did what was necessary to deliver him to them.'

'But not before the British thought you had betrayed them. They tortured me when they assumed you had taken him to the Soviets, along with your former lover.'

'I cannot forgive the British for what happened to you. My only hope is that one day Germany will be free of them, and all other occupiers.'

'It is easy for you to say this. Many former Nazis have been awarded the privileges they had under the Nazi rule. There has been no justice and where there is no justice, or accountability for crimes that were committed during Hitler's *Reich*, there can be no future for Germany. I want to go home to Scotland.'

'You know it would not be possible for me to join you there, and my own homeland no longer exists. Prussia was formally abolished by the Allies in February of this year. I am now obliged to stay in what remains of my country. I owe it to my family and my ancestors, and you are part of this. Besides, my mother thinks highly of you and she is not a woman who takes kindly to other women.'

'If Svetlana brings your children to her, I am sure she will be welcomed.'

'Svetlana has disappeared. She was being guarded by the family of my first wife, in Graz, but has escaped.'

'Am I to assume she will appear at the *Schloss* at any time? If so, should I make to leave and take our children with me to Bonn, so you may enjoy her company here? I will do so gladly.'

'When you speak as you do, I wonder at what you have suffered and endured and I do not blame you. But I want you to know that I have never loved a woman as I love you. I feel no man will ever understand or love you as I do. If you wish to leave me and take Erik as your husband, I understand why you would do so. It would be dishonourable of me to force you to stay.'

'I will think about it. But please allow me to return to my children. It is time for Róisín to be fed.'

'Of course, but I should wish to accompany you as it is now dark.'

'Do you fear assassins?'

'Not as much as my wife's temper.'

'On this occasion there is no hairbrush.'

He remembers this and smiles as they walk together to the *Schloss*. Perhaps there can be reconciliation after all.

# 48

She will not permit him into her bed. She knows he has not revealed all of his time with Svetlana on their journey to Graz. She suspects he was obliged to bed Adalie during their pursuit of Altmann; it would have been part of the deal Harrison forced upon him. The fact that the woman is now dead makes it easier to accept his infidelity. But Svetlana is more of a threat than ever before. She fully expects the woman to turn up at the *Schloss* and claim her husband. But she also knows Luisa would not welcome Svetlana; she fears and distrusts Russians, the people who murdered her family in cold blood. Erik is arriving the following day. She has missed him. It will be interesting to see the two men together. Perhaps it would have been better if her husband had never returned; it would certainly have been simpler.

She falls asleep with Róisín at her breast and dreams of France, of the *château* and her first sight of her husband as he stood at the great door and rang the metal bell pull, a tall handsome figure in the battle dress of a *Wehrmacht* general. In the dream she watches herself at the vast ornate mirror in the hall of the *château*, hastily arranging her newly peroxided hair as she prepares to welcome her feared enemy to the house which has been her home for two years. Still in the dream, she wanders into the library and sees the Bösendorfer piano by the windows which opened onto the terrace, and sees the cellos lined up against the wall close by. She knows she is dreaming because she can fly. This was something she learned as a child. Her dreams were always lucid, and in dreaming she could lie very straight and move her arms as wings and fly, never high but enough to move silently and swiftly above the ground. And it is so in this dream as she moves from room to room, looking down on her life of before. She sees Lotti and Emilia at their desks in the library and her husband at the massive mahogany desk that had once been Stefan's. She sees him look at the letters that have been put before him, which he immediately thrusts to the back of the drawer, and she watches as he gathers her up into his arms and carries her to his room.

And then the dream changes and she is at the piano and he is playing the cello, the Guadagnini cello, and she can hear the poignant strains of *Nacht und Träume*. It is then she awakens, and there is the sound of the cello. She places Róisín in her cradle and notes that her son is asleep in his cot bed. She slips a shawl over her shoulders and goes in search of the music. She finds him on the terrace of the *Schloss*. He is alone, but from the woods she can hear the trill of a nightingale. It is the Guadagnini cello and he is weeping as he plays it. She has no idea how the cello has come to be here: she had put it in a cupboard in Bonn months ago. The night is warm and she sits quietly on the parapet around the terrace and listens to him play. She knows he is unaware of her presence, but after a while, she can no longer bear to watch him weep and goes to him. She wraps her arms around him and there is only stillness between them. From that stillness comes the knowledge that despite all that has happened to them since the end of the war, the separation brought by the war, the trial that followed and the deceit and violence they have endured since, there is still love between them. She helps him place the cello in its case, takes his hand and leads him to her bed.

In the morning the mystery of the cello is revealed. Erik is at the *Schloss* and it was he who brought the cello from Bonn. He is with Luisa and Leon at the breakfast table when she and Karl join them. Their son is on Erik's knee being jigged up and down to his favourite "horsey" song. Luisa explains that their son had heard Erik's voice and had left the bedroom without waking his parents.

Later Erik and Helen walk together in the gardens. He informs Helen he will always love her but understands her life is with her husband; to attempt to take her from him would be dishonourable and neither could be happy in such a circumstance. He is to marry a fellow student at the university who has made it clear that she is enamoured of him, and this will be enough for him. They will raise a family together and be good citizens of the new Germany, the country which now promises peace and prosperity.

Both have tears in their eyes, but Helen knows he speaks with wisdom. It will never be over between them, but neither could she be with a man other than her husband. She talks to Erik about Svetlana, and he agrees she could cause more trouble between them.

'When she makes her way here, as I believe she eventually will, she should be persuaded to accompany your husband to Bonn where Major Harrison's replacement may be interested in what she has to offer. You have to accept that Svetlana will not relinquish your husband as I have been prepared to do you. She is dangerous in more ways than her sexual attractions, but it is for others to uncover her lies and duplicity. I will watch over you and your family.'

She has no words in response but wraps her arms around him. She kisses him on the mouth and in an instant she is clinging to him, not wishing to let him go. He lowers her to the ground and they are locked in an embrace; he enters her roughly but that is how she wishes it and cries when it is over. They acknowledge this must not happen again but both hope it will free them from the past and enable them to face the future, whatever it brings.

They return to the *Schloss* where Luisa informs them that her husband has taken both of his sons to the Kanal to watch the boats. Róisín is fretting for a feed and Helen puts the baby to her breast. Erik takes his leave of them; he has patients to care for at the hospital and his wedding to arrange. All are invited and he hopes his former *Kommandant* will agree to be "*Trauzeuge*".

After he has left, Luisa puts her arm around her daughter-in-law, for whom she has great love and respect.

'Whatever comes of this morning it will be our secret. It is unlikely what has passed between you and Erik today will result in a child; your daughter is at the breast and it is soon after her birth, but it would not be the first time such as this has come to pass, nor indeed at any time in a marriage. My second son was not of my husband. I know how much you love my son, and that is enough for me. The child would be my grandchild nevertheless.'

# 49

Helen is disturbed by the barking of Meg. She is proving to be a good watchdog as well as a companion for her stepson. Even Leon's reserve softens when the dog is with him, and she often joins him when he goes for walks in the woods around the *Schloss*. He does not wish for human company at these times; he has made this clear to his father, but the dog is welcome.

Helen leaves the bed where her husband is sleeping deeply, reaches into the chest of drawers by the bed and removes her gun. She wraps her shawl around her shoulders and goes down to the kitchen where the dog sleeps at night. She finds Meg agitated and barking at the window that overlooks the kitchen garden. Helen picks up the torch from the table by the kitchen door and, with Meg beside her, goes out into the darkness. A figure moves in the bushes, but Meg's attention is drawn to another who approaches Helen from behind and she barks a warning. Helen turns to see a blonde woman of around her own age closing on her with a gun raised. But the dog senses the threat to her beloved mistress and aims a sharp nip at the woman's ankle causing her to cry out in pain. She stumbles and Helen takes the opportunity to fire at the woman's gun arm. The gun drops to the ground as she attempts to staunch the bleeding from her shattered hand. Meg then runs towards the bushes yapping excitedly and the figure emerges. It is Leon.

Luisa has heard the commotion and the noise of gunshot and appears soon after. Leon is ordered to his room while Helen attends to Svetlana's wounds. Svetlana is secured to a chair while Helen removes the bullet and applies bandaging to the hand. It will be many months before Svetlana will hold a gun or indeed her husband. These are Helen's thoughts as she tends to the woman she loathes. Her husband has now appeared in the kitchen and been apprised of the drama. He goes to his car and removes a syringe containing the sedative he used on Altmann. No words pass between him and Svetlana, or indeed with his wife, as he injects the contents of the syringe into the upper arm of Svetlana. The woman collapses within seconds.

He carries Svetlana to an empty bedroom and asks Luisa to keep guard over her while he dresses. He asks Helen to dress and be prepared to drive with him to Bonn as soon as she is able. He will need a witness to the events of the night. But Helen understands that he does not wish to be alone with Svetlana; to do so would cause her to suspect his motives, such is the distrust now between them. There is Róisín to consider; there is no time to express milk for Luisa to bottle feed her, so she will have to accompany them. There are substantial risks in this arrangement, but Luisa will telephone Erik at the hospital and ask him to meet them on the road to Bonn. Leon will be questioned regarding his part in the attempted killing of his stepmother on their return. Meanwhile, he is to be locked in his room and only permitted to leave at mealtimes and for toilet.

At first light they load the semi-conscious Svetlana onto the back seat of the car and cover her with blankets. Her husband secures her uninjured arm to her body with a strong belt. Helen, with Róisín wrapped in warm blankets, sits in the passenger seat. They have food and water as well as a flask of schnapps in the trunk of the car. Helen knows her husband has more of the sedative in the glove compartment. As they make to leave, they hear a loud yapping and Meg throws herself into the car at Helen's feet. She will not leave her beloved mistress's side.

Helen strokes the dog, gently scratching under her ears which she knows the dog enjoys, and as she does so, she softly murmurs, 'You saved my life this night.'

They drive through the day, and when darkness falls, Helen takes over so her husband can sleep. She secures Róisín inside her husband's coat and both are soon asleep. She has never had driving lessons but was used to taking the wheel of her Uncle Damian's tractor during harvest time. It does not take her long to become accustomed to the gears and steering. Before she takes over, she administers more of the sedative to Svetlana. She has not stirred throughout the journey so far, but Helen does not underestimate the woman's strength. She has her child to protect as well as herself. The dog appears to sense this and sits on the rear seat at the head of Svetlana. She will be alert to any danger. Helen drives and her husband sleeps. Helen stops to feed Róisín, and when the daylight awakens her husband, she prepares breakfast for both of them. The early morning air is fresh, and they warm themselves with the schnapps. Helen checks on Svetlana. The bandaged hand is secure and there is no bleeding. The woman is conscious but drowsy. Helen gives her some water and then more of the sedative.

They reach Münster by mid-afternoon and Erik is on the road waiting for them. He takes Svetlana into his car, and they follow him to a small *Gásthaus* outside the city. Here they take rooms for the night and arrange a rota to keep watch over Svetlana. They enjoy a meal together and, after the dog has been fed and exercised, they bathe and sleep with Róisín between them. Each takes their turn in watching over Svetlana for two hours during the night. Helen insists she takes her share of the watch, despite the men's objections that she should rest. On her watch, Svetlana stirs and spits at Helen. She speaks English well enough to curse her as a "bitch from hell", but Helen is not disturbed by her words; the feeling is reciprocated, as she informs her in the vernacular.

Svetlana is awake enough to be given breakfast and, with Erik's help, Helen takes her to the bathroom to wash. She redresses her hand and, once she is settled in Erik's car, gives her a large dose of sedative, enough to ensure Erik a peaceful journey to Bonn.

They arrive in Bonn in the early evening and drive immediately to Allied Command. Helen and Erik are taken to the office of Major Harrison's replacement. To her astonishment and pleasure, she finds it is Major Mackenzie, the officer who was so kind and helpful during the days of her husband's trial in Nuremberg.

Erik explains that Helen has captured the daughter of a high-ranking Soviet general. The woman is an NKGB agent and claims to be seeking to defect to the British. She has attempted to kill Helen and her testimony may be open to doubt. The woman was one of the Soviet agents at Genoa who were planning to take Altmann before he boarded the ship to Argentina. Major Mackenzie turns to Helen.

'Altmann is now in British custody and is being very useful. I also know of your role in this. Harrison has confessed to his crimes against you. I can only apologise for what you have suffered at the hands of those who should have been grateful to you.'

'There is no need for an apology. It is enough to know the torture centre has been shut down and those incarcerated there have been released and given medical treatment. My concern is what is to be done with Svetlana Zharovskaya, the NKGB agent. I am not sure you should believe her story; that her father has fallen out of favour with Stalin and she risks imprisonment in the *gulags* if she returns. It is for your own intelligence agents to determine the truth. She is a threat to me and my children, but she knows where my husband's children are being held. Perhaps there is a deal to be done with her.'

'Where is the woman now?'

'She is asleep in Erik's car. My husband and our dog are guarding her. We drove her from Lübeck where she tried to kill me. With the help of my dog, I was able to shoot her before she killed me. Since then, she has been kept sedated, although I have tended to her wounds and ensured she is safe.'

The major smiles. 'It seems you have not forgotten what you learned during the war. Perhaps we should formalise your usefulness in capturing enemy agents by offering you a job with us.'

'Thank you, but no, I have more than enough intrigue within my family.'

Erik takes the major to his car and, with the help of two of the guards, Svetlana is unloaded and taken away. Helen joins her husband in his car. They decide they will stay in Bonn for a couple of days. There may be news of Karl's children, if Svetlana will talk.

It is good to be back in the apartment. The building is in a decent state of repair and all the apartments have kitchens and bathrooms. There is now a concierge, who complains that electricity and water supply can be unreliable and asserts that the British are deliberately making life difficult for Germans, as rationing and hunger are still a problem. She has a sister in Berlin, in the Soviet sector, where there is food in plenty and new apartments have been built with modern bathrooms and kitchens. Helen resists the urge to tell her to move there if that is what she craves.

They are welcomed by Magda and Pavel who are charmed by Róisín. She gurgles and smiles at them as they play with her on the floor, lifting her head when they call her name. They have news of their own to tell. They married in June in a quiet ceremony and

Magda is pregnant. The baby will be born in October; it is a new beginning for them after the tragedies of their former lives.

Ian and Morag come to supper and bring gifts of food and drink as well as presents for Róisín. They have been invited to the wedding of Erik and Traute which will be held at the Lutheran church in Bonn in October. Ian has met Traute and informs Helen that she seems "*a* nice enough *lassie,* though she is *nae beauty an' it's mae thinkin'* the lad just wants to *gae* on with his life."

Helen realises Ian understands how it was for her with Erik.

Her husband is quiet throughout the evening, as he has been since they arrived back at the apartment. Helen has found this oppressive. She understands the guilt he feels at Svetlana's attempt to kill her, and the knowledge that his son had been an accomplice in this.

It is late in the evening when their guests leave. Her husband clears the dishes while she feeds Róisín and settles her in the crib by their bed. He looks uncertainly at her as she undresses, but she takes his hand and leads him to the bed. She wants the cool strength of his hands; the hands that awakened her passion and soothed her pain, and which she now needs to reassure her that whatever has happened during the months they have been apart has not changed their love.

## 50

July 1947
Bonn, Germany

One week later, they are invited to the home of Major Mackenzie and his wife, Edith. The invitation instructs that the evening will be "Black Tie" with "carriages" at 11 p.m. Helen laughs as she explains to her bemused husband the archaic use of language on the embossed and ornately scripted card.

'It means you are expected to wear a black suit, tuxedo and black bow tie, and I a floor length gown.'

'And the carriages?'

'It is just a polite way of telling us when we should leave.'

'And where shall we find these garments?'

'Perhaps I should do as Scarlett O'Hara and find some old curtains to fashion into a gown, but even curtains would be hard to come by.'

'And I? Perhaps I should refashion a *Wehrmacht* uniform into a suitably abject garment. I believe these uniforms can be found on the black market. Or perhaps, as Major Harrison threatened me with "Operation Coal Scuttle", I should go to Essen, to those mines formerly of *Herr* Krupp and ask your British officers to exchange the *Wehrmacht* uniform for the garb of the miners. Many of my former comrades have been obliged to do the same. We shall make quite an impression: you in curtains and I in *Grubenhose* and *Bergkittel*.'

But there is humour as he says this; the ironic, mocking humour that had at first confused her and then come to love.

It is Edith who comes to their rescue. The NAAFI have recently established a formal dress hire service and the day following the invitation, she arranges for both to be driven to the NAAFI and appropriately fitted for "black tie". Edith chooses the gown for Helen. It is a Dior creation in green silk, cut low at the bust and back, but suitably modest nevertheless. She has loaned Helen her garnet necklace and bracelet, for which Helen is very appreciative; garnet is her birthstone and her wedding ring is of the same stone. When her husband is revealed in his "costume", which is how they regard this dress code, she is impressed by how well it becomes him; as usual, he will be the most handsome among the men.

Edith has insisted they bring Róisín with them; she would like to meet her, as she did their son. Their own children's nanny will take care of her while Helen is at their home. Meg will be taken into Magda's apartment for the evening.

A Mercedes car bearing the British flag collects them from the apartment building. Major Mackenzie and his family have requisitioned a villa close to that of Colonel Oakley and his wife. A uniformed maid ushers them into a vaulted entrance hall and, for a moment, Helen is unsure of how it will be arranged for Róisín. She can hear the polite murmuring of guests from a nearby room; should they enter, together with the shabby bag containing a bottle of expressed breast milk and a change of nappy? Or go in search of the nanny? But Edith is there immediately and takes Róisín in her arms. She exclaims over her red-gold curls and ivory skin but also her resemblance to their son.

They are the last to arrive, and the guests are already assembled in the salon and on the terrace overlooking the Rhine. The salon is magnificent, with oak-panelled walls that reach to a high, ornately gilded ceiling. The floors are marble, and Helen is conscious of the noise her heeled shoes make as they enter the room. She is more accustomed to wearing sturdy boots and sandals. While Karl and Helen are introduced, Edith insists on showing Róisín to the ladies of the party who are seated on sofas around the salon. All the assembled women remark on the beauty of Róisín, all except one guest: Sybil Oakley's social smile of welcome freezes when she sees who the new arrivals are. Edith leads Karl and Helen onto the terrace, where more introductions are made and Róisín the subject of even more admiration. Edith takes Helen to the same nanny who took care of her son during the days of her husband's trial at Nuremberg. Róisín will be in good hands.

Helen is introduced to the guests who are now mingling on the terrace. Champagne is served by British staff officers. She is introduced to the wife of the French High Commissioner, Odile François-Poncet. She notices her husband in conversation with an older man, and Major Mackenzie is approaching him with another older man. Odile is very friendly and requests that they speak together in French as she does not feel her English is good enough, nor her German.

'We spent many years in Berlin and as with many political wives, I spent too much time with my French compatriots and did not learn more than a few words of German. That is my husband, André, over there, and he is coming to speak with *Monsieur* Adenauer and your husband. He is very handsome your husband is he not? I understand you met him under most unusual circumstances. Do not fear, my dear, we know of your exploits. You have been overlooked for far too long. We also know how hard it has been for you here.'

'That is over now, and I have been fortunate to find good friends among German people.'

'Come with me, I shall introduce you to *Frau* Adenauer. She is a good friend of mine. Fortunately, her French is excellent.'

Helen is taken by the hand to be introduced to "Auguste", who is charmed when Helen greets her in perfect German, but for the sake of Odile they continue in French. Edith, who has been busy circulating among the other guests, joins them and reports that Róisín has settled to sleep having been fed the bottle that Helen brought with her.

After a while the serving of dinner is announced. Edith whispers, 'This is a very formal occasion, and we are escorted to the table by the men among the guests.'

Helen is immediately approached by the husband of Odile, who bows formally in front of her and requests the honour of escorting her to the table. She notices that her husband is with Edith and Major Mackenzie with Auguste Adenauer. Odile is escorted by *Herr* Adenauer. Colonel Oakley is escorting a very elegant woman, who seems familiar to Helen, and Sybil is accompanied by a man in French army uniform.

They are led into another magnificent oak-panelled room where a mahogany table is set with twelve place settings. The flags of three nations are placed at precise intervals on the table, the silver glistens and the crystal glasses sparkle in the reflected light of an enormous chandelier. Major Mackenzie and Edith take their places at opposite ends of the table. Auguste Adenauer sits to his left and to his right, Karl. Edith has *Herr* Adenauer on her right and Colonel Oakley to her left. Helen finds herself seated between Adenauer and André François-Poncet, and directly opposite the woman who she is certain she recognises but cannot at this moment recall from when and where.

The meal is delicious and notably without the restrictions of rationing. Helen finds the protocol of conversation very irritating. It appears she is only permitted to address those around her at designated times. She finds this absurd. Of course it would be impolite to shout across the table or speak with her mouth full of food, but it seems the other guests have also been instructed in this bizarre etiquette. Her Scottish family are aristocrats of some note, but she does not remember *Maman*, or one of her Gordon aunts, signalling her guests to instruct them when it is time to address another. It appears to be a form of conversational musical chairs, and she has to suppress a giggle at the inanity of what she considers a very English idiosyncrasy.

She finds herself alternatively in conversation with both Adenauer and François-Poncet. She exchanges a few pleasantries with both, at which time they each, alternatively, ask her how she views the future of her family in post-war Europe. She decides to break with this annoying protocol and tells them both, simultaneously, that she is perfectly happy to be in Germany. At the present time neither she nor her husband are welcome in France, she because she is considered by some as a collaborator.

Helen has raised her voice as she says this and notes Sybil's pursed lips and nod of her head at her neighbour, but she continues, 'And as my husband was part of the occupying force in France, we feel that France will not be happy to host any such as he for many years to come. Sadly, the same is true of my village in Scotland. Too many young men did not return from the battlefields of Europe, and should it be discovered that I am married to the former enemy I will not be welcomed. The Allies feel Germans must be punished for their misdeeds and I am happy to share in this punishment. I am married to the man I love, and I have his children. Either I can be considered a citizen of nowhere or as a citizen of the new Europe; frankly I would prefer the latter.'

She then translates all she has said into French and German. When she has finished speaking, and all at the table have been most attentive, Odile claps her hands, and to her great surprise, so do most of the other guests, including the Adenauers and the François-Poncets.

It is time for the ladies to withdraw and leave the men to their port and cigars. Helen has explained this ritual to her husband. She excuses herself and goes to check that Róisín is comfortable. She finds that her daughter has awoken and is working herself into a rage as the bottle is empty. The nanny appears exhausted; perhaps the major's children are more placid than her daughter. She loosens the straps of her dress and Róisín suckles voraciously. Helen tells the nanny to go to bed; she will not be returning to the party until "carriages".

Edith appears soon after 11 p.m. She finds Helen asleep with Róisín at her breast. She gently rouses her and informs her that the car is waiting to take them home. Helen apologises for any perceived lack of manners in absenting herself from the gathering, but Edith places her arm around her.

'Not at all and quite to the contrary; the Adenauers and Odile and her husband are all close friends of ours, and they were most impressed by you. Your courage and forthrightness are just what we need at this time of great change in our world; you have more friends than you could possibly imagine.'

She wraps a wool cape over Helen and Róisín and accompanies them to the waiting car. As they approach the car, she notices her husband in conversation with the woman she had struggled to place in her memory earlier in the evening. They part when Helen and Róisín appear, and her husband helps her into the car.

Once Róisín has settled, they discuss the evening. Karl informs her how proud he was when she spoke so honestly about their situation. He also tells her how beautiful she looked as she did so, and that her courage and beauty never cease to enchant him.

It is he who initiates their lovemaking, although her desire matches his. When he enters her he is not gentle, not as he was the first time he took her, but it is what she wants: to feel he possesses her completely as he did before, before all that has passed between them, the women she knows he has enjoyed and they him, and for her, before Erik.

They lie together, his arms enfolding her, and she is at peace. After a while he sleeps, and she hears Róisín stirring. Her breasts fill with milk and she lifts her daughter to her breast. She falls asleep as Róisín feeds and she dreams. In the dream she remembers the woman. It was the night of the recital, a July evening at the Château des Tilleuls. She was called to the kitchen by the cook but had noticed her husband in conversation with Hans, the *Oberfeldkommandur*, who was accompanied that night by a very elegant and beautiful woman. She struggles to remember the language in which they spoke. She is drifting in and out of sleep; exhausted by the events of the evening and her daughter's hunger. But then she is dreaming again. She can see the salon and the piano, the cello placed carefully beside it. The cook speaks to her in French; she is required in the kitchen urgently. She hears again the conversation of her husband and Hans with the woman; they spoke in German, as she had heard them speak this evening as Edith helped her to the car.

## 51

She waits until they are eating breakfast before she asks him about the woman.

'Surely the woman you were speaking to last night is the same woman Hans brought to our recital, after which I had to go to Paris, the night before the *Vel d'Hiv rafle*.'

'I do not recall. Hans had so many women, any one of which could have been with him that night. I am sure you are mistaken, the woman I was speaking to is French and works as an *attaché* at the French High Commission.'

'And the man with her?'

'He is a French army colonel.'

She knows this as she had been introduced to him on the terrace. He spoke with a Normandy accent, which she had recognised immediately, and they had spoken of the destruction of Caen. He is a Catholic, and regularly attends mass at Église Saint-Pierre. He knows her dear friend, *Père* François and promised to pass her best wishes to him the next time he has "*congé du service*".

'So this woman is unconnected to the colonel, romantically I mean. She is French and speaks German but is not from Alsace. When she speaks French, it is not with an accent that I recognise.'

'Perhaps that is because she has been in Germany for so long.'

'Perhaps that is what I am trying to say.'

'*Liebchen*, I do not understand why you have such an interest in this woman.'

'And I am asking why you should have such an interest in her.'

'I was merely bidding her goodnight. It is polite to do so is it not?'

She does not believe him. She decides to change the subject. They agree they will send a letter of thanks to the Mackenzies. He tells her again how proud he was of her at the dinner.

'Not only was my beloved wife the most beautiful woman there, but also her little speech was extremely well received.'

'I was concerned it may have caused offence, particularly to the British.'

'To *Frau* Sybil and perhaps her colonel husband, but all others were most impressed.'

She considers this.

'Who is André, the husband of Odile?'

'He is André François-Poncet. He was the French ambassador to Germany through the years of Hitler. He resigned his post after the Munich agreement and was reassigned to Rome, as ambassador to Italy. He resigned from this post in 1940, when Italy declared war on France. He is a man of principle. He returned to France, where he was arrested by the *Gestapo* and spent three years in prison during the occupation of France. Odile was also arrested but managed to escape to Switzerland, where she had family to support her. André is now the French High Commissioner, ambassador if you prefer, to the British and American Zones.'

'Who is *Herr* Adenauer? I realised he must be a person of some prominence, but he did not enlighten me during our conversation.'

'*Herr* Konrad Adenauer is also a most interesting man. He is Catholic and Prussian as I am, but we differ. He was born in Köln, in Rhineland Prussia, and the people of that region did not wish to be part of Prussia. They disliked the militarism of Prussia and the discipline and power of the Prussian ruling class. He is a man with a strong moral conscience both in his personal life and in public service. For over twenty years he was the elected mayor of Köln, but he always opposed Adolf Hitler. When the Nazis came to power in 1933, he was dismissed from his post and his bank account was frozen. He became a pauper and had to rely on the help of friends to survive and to ensure the safety of Auguste and their eight children. He was imprisoned following the assassination attempt on Hitler, the so-called "Valkyrie Plot", and became very ill. A former political rival, a communist, who was a *Kapo* at the prison camp, saw Adenauer's name on the list of those to be deported to the East and managed to get him into the camp hospital, where he remained until he was released, in November 1944.

'The Americans installed him as mayor of Köln, but when the city was transferred into the British zone of occupation, he was dismissed. He considers himself a political equal of the occupying Allies and is determined to build his new political party, the CDU, or Christian Democratic Union, which he hopes will unite Catholics and Protestants in a single party.'

'I had no idea that religion could play such an important role in politics. In France, there has been a complete separation of the church and the state for many years; so *Maman* informed me at least.'

'It has been so in Germany, except during the time of Hitler. Since 1946 Adenauer has been the leader of this new party and the British now regard him as a future Chancellor, as he had been considered in the years before Hitler. Unfortunately, he has low regard for my people, we of East Prussia. He blames our "Prussianism" for the rise of National Socialism. For this reason, some say, he opposes any idea that Berlin could be the capital of Germany again.'

'But surely he regards the Soviets and Communism as the greater threat now.'

'Naturally, and we spoke of this on the terrace. We have our differences as you will imagine, but he has been very forthright with the Western Allies; should the Soviets become hostile they will need help from Germany. He envisages a German Army led by senior German officers, and the heavy industry to support such an army. This will take time. The Allies wished to completely demilitarise Germany, remove all our heavy industry and reduce us to an agricultural society; a return to "*Heimat*". Many Germans would welcome this, with the sentimental yearning which omits the memories of the hardships and uncertainties of those times.'

'It is the same for many people; they want to believe the past was a better place, where the sun was always shining, there was food in plenty, and they were young and their children biddable. Perhaps such a time will come for us.'

'The struggle we have in Germany is to persuade people that life under the rule of Hitler was not the utopia many wish to remember it as. For some it was, including my family. We despised Hitler and knew him to be a purveyor of lies and brutality. If you were not a Jew, considered an *Untermenschen* or not courageous as *Herr* Adenauer, life was good: there was work for all, food on the table and the feeling of pride in being German. Now we are a defeated people, despised and humiliated. At your movie theatres in Britain, they show film reels of Germans being humbled at the *Fragebogen,* and former military commanders forced into menial labour under the orders of... "squaddies", I believe this is the word to describe such soldiers. People in Britain enjoy seeing how we live in buildings such as this, or as our home was, among rubble with no water or electricity. They watch and gloat, and say we are being punished as we deserve to be punished.'

'And do you not believe that the victory was an honourable

one? If Hitler's Germany had been victorious, there would not be a Jew left alive, Slavic people and others would have been enslaved and worse; and I would most certainly not be alive.'

'You know I would have protected you to the death.'

'That is ridiculous; you would have been forced to divorce me or be executed.'

'*Liebchen*, it is as I said, to the death. But laying down my life for you is not what I wished to speak of today. It is of my conversation with *Herr* Adenauer. The Allies are now agreed that the industries of Germany must be restored after the destruction of the war. The Allies will benefit from this in trade and reparations, but so will Germany, if not immediately then certainly in the future. As I spoke of earlier, there will eventually be the need for a German military to counter the Soviet threat. *Herr* Adenauer has made it clear he will be prepared to overlook my "Prussianism" and invite me to be part of this new army, as a general.'

'I am happy for you, but surely this means more time when we are apart. I do not feel our marriage flourishes in separation. You, for one, have too many... distractions.'

She endeavours to put as much ironic humour into these words as she can.

He laughs.

'*Liebchen*, you know I love you above all women. Part of my appeal to such as *Herr* Adenauer and *Monsieur* François-Poncet is my exceptional, incomparable wife. You charmed them all, and they are in awe of you.'

They are interrupted by Róisín's demands for attention.

'She has her mother's temper, and also her way of attracting attention to herself.'

'I would not be with you if that were not so.'

Róisín pulls hard at her breast until she is certain she has her mother's full attention and then feeds more gently until she sleeps. Helen allows her mind to drift over the conversation she had with her husband. She is happy for him; he was born to be a soldier, but she cannot banish her disquiet regarding the woman she recognised at the supper party.

Later they discuss when they should return to Schloss Mariendistel. They miss their young son, and there is the uncomfortable issue regarding Leon; his treachery cannot go unexplained, and possibly unpunished. There is also the matter of her medical studies; she has to make up the clinical sessions required to complete her training, and for this she must remain in Bonn. They agree that he will return to Lübeck to be with Leon. The dog, Meg, will return to Lübeck with him; the heat of the city in summer will be uncomfortable for a dog. As soon as he feels Leon is safe and of no risk to himself or others, he will return to Bonn. Luisa has offered to come to Bonn to help care for Róisín, and will bring their son with her.

## 52

Luisa arrives to care for Róisín while Helen is working at the hospital. It is both a blessing and a curse. Luisa believes in strict routines for babies. Róisín's demands for feeding go unanswered when her grandmother is in charge. Luisa has drawn up a timetable for Róisín; this schedules the times when she is fed, the times when she is entertained with songs and rhymes, in three languages, and when she sleeps. This very Prussian regime does not suit Róisín, at all, and each evening Helen returns to a disgruntled daughter, who punishes her mother for her absence with baleful looks and clamorous claims to her breast throughout the night. This is how it seems to Helen.

But in every other respect, it is a good arrangement. When Helen returns in the evening her son is ready for bed, having been fed a nutritious meal and entertained with folk tales and songs. The apartment is in good order and Luisa is much loved by their neighbours. She does not make any attempt to endear herself to the concierge, who she regards as stupid and over fond of interfering in the lives of the residents. Luisa suspected her of tampering with the mail and one day witnesses her steaming open a letter addressed to a neighbour. She challenges her about this, informing her that if she wishes to spy on the residents she should take the train to the Soviet Zone where there are opportunities in plenty for such as her. Furthermore, she will report her to the authorities and have her removed from the building; she will then be homeless. Luisa has the manner of one used to giving orders and being obeyed; the neighbours address her as *Gräfin* Luisa.

Erik is also working at the hospital. He is doing his training in surgery and she is working on a medical ward, but they occasionally meet at meal breaks. Helen has been introduced to Traute, who is always with Erik at these times. Helen feels that Traute does not wish her to be alone with Erik, and wonders whether he has told her of what has been between them. She has the opportunity to ask him at a time when Traute is summoned to attend to an emergency on her ward and they are left together in the dining room.

'I feel Traute does not trust me in your company. Have you told her of how it was between us?'

'No, I have not and I will not. I have to make this marriage a success. Both sets of parents have met and are pleased at the prospect of the union of two prominent medical families. Traute's father is a Professor of Surgery here and my parents feel my career will benefit from the connection.'

'I know I should not ask this; do you love her?'

'No, for me this will always be a marriage of convenience and duty. It is you that I love, as well you know.'

'Perhaps we should not meet. When my clinical training is completed, I will move to another hospital, in that way, it will be easier for both of you.'

'It will not be easier for me, but for Traute, yes, it should be so.'

'And your other duties?'

'They are the same. I am still useful. There will soon be news of our "Russian Doll".'

He says no more as Traute has returned. Helen takes her leave of them.

So there will be news of Svetlana. She wonders if her husband will be part of this.

# 53

Her husband returns to Bonn with both Leon and the dog. He asks to speak with her in private. Luisa takes charge of the boys while they put Róisín in her baby carriage and go to a nearby park. It is the evening and the streets are cooler so they take Meg with them. He explains to Helen that he has missed her and that Leon could not be left unattended.

'And how was it with Leon?'

'It is very complicated. My son is angry on account of the destruction of his country and continues to apportion blame to me for this. I can understand how he feels; children have endured much suffering both during the war and in defeat. Many are orphans and live on the streets as beggars. Leon is fortunate as he has a home, but he is angry and resentful nevertheless. He also fears for his siblings and cousins; he feels guilty that he is safe and they are not. He has admitted how he was persuaded to assist Svetlana in her attempt to kill you. She knew where to find you; how she found this information, I do not yet know. She met with Leon in the woods of the *Schloss* and promised that his brother, sister and cousins would be returned to Germany, to their father, but in order for this to be achieved, you should be killed. She persuaded him that your actions played a part in Germany's defeat and you would cause further ruin for Germany and our family.'

'There is some truth in what he says, as you know well.

Perhaps it will be easier for him when your children are returned. I should then live apart from you, to allow you to enjoy your family, without the resentment and disharmony my presence provokes.'

'You know that is not want I want. I love you and you are my wife, and we have children together. Leon will have to accept the situation. He needs to go to school. His tutor left their home in December 1944. Since then, my children have had no education.'

'They learned how to survive in a forest; that is an education. But I understand that this situation cannot continue. It is the summer recess for schools. We have time to plan for the new school year.'

'Now, *Liebchen*, we must return to our family. I brought the Guadagnini cello with me. We will play together this evening. "Music has charms to soothe the savage breast". Perhaps we can charm Leon with *Nacht und Träume*, and even our daughter to sleep. My mother tells me that she keeps you awake all night as a punishment for leaving her to the stern dictates of a Prussian matriarch.'

'It is good for Róisín. Luisa loves her, but she recognises her wayward and rebellious spirit.'

'She is as her mother and will be as beautiful. I fear we will have many challenges with our daughter.'

'We will enjoy them together.'

She leans into him as he pushes the pram. He whistles for Meg, who returns with a tennis ball in her mouth. She has evidently stolen this from two children who are using the ruins of a former tennis club to play a game. The club house is an empty shell which, according to their neighbours, is used by older children, some as young as twelve, to barter amphetamines and tobacco for sex.

This is what war has brought to these children; their childhoods were taken from them and they are old before their time. The two children whose ball Meg has stolen are playing on a rutted clay court with a piece of wire for a net. Helen retrieves the ball from Meg and returns it to them. She asks their names and promises to appeal to the British Control Commission to restore the tennis court and make a playground for local children. The ruins provide scope for war games and hide-and-seek, but the rubble is dangerous and buildings near to collapse are still a feature in this district.

It is good to make music again together. She struggles to keep the tears from flowing as they play the *Arpeggione Sonata*. The second movement, in particular, evokes memories of their time at Château des Tilleuls. They end the recital with *Nacht und Träume* and, for the first time, Leon shows emotion. He tries to conceal this and soon after excuses himself to go to bed, but requests that Meg be permitted to join him. He will sleep in their son's small room and Luisa has insisted that she will make her bed on the sofa beside the *Kachelöfen*.

The bed is large enough to accommodate their son, and Róisín submits to being placed in her cradle. As they lie together he describes how Leon enjoyed listening to him play *Nacht und Träume* in the orangery at Luisa's villa in Kranz, and would request it before he went to bed. Perhaps music and the dog can help reconcile Leon to his new family.

They both wish to make love but their son is in the bed and their daughter is easily disturbed. Helen believes her daughter is awake even when she sleeps, so aware she seems to be of the slightest movement or sound. But slowly and silently they move closer to each other. Her lips search for his; she wants to breathe his breath and taste his mouth. His hands move over her body and seek out the place he knows gives her so much pleasure. It is exquisite, tantalisingly so, but she knows she must remain silent. She moves over him, kissing every part of his body and it is he who struggles to be silent. She wants him inside her and she draws him close to her again so their eyes meet. He lifts her onto him and it is as always; even better. There is the same desire and passion, but equally, there is the acknowledgment that they must reset the love between them. There has been infidelity, and she is certain he has not revealed all that is between him and Svetlana, nor what there was with Adalie. On her part, there has been Erik and she cannot easily banish the memories she has of those months when they lived together and slept in this bed. Róisín is stirring and murmuring in her sleep. Luisa has noted how precocious her granddaughter is, that her eyes seem to see more than there is to see and her ears hear more than there is to hear. But she does not cry, so they whisper together.

'*Liebchen*, when I spoke the words of William Congreve, "Music hath charms to sooth a savage breast" I was reminded of other words in the same play.'

'You are talking about "The Mourning Bride". I know this play, and also that many of its best-known lines are wrongly attributed to Shakespeare.'

'So you will know how it was written "Hell hath no fury like a woman scorned".'

'Of course I know of these words, and presume it is Svetlana you wish to speak about. But her "Love to Hatred turned" is directed at me. She tried to kill me and not you. Perhaps she imagined she could replace me in your affections.'

'That could never be, but in our time of travelling to Graz, we were together.'

'I imagined you would not be able to resist her. Erik told me how it was between you.'

'You must know that it was not love. I had been away from you for months and without any contact from you. I did not know you had been forbidden to enquire after me. Adalie told me you had found another, of which Harrison must have informed her in some way. I now realise how we were both much deceived by Harrison. Svetlana was available to me and, yes, I enjoyed her, but she is a woman who uses men for her own pleasure and does not care to give in return. With her, sexual relations between a man and a woman must be brutal. I have known many women such as she; they cannot love but they will take all they can from a man. For men, there is pleasure and excitement with such women, but afterwards there is only emptiness and uncertainty. I am asking for forgiveness, not so much for what happened with Svetlana on the journey, but for the threat to your life that came of it.'

'There is no need for forgiveness; we should leave that to priests in the confessional. I am aware Svetlana is a threat to my life and the lives of my children. I will be on my guard. I have a gun and will use it to protect my family.'

'You truly are a remarkable woman.'

'I have said these words before but will repeat them: I would not be with you if I were not such a woman.'

She moves closer to him again. Róisín seems to have settled to a deeper sleep. They start again; the furtiveness makes it all the more exquisite and exciting.

Róisín sleeps; she is aware of what is between her parents, but her dreams are full of foreboding.

## 54

Early the following morning the concierge is at the door. With an air of immense self-importance she hands Helen a letter which she says has just been delivered by a British army officer. The letter bears the stamp of British Military Command. The woman is slow to leave the doorway, and Helen wonders if she expects her to open the letter and read its contents to her or give her a tip. She does neither, but thanks her politely and closes the door.

The letter is brief but requests that *Herr* von Werstein and *Frau* von Werstein attend the office of Major Mackenzie by 9 a.m. A staff car will be sent for them.

Major Mackenzie's greeting is friendly and both are offered coffee, which they are grateful for. Real coffee has been in short supply at NAAFI, and what little Helen is able to obtain she shares with her neighbours. She suspects that the likes of Sybil and her friends have found ways of circumventing rationing and have been stockpiling it.

He comes straight to the point of their summons to his office. The Soviet agent in Military Command has been "turned" on the threat of being handed back to the Soviets. He has been very useful and imparted valuable intelligence to his new handlers. Major Mackenzie turns to Helen.

'I can assure you the techniques used to extract this information were not in any way comparable to those you and others suffered at Bad Nenndorf. Furthermore, from what we have learned, I will be obliged to request your participation in a mission which will put you in danger, but if successful will ensure the safe return of your husband's family. You will, of course have the option to refuse.'

'If it means my husband's children can be returned to us, it would not be an option, it would be a necessity. Of course I would not refuse.'

Karl is not so positive.

'My wife has been placed in more than sufficient danger over the last six years. I would wish to know of the risks she would be taking and that she can trust British Intelligence. Her experience with your predecessor, Major Harrison, does not give her faith in your organisation.'

'Of course, I understand your apprehensions, absolutely. What she suffered was an outrage and without any justification. I should not speak ill of my former colleagues, but it is my opinion the man is a sadist and that he took great personal pleasure in humiliating Helen. So I will tell you what I know and clarify the reason for asking you here.'

The major goes on to explain that Svetlana's claim to be seeking refuge in the West on account of her family's fall from favour was a lie. The agent has revealed that Svetlana had hoped to work as a double agent, ostensibly working for British Intelligence, while passing information to the Soviets.

Helen smiles as she remembers that Erik has been feeding this "useful" agent nothing but trivia and fabricated military "secrets". She can only hope his information on Svetlana is reliable; her life could depend on it.

'This seems credible. It is clear, to me at least, that Svetlana was at the port of Genoa because she knew my husband would be there. Has your newly recruited agent explained how Svetlana knew this and what she hoped would come of it?'

'According to intelligence he informed the NKGB, for which Svetlana has worked as a senior officer since its inception, of the names of the British agents who were tailing Altmann. He also arranged for the photographs to be sent to you by one of his junior agents.'

She has further cause to smile as she ponders the major's words. *So, perhaps he does not know of Erik's role in sending the photographs. Does Mackenzie know Erik works as a double agent, or has his cover been blown by denouncing the "useful agent"? It would be interesting to find out.*

She replies, 'But what would her plan have been if she and her fellow agents had managed to capture Altmann? Would she have tried to save my husband?'

'Svetlana is a consummate opportunist. When she saw her comrades killed by the Italians, and that Karl had captured Altmann, she moved swiftly into another role; that of the supplicant defector and persuaded your husband of this. He eventually saw through her lies and arranged for her to be kept as a prisoner of his family in Graz while he returned to Bonn.'

'This makes my husband appear more of a fool than a hero. I can assure you that he is no fool. He took her with him to Graz and gave her every reason to believe he had been duped by her, to the extent that he had sexual relations with her on the journey. It is what she wanted and believed he wanted from her.'

Her husband looks uncomfortable.

'It is true and because of this, Svetlana considered that she could kill Helen and take her place in my life.'

'She believed you had fallen for what we call a "honey trap".'

'But for some of our time together, I did believe her, I wanted to believe her.'

Helen interrupts. She is losing patience with the interview.

Surely a dissection of her husband's sexual relations with Svetlana is not the purpose of this meeting.

'You did not answer my question. If the Soviets had captured Altmann, would she have allowed them to kill my husband and left with them, or would she have attempted her scheme to persuade my husband she wanted to defect?'

'I do not believe she would have allowed him to be killed. He had failed in his mission and would be suspected of treachery by the British. She would know there could be no bogus defection. It is more likely she hoped that Karl would join her. But this is speculation and distressing for Helen. We have Altmann and we have Svetlana; "two birds with one stone" as we say.'

The major orders more coffee to be brought to the office and then continues, 'According to our intelligence, the Soviets believe Svetlana was abducted by your husband and they want her back. They have offered the return of Karl's children, including the two cousins, in exchange for Svetlana. It is not normal for the Soviets to allow the abandoned children of East Prussia to be returned to the West, despite the pleas of the Red Cross. This is a significant concession by the Soviets; Svetlana must be very important to them.'

'On whose intelligence do they believe she was abducted? If it is your newly useful agent, how can we be certain he can be trusted?'

'He has no wish to be returned to the Soviets. He knows he would be executed.'

'How is the exchange to be arranged?'

'As we do not trust the Soviets to return the children, it has been suggested by an intermediary that Helen is given safe conduct to Dresden, where the children are being held. She will have papers to authorise their release and she will bring them, under the same escort, to Checkpoint C, where we will be waiting with Svetlana, and the exchange will be made.'

Her husband speaks up, 'Under no circumstances will I permit my wife to take such a risk. I will go to find my children.'

'Then that is a problem. The Soviets will arrest you immediately and you will spend the rest of your life in the mines of the *gulags*.'

'And why is that? I have committed no crimes.'

'They wish to please the Poles. There has been discontent in Poland following the elections in January of this year. In the Yalta Agreement, Stalin promised a "free and unfettered" electoral process in post-war Poland but knew full well that in such circumstances the result would be overwhelmingly anti-Soviet. Politicians opposed to the Soviet occupation were persecuted during the election campaign and the results were falsified in favour of the party supported by the Soviets. Many politicians fled the country and anti-communist Poles have felt betrayed. To appease this resentment, Stalin promised to bring to justice Germans accused of perpetrating war crimes on Polish territory during the war years. You, Karl, are on his list of perpetrators.'

Helen feels her temper rising.

'This is ridiculous. I know of what happened at Czatków. My husband tried to save the woman and her children. He was appalled by the atrocities he and his men discovered as they crossed Poland.'

'Nevertheless, Karl would be at risk of arrest and worse. Our intermediary has advised that it must be Helen who brings the children to the British sector.'

'And if I do not return with the children?'

'Svetlana will remain imprisoned here in Germany.'

'Until a better deal is made for her release, I am sure.'

Major Mackenzie looks affronted.

'Helen, surely by now you understand how much we value

you and that we are proud to have you among us.'

'There was a time when I thought that might be so, but in these past eighteen months I have learned otherwise; my worth and that of my husband lies in our usefulness to the British. You and Edith have been exceptionally welcoming to us and we are grateful. But I will go. Please tell me how I can do this.'

# 55

## August 1947
## Bonn, Germany

Luisa will return to Schloss Mariendistel with Róisín, young Karl, Leon and Meg. Luisa now has a substantial number of people to assist her at the *Schloss*. There is a nurse for Róisín and Karl, a tutor for Leon, a cook, housemaids and gardeners. Luisa's inheritance included several lucrative investments in the coal and manufacturing industries, which are now flourishing again in the Ruhr. These were, of course, Scottish investments and under the protection of British law.

Karl will accompany Helen to Berlin, where she will be helped into the Soviet sector by the British military. She will be passed directly into the care of the Soviet military, who will take her to Dresden, where the children have been located in an orphanage. At each stage of her journey from Berlin to Dresden she will be accompanied by a designated Soviet military interpreter, fluent in German and English. Amongst a few personal possessions, she has also packed clothing for the children and several photographs of their father and brother, as well as of the Schloss Mariendistel with Luisa in the foreground. Louisa supplies a photograph of the children on the beach at Kranz with their father, and one of Leon with Meg, the dog. There is also a large supply of chocolate.

She has papers attesting to the children's parentage, which are stamped by Bizone Command, as well as by the International

Tracing Service, who have confirmed that the children are being held at the Leuben Institute in an area of Dresden by that name. The institute was used as a workhouse and correctional facility for "deviants and asocials" from the late 19th century. It survived the bombing raids and firestorms and is now used to house the hundreds of orphaned children found wandering in the ruins of the bombed cities, as well as those captured in the forests bordering Lithuania. She is warned that the conditions at the institute are grim. A Red Cross inspection of the institute late in 1945 had reported the harshness of the regime for the children, and the poor quality of the accommodation and food. As Dresden is now under Soviet control it would not have improved.

An RAF plane flies them to the British Air Force base at Gatow, and from there they are taken in a military car to Checkpoint C, the official crossing point to the Soviet sector. Karl embraces her and assures her he will wait in Berlin until she returns, which will be in three days at the most. Her papers are checked and her bag is searched by a severe female guard. She is led to a jeep occupied by two Soviet soldiers, where her papers are checked again and she is helped into the rear seat of the vehicle. She keeps her possessions close to her, her peggybag and water flask on her shoulder.

Her escorts make no effort to engage her in conversation and she does not understand Russian. She asks in German how long the journey will take and is ignored. They drive through the day until nightfall. She knows Dresden is nearly two hundred kilometres from Berlin and the journey is delayed by the destruction of bridges and damage to the roads. She is concerned when they stop the car by an area of woodland and remove bottles of vodka and food from a box on the seat beside her. They indicate that she must leave the vehicle and accompany them into the woods. She is offered the first *glotok* of the bottle but refuses. She asks in English for water but it appears there is none. She realises that neither speaks English nor German. They are not the interpreters she was promised; she has fallen into a trap. She now fears for her husband. He is in Berlin waiting for her return and is close to the Soviet checkpoint. He could be abducted by the Soviets, as she has learned has been the fate of others.

The men continue to drink and eat, and after a while sing raucously. One attempts to kiss her, but she pushes him away. This angers him and he makes to grab at her, but she is too quick for him and runs for the protection of the trees. They stagger to their feet and shout, *"Komm, Fräulein"* and pursue her. She stumbles through the undergrowth and takes refuge behind a tree. She can hear their drunken shouts as they search for her. She slips the peggybag off her shoulder and removes her water flask. She releases a clasp at the bottom of the flask and removes the gun secreted there. Her pursuers will also have weapons, guns that will be more powerful than hers; she will need to at least disable both men simultaneously to survive.

They are getting closer and she snaps an overhanging branch. They immediately move towards the sound and she is ready for them. She takes aim at the man closest and fires at his chest and he falls to the ground. His companion reaches for his gun, but she calmly takes aim and fires between his eyes. He too falls to the ground and is motionless. Meanwhile, the first man is struggling to his feet, but a bullet between his eyes finishes him. She quickly gathers their weapons and the keys to the vehicle. She covers their bodies with brushwood and places the vodka bottles beside them. She takes a moment to appraise the macabre "picnic". It is possible others may follow so she finds more branches and brushwood to cover the area. When she is satisfied the bodies will not easily be found she returns to the jeep. She takes the food with her.

She has no idea where she is but at least the fuel tank is full. She looks in the compartment in front of the passenger seat. There is a map of Germany and the route they have taken is marked on it. She estimates she is within thirty kilometres of Dresden. She will follow the map but avoid the main routes, which could be guarded. The fact that whoever set the trap will assume her to be dead provides little comfort. She will not find the orphanage without assistance, and it is possible the orphanage does not exist, or the children moved elsewhere. She drives through the dark and follows signs in both Russian and German to Dresden. It is still dark when she reaches the outskirts of the city. It is a full moon and she can see the utter devastation of Dresden. She parks the jeep in the ruins of a church and goes in search of help.

There is a light within the ruins of the church and she goes towards it. She looks through the window of what appears to be the remains of the vestry and sees an elderly man in a priest's robes writing at a desk. The room is in a poor state; the walls are scorched and large pieces of plaster have fallen from the ceiling. A crucifix hangs on one pitted wall and on another is a picture of the Madonna, but not one she is familiar with. She knocks tentatively on the window and the priest swivels round with fear on his face. When he sees it is a young woman and not the dreaded Soviet military, he immediately stands up and comes to the door.

She explains her situation as best she can in German, but he interrupts her to ask if she would prefer to speak in French.

'It is my mother tongue and I am happy to be able to speak it freely once again; it has been many years since I have been able to do so.'

'How is it you speak French?'

*Père* Gerard Schroeder explains that he was born in Kruth, in Alsace, in 1876. His mother, Grita, was the daughter of the local *maréchal-ferrant* and his father a *Reiter* in a Prussian cavalry regiment that had taken the village in the early stages of the Franco-Prussian war in 1870. His father had come to the forge to have his horse reshod and he and his mother had met and fallen in love. Following the defeat of France and the subsequent annexation of Alsace and Lorraine to Germany, they married and settled in the village. There had been a great deal of local opposition to the marriage, but as many such unions were formed in the years following the defeat of France, they were left in peace to raise a family. *Père* Gerard was their third son and from a young age, he had been determined to be a priest. They spoke French and German at home, as did many of that region.

'I do not recognise the Madonna in the picture. Who is she?'

'She is Our Lady of Kruth. From 1872 to 1877 she appeared to four children on many occasions, in a cloak of golden threads with a golden crown on her head and a black cross on her chest. She was often seen holding a sword in her hands, as you see in the picture. A shrine was built at the place where she appeared. There were reports of miracles and thousands of pilgrims visited. When I was ordained as a priest, my parents gave this picture of the Madonna to me.'

'How did you come to be in Dresden?'

'My father's family is from this city. I came here in 1899 as a young curate and became a parish priest in 1919. I was very happy until the time of Hitler, but with the help of friends I survived, along with a number of Jews who were hidden in the church. I now fear the wrath of the communist Soviets. But I will stay here and continue to administer to the few of my parish who have survived the war.'

'I need your help, father, and I have to trust you.'

She explains her situation: that she is in Dresden to rescue the children of her husband whose second wife she is. She has been informed that they are in The Leuben Institute. She has papers authorising their release and return to their father and family in the British Zone. She had been promised an escort to Dresden with a military interpreter, but she was betrayed The men into whose care she had been placed by the Soviets spoke only Russian and had been instructed to kill her.

'And where are these men now?'

'They are buried in a forest. I killed them.'

'You have courage, a great deal of it. And it is no sin to kill those who wish to dishonour and murder you.'

'It is not the first time I have had to do this.'

'How did you get to this church?'

'I took the vehicle they used and drove it here, but only by chance did I find the church.'

'So you have papers and a vehicle. To find the children, in that I can help you, but it will be difficult to get them out of Soviet territory. You say there has been a betrayal. This means you have enemies who will be looking for you. You are in a very dangerous situation.'

'Is there a way I can contact my husband to inform him of what has happened? He is expecting me to return to Berlin within 48 hours.'

'He will have to wait for you. For this night you will stay here with friends. Is your vehicle well hidden?'

'For tonight it is but my pursuers will soon be looking for it.'

'Follow me and do not be afraid. You are safe here. Are you a Catholic?'

'Yes, as are my mother's family and that of my husband. I have not been to mass or confession since the end of the war. I have begun to feel that a God who permits such cruelty and devastation in the world is not one I would wish to continue to worship.'

'Perhaps the same God brought you here tonight. Now, I need your help; when I roll back this rug you will hold it while I open what is beneath.'

He rolls back a tattered rug on the floor behind his desk and reveals a trapdoor. She watches as he pulls hard on the metal ring and the door opens to reveal steps that appear to go deep underground.

'You must go ahead of me with this torch, and I will close the trapdoor and replace the rug as I follow you.'

She descends the steps and follows the corridor at its base. This leads to a room in which three men are sitting on bunk beds reading by torchlight. *Père* Gerard introduces Helen and explains her situation. They, in turn, relate their own predicaments. All are former concentration camp prisoners who had the misfortune to become trapped in the Soviet Zone at the end of the war. There is a network that *Père* Gerard and other priests of all faiths have organised to smuggle those in this situation into the British and American Zones, where they hope to find their families. The Soviets have tightened their grip on their zone and without the right papers, it has become difficult, if not impossible, to travel between the zones.

She accepts the spare bunk bed with gratitude. There is a lavatory with a washbasin close by. She is not hungry but accepts the bowl of soup which is warmed for her over a small Primus stove in a corner of the room. She is told this room was used to shelter Jews during the times of persecution and deportation.

*Père* Gerard wishes them all a good night and informs Helen that a "runner" will be sent immediately to contacts in Berlin. Her husband will be informed of what has happened.

She finds it difficult to sleep. She worries about Róisín who will be missing her, and her breasts ache with milk. She is able to express the milk from her breasts in the bathroom, which relieves the pain and leakage into her clothing. She worries for her husband who could be in mortal danger, and she worries how she will be able to get the children to safety. She is too exhausted to consider the betrayal that had been the attempt on her life.

It is first light before she eventually falls into a deep sleep. Her dream again takes her back to France. She sees the *château* on a July evening where she and her husband are to give a recital. She can smell the musky fragrance of the night-scented stocks and the roses she and Lotti have arranged in the salon where the recital will take place.

She sees the woman who arrived with Hans. Her long dark hair is in a chignon arranged low over the back of her elegant neck. Around her neck is a diamond collar. She is wearing a black velvet dress which is cut low over her bust. Both men, her husband and Hans, appear to be captivated by her, just as her husband was on the night of the Mackenzies' supper party. She then falls into a deeper, dreamless sleep before she is awakened by *Père* Gerard, who informs her she must wash and be prepared to leave within the hour.

It is as she dresses that she remembers the dream and considers its significance. The woman is the one who betrayed her. It is she who "arranged" the exchange. She is Major Mackenzie's "intermediary". The woman is working for the French High Commission. Perhaps she was tasked with punishing a former collaborator, as many may still consider her to be, and perhaps she will organise Svetlana's repatriation as part of another deal between the Allies and the Soviets. Whatever the conspiracy or motives, there will be no exchange at Checkpoint C. She and the children will be murdered if they approach the border.

## 56

August 1947
Dresden, Germany

*Père* Gerard drives a 1934 Mercedes saloon. It is very slow and the bodywork shudders as they pass over the ruts and holes that are the roads to Leuben. As they drive, Helen explains her suspicions about the plot to kill her and her anxieties for the children. He allays her fears as best he can.

'It is important we get the children released from the institution. They will be hidden in the church until we have news from Berlin. In a few minutes, we will be intercepted by another car. You and I will change places with the driver and passenger. We will do this again before we reach the institute. In this way, my vehicle cannot be traced to the church. It is a normal precaution which we learned during the time of the Nazis and *Gestapo*.'

In the third car, they are joined by a young woman. She does not reveal her name but explains she will take charge of the papers authorising the release of the children. Helen should not be seen at the institute.

'There will be people looking for you and they will come to the institute and question the staff. It is better for them if they have not seen you. It would go badly for them if they were interrogated. I am sure you understand. You must lie in the well of the car while I enter the building and remove the children. I have a contact at the institute who will ensure the children are released into my care.'

They arrive at Leuben and a sign directs them to the institute. Helen is shocked by the dilapidated buildings that are home to her husband's children and their cousins. The main structure is a former farmhouse, but pig pens and cattle sheds have been incorporated to house the inmates. It has survived the bombing raids and firestorms, but there are gaps in the walls and part of the roof of the main building is missing. A forbidding barbed wire fence surrounds the site. The woman leaves the car and rings a bell on the massive metal gate that is the entrance to the institute.

It is one hour later when the gate opens and the woman returns, accompanied by two girls of around nine years of age and two boys who look to be around fourteen. All are pale and their ragged clothes hang from their frail bodies.

There is little space in the car, so Helen remains in the well of the passenger seat and the children are bunched together on the rear seat of the car. There is no time for introductions or explanations as they speed away from Leuben. As before, they change vehicles twice before they arrive at the church, where they are quickly ushered into the vestry and down into the secret rooms beneath.

There is hot soup waiting for them and as they eat, Helen tells them who she is and that they will be taken to join their father, the uncle to Johanna and Felix. They are able to wash and dress in the clothing she has brought for them. They are silent throughout this time and look around furtively as though they cannot trust those around them or the situation in which they now find themselves. Helen is anxious they might try to escape; they have become feral during their time in the forests and incarceration in the institute.

After a while, she shows them the photographs she has brought with her and for the first time the children look animated. It is the fortress of sand on the beach that prompts Alexi to exclaim, 'It is

Papa and there is Leon. I remember now, and *Oma* Luisa used to bring the picnic to the beach.'

Maria-Sophia tries to snatch the photograph from him and cries when she sees that she is not in it.

'You were just a baby. Your nurse used to bring you down to the beach, and you would cry all the time.'

Maria-Sophia throws herself at Alexi and pulls out a chunk of his hair. The other children join in, scratching and tearing at each other. Helen has never witnessed such savage behaviour in children but understands this is due to the trauma they have witnessed and endured. She restores order by telling them she will not show them the other photographs she has, including another of their brother, Leon, if they continue to fight. Furthermore, she has chocolate with her and they will only receive it if they behave.

Helen has found it difficult to explain all of this in German, but they have understood her well enough. Soon they are calm and enjoying large pieces of chocolate, which she encourages them to share with the three men in the adjoining room. It is clear that sharing was not something they were accustomed to doing at the institute or in the forest; it would have been survival of the fittest, or the most determined and ruthless. They immediately stuff the chocolate into their mouths before Helen can enforce this. Soon after, Maria-Sophia announces she is going to be sick, and Helen tells her this is due to her having eaten the chocolate so quickly. She takes her to the small washroom, but it is too late and Maria-Sophia vomits over Helen.

They both wash at the sink and Helen notices for the first time the small gold birthmark on the left arm of her stepdaughter; it is identical to the one on the arm of her daughter, Róisín. Helen does her best to explain that she has a half-sister with the same mark, but Maria-Sophia is not interested and asks for more chocolate. This is denied and Helen can see the beginning of another tantrum. Perhaps Róisín's temper is not only inherited from her mother, and then she remembers that she and her husband share a common ancestor. Life at Schloss Mariendistel will not be a haven of tranquility.

They settle to sleep at around 11 p.m. after more soup and chocolate. She will stay with them and lock the door. She still worries they may try to escape. In the early hours of the morning, she hears a tap at the door. It is *Père* Gerard. She joins him in the corridor outside the room and they speak in whispers.

'The runner has returned and the news is not good. The bodies of the men have been found and there is a search for the jeep, and for you and the children. Your husband has been made aware of the betrayal and is most concerned for you.'

'Is there any way we can escape, perhaps across the border to Czechoslovakia; it is not too far from here?'

'That is not possible. The government of Czechoslovakia is sympathetic to the Soviets, they dare not be otherwise. There will be guards on both sides of the border looking for you. For the moment you must stay here with the children. We are moving the jeep further into the ruins. We have changed the number plate and made a few adjustments to the vehicle so that it is not immediately recognisable. Another runner is in Berlin with your husband, where they hope to make a plan for you and the children. Now return to the room and get as much sleep as you can. There will be difficult times ahead.'

# PART FOURTEEN


## Karl

# 57

August 1947
Berlin, Germany

I knew there had been a betrayal when Svetlana did not arrive at Checkpoint C at the allotted time. The plan had been to bring her under armed guard in a British Staff car. The car arrived and a very apologetic Major Mackenzie climbed out. He took me into the Border Control station, and I was invited to sit at a table where two RAF officers were already seated. There was a large map of Germany on the table with circles of different colours imposed on it. After introducing me to Wing Commander George Vartis and Squadron Leader William Dixon, the major explained the situation to me.

'I regret to inform you that your wife's concerns were correct. Our intermediary has proved to be unreliable...'

I interrupted him at this point.

'Unreliable! You English have a strange way of describing the person who organised the murder of my wife. She is a duplicitous killer who I knew to be part of Himmler's SD, and who has now aligned herself with the Soviets.'

'How do you know of this?'

'I made my own enquiries as to the identity of your intermediary but by the time I discovered her identity and her recruitment, my wife had already left for Dresden. I know this woman from my time in Normandy. In those days, she was working for Himmler, for his SD or *Sicherheitdienst,* his security service. Many young women assigned as secretaries to the *Feldkommandurs* had been recruited by him. Fortunately for my wife and myself, my secretaries were not spies and murderers. I have already had to deal with one of your trusted recruits and now you have another in your midst.'

At that moment I would have gladly shot Mackenzie for his naivety. He had invited the woman to his home. I had recognised her immediately and realised how easily she had ingratiated herself into the occupying hierarchy. I suspected she would be part of some espionage organisation, whichever paid the most. By working for the Allies and the Soviets she was in the pay of both. My wife had been correct in recognising her, but I could not tell her of my suspicions. She had also been very flirtatious with me, which caused me great embarrassment as Helen had noted our conversation. My wife is often more watchful of me than I feel comfortable with.

'*Herr* von Werstein, Karl, please calm down. Anger will not solve the situation. I agree we have been duped by this woman and I now have to tell you what we know. Svetlana escaped from captivity as we were preparing to bring her to Berlin. She begged the guard to release her, expressing an urgent need to use the lavatory. As there was no female guard available, she was permitted to go without an escort. When she did not return, the toilet block was searched and we found an open window. It was clear she had been assisted in her escape; a delivery vehicle had been close to the block and was seen leaving soon after. No deliveries had been scheduled for that time, so we can assume this was how she escaped. We then knew that no exchange would take place at Checkpoint C. At that time, however, we did not know of your wife's fate. We learned of this today from a "runner", a person engaged in assisting those trapped in Soviet territory to escape, and pass information between the zones.'

'So my wife is dead and my children remain lost to me.'

'No, that is not the case. As you have learned, your wife is a woman of immense courage. She was taken from the Soviet checkpoint by two thugs whose remit was to kill her, but not before enjoying themselves with her. Their bodies were found in an area of forest approximately thirty kilometres from Dresden. Both had been shot. The Soviets identified the bullets in the dead as those of an Enfield No.2, the gun given to Helen by Major Harrison. How she managed to hide the gun as she passed through the security checkpoint is a mystery.'

'It is the gun she used to disable Svetlana. I knew of it, but we do not discuss it.'

'Your wife then drove the Soviet jeep to Dresden where by the most incredible good fortune she met a priest who is part of an organisation helping those who do not wish to live under Soviet rule. I am not permitted to know the name of the priest or the whereabouts of the hideout the organisation uses.'

'And of my children, and the children of my brother?'

'We have just received news from a contact in the institute that they were collected this morning and are in the care of your wife. The problem now is to get them out of East Germany. There is a search of Dresden and the surrounding countryside for her. Her life, and the lives of your children, are still in grave danger, but there is a plan. I will leave it to Wing Commander Vartis to explain the plan to you.'

'Good evening, *Herr* von Werstein. We have not met before, but I was a guest at your *château* for a while in 1941, although you were on the Eastern Front at that time, as I remember.'

Despite the gravity of the situation, I could not help but smile at his choice of words. He must have been the "guest" who took the letter and photographs to Helen's *Maman* and, in so doing, had been able to identify the spy, Auriole Ritter. In many respects, I owed the life of my wife to this man.

'What we propose is extremely dangerous for all concerned. I cannot emphasise this enough, but it is the only chance we have of getting Helen and your children out of enemy territory, which is how we now regard the Soviets, as our enemies. The plan is for Squadron Leader Dixon and I to fly a plane, a Douglas Dakota, from Gatow into Soviet airspace. Once we cross into Soviet-held territory, we will fly at low altitude, under the radar as we say, to pick up Helen and the children, and I believe there are three others, from an appointed place tomorrow night. There is much at stake here. We have to fly low enough to evade the Soviet radar and air defences, but at that altitude we risk collision with trees or other structures on the ground. On the positive side, a good cover of trees and shrubs, ground clutter as we call it, will shield us from radar detection, but only for so long; timing is essential in this operation. Also, we will pass over an area of heathland, with no ground clutter. In this area, we will have to fly even lower; the closer we are to ground level at this point, the curvature of the earth will shield us from radar detection, but we will be more at risk from observers on the ground.'

As George spoke, he used a stick to point out on the map the route he proposed to take over the Soviet Zone, as well as the air defences he would have to avoid.

'To reiterate, timing is crucial; we have a maximum of 20 minutes to land and take off. Helen and the children will have to be waiting close to where we land the plane. The Douglas Dakota is not as easy to manoeuvre on landing and takeoff as the Lysander I flew on missions over France, but it has the capacity to carry your wife and family, as well as those who hope to return with her.'

'I will only agree to this if I can come with you. If Helen and my children are lost to me, I should not wish to live. My young son and baby will forget us and have happy lives with their grandparents. Leon will have his grandmother and learn to be the man in the family. I must be part of this; it is my duty to Helen, as well as to my first wife and my brother.'

So it was agreed. We arranged to meet at 8 p.m. the following night on the airfield. A newly waning gibbous moon would provide good light for landing and take-off.

# 58

We took off from Gatow soon after 8 p.m. The weather conditions were good with a light breeze and cloudless skies. The moon cast a silver glow over the runway and the breeze would provide a good tailwind. Before we boarded Major Mackenzie handed me a gun.

'You may need this.'

'I understood that Germans are no longer permitted to bear arms.'

'We make exceptions, as well you know.'

We shook hands and he wished me, 'Godspeed, my good friend. We will be waiting anxiously for the return of this plane tonight.'

George gave regular updates from the cockpit. The route he was taking was over large tracts of woodland and rough ground, avoiding the urban areas. At times we seemed so close to the ground that the plane would shudder and threaten to stall, but George assured me this was to be expected and he would gain some height for a while before descending again. After 45 minutes, he drew my attention to a flash of light from among a clump of trees.

'That is the beacon. I can see our landing place. Hold on to the strap above you, there will be some "chop" as we will be facing a headwind as we land.'

I looked down and saw a vehicle parked on the edge of the woods. A group of people stood close to it. There were no children among the group.

The plane bumped to the ground and the co-pilot rushed to open the door to release the steps. Three men ran towards the airplane and clambered on board and a fourth person followed them. I asked her where my wife and children were.

'Helen and the children have not yet arrived. There is no way of knowing where they are. They left soon after 7 p.m. and should have been here by now. The roads were clear.'

George left the controls and joined us.

'We need to leave on time. If Helen is not here within fifteen minutes, we will have to return to Berlin.

'I will not leave without them.'

'That is your choice, Karl, and I respect it, but there is still time so we will wait as long as we can. But there may be Soviets looking for her, and the longer we wait, the more dangerous it is for all.'

The three men were given blankets and tea from a flask. They looked very nervous. All understood the consequences if they were discovered by the Soviets.

Suddenly lights appeared in the distance, but the lights were from two vehicles and not one. The Soviets had found the landing place. I had my gun ready but knew it would be ineffective against the weaponry the Soviet soldiers would have. George returned to the cockpit and took the controls.

'We are leaving now and that includes the driver of our three refugees.'

# PART FIFTEEN

## Helen

## 59

August 1947
Dresden, Germany


*Père* Gerard comes to the room in the early afternoon where she is struggling to mediate another outbreak of fighting between the children. On this occasion, it is over ownership of the photograph of Leon and the dog, Meg. Maria-Sophia, whom Helen now realises is as much of a tyrant as her own daughter promises to be, has claimed it for her own; it is her brother in the photograph and she is determined to keep it under her pillow. Johanna wants the photograph because the dog reminds her of one she used to play with at her grandparents' house in Marienberg. The photograph is in danger of being ripped into shreds. Helen goes into the adjoining room and asks for scissors, which she uses to cut the photograph in half; Maria-Sophia has Leon and Johanna has the dog. She has not asked Johanna how she came to be reunited with her brother and cousins. Leon had been told Johanna would be taken to safety and for possible adoption in Lithuania. There are many questions she would like to ask, but now is not the time.

She is instructed to prepare the children to leave at 7 p.m. She will be given the uniform of a Soviet soldier and will drive the children in the jeep to a field close to a forest outside of Dresden. An RAF crew will collect them from there and fly them to Berlin. They must be at the landing place by 9 p.m. as the plane will only have 20 minutes to land and take off.

She has a map of the place and clear instructions on how to get there. She explains as best as she can to the children how it will be and that they will soon be with their father, grandmother and Leon. She explains that they must be calm and quiet at all times while they are travelling to the plane, and that if they see soldiers they must stay hidden under the seats and allow her to deal with them.

'Will they be Russian soldiers?' asks Felix.

'Yes, they will be the soldiers guarding the Soviet-occupied zone and they will be Russian.'

'Will you shoot them?' asks Alexi.

'Only if I have to, to protect you all.'

'Are you now our mother?' asks Maria-Sophia.

'Yes, if you are happy for me to be your mother.'

'I will think on it,' she replies.

By 7 p.m. they are dressed and ready to leave. The children are in warm clothing and each carries their favourite photograph. Helen has the remains of the chocolate supply in her peggybag, as well as the water bottle. She feels uncomfortable in the Soviet field dress and beret, but she has the guns she removed from her attackers and has been taught how to use them. She has been taught some basic Russian words of greeting and commands which it is hoped will help her at any checkpoints on the road. Their three companions left at 6 p.m. They will be loaded onto the same plane, but their journey to the landing site necessitates three changes of vehicle to avoid detection of the hideout in the church. The woman who brought the children out of the institute arrives soon after 7 p.m. and takes them to where the jeep is hidden. The children are told to lie under the rear seats. As there is only space enough for three children, Maria-Sophia will lie next to Helen, in the well of the passenger seat. Helen has the map on the seat beside her and a Soviet Tokarev, the TT-30, a common Soviet semi-automatic pistol. Next to that is a much larger weapon, a PPSh-41 rifle. She warns Maria-Sophia that there will be no more chocolate if she touches the weapons, and she meekly curls into a ball but not before pinching Helen's leg painfully. If they survive the journey, she hopes her husband is not distressed by his daughter's behaviour. Surely this wild creature is not the beloved child of his memories.

She takes a route through the ruins and backstreets of Dresden. People on the streets lower their heads when they pass them in the Russian vehicle; the Soviets are feared as much as the *Gestapo* used to be. After a while, the ruins of Dresden are behind them and they are in open countryside, heading towards the place from where she prays they will be taken to safety.

They are overtaken by two Soviet vehicles on the road and she uses her horn as instructed to indicate a salutation. It is now 8:15 p.m. and they are making good progress. The children are quiet, and Maria-Sophia has fallen asleep holding the now very crumpled photograph of Leon. Darkness falls early in August in Eastern Europe, but it is a cloudless night and the moon lights up the road ahead. She can already see the outline of the forest that is their destination.

## 60

She can see the plane on the ground; two Soviet vehicles are approaching it. They are close enough for her to read their number plates. They are the vehicles that overtook her on the road from Dresden. Either the plane has been spotted by radar or someone on the ground or there has been a betrayal. Whichever is correct is irrelevant; she has to get to the plane before they do and disable them. She sees a tall figure on the steps of the plane and realises at once it is her husband.

She turns to the children, who are now trying to sit up to see what is happening, and tells them to get back under the seats as far under as they can go and to hold on tight; she will be driving fast and it will be a bumpy ride.

To Maria-Sophia she says, 'I know I told you not to touch the guns on the seat, but in a few moments I am going to ask you to pass the smaller one to me.'

'Does that mean I will not get more chocolate?'

'If we get on the airplane, there will be plenty of chocolate, for you especially.'

She presses hard on the accelerator and heads towards the plane. On her instruction, Maria-Sophia passes her the Tokarev, which she holds in her left hand while steering with her right. She can see the Soviets getting closer to the plane; they are doubtless more interested in capturing it and its passengers than looking behind them. She has the advantage of surprise. The propellers are already moving and the engines have fired up. She speeds towards the Soviet vehicles and aims her pistol at the driver of one; he slumps over the steering wheel. She stops the jeep and asks Maria-Sophia to pass her the rifle and she turns the weapon on the Soviet soldiers. One has time to reach for his gun, but she scatters several rounds and he is caught by a bullet. By this time, her husband has come from the plane. She gives him cover with the rifle while he plucks Maria-Sophia from beside her and rushes her onto the plane. He then returns and takes the rifle from her; his aim is better than hers and, before long, all the Soviets lie dead or wounded around their vehicles. Alexi, Felix and Johanna are boarded onto the plane. She goes to retrieve her peggybag, water bottle and the chocolate, but in that time she sees more vehicles approaching the plane. The woman who had driven the three men is agitated.

'They will identify the car and trace it to the church.'

'Is there a fuel can in the jeep?' asks her husband.

'Yes, there is a can in the back behind the seats, but there is no time', she replies.

'There is time.' He rushes down to the jeep where he removes the fuel can. It takes a few seconds to pour the gasoline over the car and fire a few rounds onto it. It explodes in a flash. Karl mounts the steps, closes the hatch door and in a moment they are in the air.

There is no time for greetings and reminiscences, even though it is a wonder to Helen to see George at the controls of the plane. But they are not out of danger yet, as he explains.

'If we have been detected on radar, the Soviets will send fighter planes to shoot us down as an enemy plane. If we have been betrayed or they suspect that defectors have organised the plane to escape, they will try to shoot us down from the ground.

Unfortunately, to avoid this, we will have to fly high and by doing so we risk detection by their radar.'

One of the men laughs.

'So either way we are fucked!'

George also laughs.

'You are right, but I will do all I can to avoid... I am mindful there are children on board... them shooting us down.'

She feels as though her eardrums are bursting as they soar into the night skies. She looks down to see flashes of light from the ground, but they are too high and far away for them to hit the plane. She wonders if they have been detected on radar yet and looks out of the small window by her seat for approaching aircraft. The plane seems to be flying at greater speed than before and she asks George whether she is correct,

'Yes, the wind is now behind us and has picked up. Now hold onto the children. We are approaching the outskirts of East Berlin, and I am going to rise high to avoid the air defences here.'

As he says this, the plane climbs into the sky and then seems to plummet. Helen's ears pop and her stomach turns over. The children are clinging to her husband, who has Maria-Sophia on his knee. All are eating chocolate. The plane rocks and shakes before assuming a gentle descent. George's voice comes from the cockpit.

'You can relax now; we are coming into land in the British sector of Berlin.'

All start to clap their hands. She hears Maria-Sophia say to her father, 'Helen told me to pick up guns. You told me that I should never pick up a gun. That was naughty of her wasn't it, Papa? She should not get any chocolate.'

Her husband laughs as he holds his daughter close to him.

'I will be sure to withhold the chocolate from her and she will be punished. She has a very large hairbrush in her room.'

Major Mackenzie boards the plane as soon as it lands. He takes Helen in his arms and kisses her on both cheeks.

'I cannot describe the relief when we saw your aircraft approaching. After you have had time to recover, we can talk about what happened. George and William will be debriefed immediately. I see we have other passengers?'

'Three are Jewish survivors of the camps. They became trapped in the Soviet Zone and have been hidden where I was hidden along with the children. They must be allowed to stay and hopefully find their families. The woman is one of the group helping such people escape from Soviet occupation. She may also need to be helped to make a life in the West, if that is what she wishes.'

'It will be arranged, do not worry.'

# 61

They are given rooms at a *Gásthaus* close to the airfield. Helen is astounded by the change in the behaviour of the children when in her husband's company. They do not fight over food and sit quietly at the table while they are served by *Frau* Becker. They hold their cutlery as though they had never torn whole loaves apart and guarded each crumb to the death, as Leon had described. They question him politely about the war and the *Schloss* where they will live with their grandmother. They completely ignore Helen. It is as though she is not there. She realises they consider her to be the enemy, one of those who destroyed their country.

Maria-Sophia announces that she wishes to share the bedroom with her father, and Johanna joins her in this request. Alexi notes the resemblance of Helen to their favourite cousin, Isolde.

'It is because Helen is a distant relative of *Oma* Luisa. She and Isolde inherited the beautiful hair from *Oma* Luisa's Scottish grandmother. You all have this Scottish blood in you. I think you should consider the wife I love more favourably. She is not only your mother by my marriage but also part of our family by blood. She is brave, a warrior, as were the Teutonic knights that you were always so proud of. She fought off the Russian soldiers and brought you to safety. She is not to blame for the catastrophe that befell our country. I fought for our country as it was my duty

302

to do so, although I knew that it was not an honourable war. But we are Prussians and we fight to defend the Fatherland. We will do so again one day, but not with dishonour, murdering innocent people because they do not share our religion or heritage. It is the same for Helen. She is proud of her Scottish blood, as you should be. Perhaps one day she will stand with you, to preserve peace and unity in Europe.'

Maria-Sophia makes a very vulgar sound in response to this and encourages Johanna to do the same.

Alexi continues, 'Is it possible Papa, that one day I will be able to fight as a soldier for my country? At the institute, they told us Germany will never again have an army, that Prussians and all Germans will never again be permitted to be soldiers.'

'Yes, Alexi, it is already being debated and I am part of it. You will have to be patient, it will take some years, but when it happens, I may again be a general, but in an army to preserve peace, not as an aggressor nation. You wish to be a soldier but first, you need to go to school. When we return to your grandmother's *Schloss,* which by the way is legally part of Scotland, we will discuss your education. But now it is time for you to sleep. Tonight, the two girls will share one room and Alexi and Felix another. Helen and I will have our own room, as your mother and father.'

'As long as she does not get any chocolate,' says Maria-Sophia.

# 62

September 1947
Berlin, Germany

He takes her in his arms and they lie together. It has been a day of wonders, fear and danger, and both are exhausted. For his part, Karl will never forget the image of his wife, her red-gold hair escaping from the Soviet cap as she drove towards the plane, firing at those who would have killed his children. He has loved many women, but none compare to his wife. He resolves to honour her more than he has done over the time of their marriage.

He had never been a man to bed a woman lightly. He had been faithful to Sophia until war and her illness separated them. It was war and what followed that caused him to dishonour the vows he had made to Helen at their marriage. But she has also been unfaithful, and he finds it hard to reconcile the admiration he had for Erik as a soldier under his command to the jealousy he now harbours for the man who loves his wife, made love to her in the bed of their apartment in Bonn, and has been more of a father to his son than he has been able to be. It will not be easy reconciling his children to his new family with Helen, but he is confident that in time this will be so. There is also the fact of Erik's marriage. He will be happy to be his *Trauzeuge*. Erik will have a wife and family of his own to care for. He will no longer feel Erik to be a threat to his marriage and his love for Helen.

Helen lies close to him, taking comfort in his strength and

the warmth of his body next to hers. She will never forget how he ran from the airplane, ignoring the risk of being caught in the crossfire, to take his daughter to safety and returned to take over the rifle, enabling her to get the other children to safety. Nor will she forget the risk he took in destroying the car that would have betrayed *Père* Gerard and his group of courageous rescuers. They are too exhausted to attempt to make love. Helen's breasts are tender and ache with milk. She longs to be back with Róisín and her son.

Each in their own thoughts and memories, they sleep.

## 63

September 1947
Schloss Mariendistel

They fly to Lübeck the following day and a British staff car drives them from the airfield to the *Schloss* which is now their home. Luisa and Leon are on the driveway as the staff car sweeps to a halt. Leon has his young brother in his hand and Luisa holds Róisín in her arms. The dog, Meg, barks excitedly around them.

The children rush out of the car to hug their grandmother and Leon. Johanna fusses over Meg who immediately goes in search of a ball; Johanna will be kept busy playing "fetch" with her.

Karl picks up their son and Helen takes Róisín and puts her to her breast. As she expected, Róisín initially feigns disinterest: Helen is certain that she is being punished for her time away from her daughter. But after a while, she suckles voraciously, and the pain of engorgement Helen has suffered during the days away from her daughter is eased.

Later they walk together in the woods. Johanna, with Meg chasing a ball, runs ahead of them, Maria-Sophia holds her grandmother's hand, Karl and Helen are with their son and daughter, and the three boys chatter excitedly. Snatches of their conversation drift towards them.

'She was driving so fast, faster than even Papa ever drove us, and she was shooting the Ivans as she drove and then she got one of the big guns and shot more of them until Papa came to rescue us. Then he was shooting them. And then more Ivans came and we had to fly away, but Papa went back to the jeep and threw gasoline over the car the other men came in and shot at it and *Boom* there was a massive explosion. Then we flew high up into the sky. It was so bumpy, but we were not scared, were we, Felix?'

Maria-Sophia has heard them and leaves her grandmother to inform Leon, 'And we had so much chocolate. One night, I was sick all over Helen, but she let me have more chocolate on the airplane.'

It is clear to all that Leon feels he has missed out on an adventure. His own journey pales in comparison to tales of shootouts with the Ivans and fast driving to an airplane to escape from the enemy. It is straight from the adventure books they used to read as children. But he is smiling, and more animated than they have seen him since his return to Schloss Mariendistel.

'She is our mother now and she is a hero. Perhaps she will be a soldier too,' says Alexi.

'She is going to be a doctor,' says Leon. He continues, 'But I have seen her shoot too. She shot a spy who was going to kill her, right here at the *Schloss* in the kitchen garden. Afterwards, she and Papa took the spy prisoner and drove her to the British in Bonn.'

Silence while the other children absorb this story.

Then Maria-Sophia is heard to say, 'I still don't think Papa should permit her to have chocolate. She told me to hold guns and Papa said I should never do that.'

'That is because you are a baby and wouldn't know how to hold one,' says Alexi.

'I am not a baby. I can hold a gun as well as you.' Maria-Sophia then throws herself in a fury at Alexi tearing at his hair, just as she had done at the hideout in Dresden.

Karl and Luisa are shocked by this.

Helen laughs. 'I have witnessed this before.' She passes Róisín to Luisa, marches up to the two combatants and pulls them apart.

'Maria-Sophia, if you ever attack your brother again, I will ensure that you never eat chocolate again. You will be sent to your room while the others enjoy it. Now apologise to Alexi and return to your grandmother.'

Maria-Sophia meekly takes her grandmother's hand but not before making a very rude gesture at Helen. Karl notices this but Helen advises him to ignore it. The child will have witnessed worse during her time in the forests and at the institute.

They discuss the children's education. It is many years since they were tutored. Helen believes the boys should attend school in Lübeck and that they should take advice on which school would be suitable for them, taking into account the trauma they have suffered. Luisa considers the girls should be tutored at the *Schloss* until they are eleven years old and then a school found for them. She already has two tutors she feels would be suitable. They will also have a piano teacher and the option of violin or cello teachers. Both Helen and Karl agree this is a good plan.

There remains the issue of Helen's medical training. She has another six months of hospital experience before her final examination. For this, they will return to Bonn with their son and Róisín. Their son will attend kindergarten in Bonn, and she will find a girl to care for Róisín while she is at the hospital. Karl is silent at this point. Helen realises he has news that he cannot divulge at this moment. They will speak later.

# 64

Five weeks later they return to Bonn. They are invited to supper with Pavel and Magda. Their baby's birth is imminent, but both hope to attend the wedding of Erik and Traute the following weekend. In the excitement of the rescue of the children, Helen and Karl have forgotten the invitation, and more importantly Karl's role as *Trauzeuge*. They have nothing suitable to wear for the event. Helen cycles to the home of Major and Edith Mackenzie where she is greeted warmly. Edith has heard of her courage and the safe return of the children. Helen explains their predicament and Edith immediately makes appointments for both Helen and Karl at the formal dress hire at NAAFI.

Helen is fitted for a costume which Edith explains is a copy of Christian Dior's New Look: a fitted silk jacket in a shade of golden brown with a matching full skirt. As Edith is helping her into the skirt, Helen notices the slight swelling in her lower abdomen. She had regained her slender figure after the births of her son and daughter very quickly, without stretch marks or varicose veins; she knows how fortunate she is in this. Luisa, ever the *raconteur* of family history, assured her that she and her grandmother and other women of the family had borne several children "without pregnancy leaving a mark on their bodies".

This gain in weight cannot be explained, particularly as she has been so active since the birth of Róisín, and has had little appetite for food, despite the constant needs of her daughter. She recalls the nausea she has felt the past few mornings, and her exhaustion which she has attributed to the rescue of the children and the numerous interventions she had to make to ensure peace between them. Maria-Sophia is the darling of her father and he overlooks her fierce temper and rebellious nature, traits she can see in her own daughter. She had become weary of mediating and compromising in the battles which were a regular feature at mealtimes, and whenever the children were together in the presence of Karl and Helen.

Luisa had assured her that they were trying to compete for their father's attention. With their consent, Felix and Johanna will be officially adopted by Karl and Helen, as it seems no other family members have survived the war. Luisa was wise enough to understand that Helen and Karl need time apart from this "blended" family to rebuild their marriage and have time with the children born of it.

She looks again at her stomach and at her pallid face in the mirror. A wave of nausea assails her, and she feels she is going to faint. Edith is at her side immediately and finds her a chair. The nausea passes and she feels well enough to request a glass of water. Edith has four children of her own and the question comes naturally to her.

'My dear Helen, are you expecting again?'

# 65

Edith can be trusted to keep the fact of this pregnancy a secret. Edith also knows that Karl is in regular contact with the former Prussian general, Hasso von Mantueffel. Karl had met Von Mantueffel on various fronts during the war; both had despised Hitler and his coterie of fanatics and sadists. Mantueffel is actively involved in the politics of post-war Germany and a proponent of a new German army, and Karl is part of this. Helen will not have the support she needs from her husband at this time, especially as she is struggling to complete the final stages of her medical degree. Furthermore, she has two young children as well as her husband's children and a niece and nephew. Helen has told her that despite the stern regime of Luisa, they continue to be wayward and resentful, that even Luisa despairs of Maria-Sophia at times.

They have been informed that Svetlana and the "intermediary" who masterminded her escape from British captivity are in Moscow, having been "spirited" through the checkpoints to the Soviet Zone. Helen knows that the intermediary informed Svetlana of her involvement in D-Day, and of the location of the *Schloss* where Svetlana attempted to kill her. Helen also knows that the same woman plotted her murder by the Soviet soldiers. Helen has little faith in the Allies' recruitment of spies, or the ability of Intelligence personnel to keep secrets. The woman had been given access to the same highly confidential material that

Helen had been obliged to protect when she signed the Official Secrets Act in 1945. Svetlana and the "intermediary" remain a threat to her and her family, as well as to Allied Intelligence.

Magda and Pavel are at the wedding of Erik and Traute, which is held on Saturday the 25th of October at the *Lutherkirche* in Bonn. The civil ceremony had been held at the *Standesamt,* the civil registration office, three days previously. Karl had been a witness to the official signing of the marriage register. The church wedding is a more extravagant occasion. In former times, Karl, as *Trauzeuge,* would have worn the uniform of a general in the *Wehrmacht,* but today he is dressed as he was on the night of the supper party at the Mackenzies, in a suit and tuxedo. The church is full to capacity with family and friends of the bride and groom. Erik's brothers and sisters are to be "pages" together with Traute's younger sisters.

They hear the sound of horses' hooves, and at once the organ starts up. Magda has explained that it is traditional for the groom and bride to arrive together in a horse-drawn carriage. Karl waits by the altar, and the pages, the girls with wreaths of autumn flowers in their hair, wait at the back of the church. The doors open and Erik and Traute enter the church. Traute wears a long white silk gown with a high neckline and a lace veil which covers her face. They are followed by Traute's sister, who holds a bouquet of calla lilies, roses and autumn leaves. Erik looks very handsome in a suit similar to that worn by Karl. The ceremony is short: a few prayers and hymns, a blessing of the rings and a blessing for the future of the couple. Traute pushes the veil from her face to receive her husband's kiss. The congregation all clap, and the couple walk together down the aisle to exit the church. A number of guests have already left the church and are waiting outside to throw rice over the couple for good luck. A photographer is also outside, and photographs are taken of the married couple and their immediate family. Erik and Traute are then helped into the waiting carriage, which will take them to a nearby restaurant for the celebratory meal, where Karl will give a speech.

Magda's labour starts during the wedding meal. She tells Helen she had felt a few pains in the church but now the pain has progressed to contractions which are strong and coming at shorter intervals. Helen goes to where Pavel is seated and informs him that Magda needs to be taken immediately to the university hospital; the baby's birth is imminent. Erik offers them the use of his father's car, for which they are grateful, but Karl cannot drive them as he has yet to give the traditional speech. None wish to disrupt the wedding, so it is Helen who will drive the car to the hospital. Pavel needs to be on the rear seat of the car to support Magda, who is now in extreme discomfort and certain that she can feel the baby's head descending. They are approximately three kilometres from the hospital when Pavel instructs Helen to pull over to the side of the road and assist him in delivering the baby. It does not take long. After a few strong contractions and much effort on Magda's part, a healthy baby boy is born on the rear seat of the Volkswagen Sedan. Helen briefly thinks she will inform Hans of the car's usefulness as a maternity vehicle. It may increase his sales.

Helen tears strips off the rented skirt to tie the umbilical cord and uses her cashmere shawl to warm the baby, who is now suckling voraciously at Magda's breast. Pavel ensures that the placenta is delivered. They continue their journey to the hospital to have the baby examined and weighed. As Helen drives, she asks if they have named the baby. They tell her his name is Josef, which in Hebrew means "God increases", a symbol of the survival of Pavel. His first family, murdered by the Nazis, will be honoured by this choice of name. The baby's middle name will be Daniel and he will be circumcised on Sunday the 2nd of November. Magda has converted to the Jewish faith and the child, and those who may follow, will be part of the Jewish community in Germany.

Helen waits while mother and baby are checked at the hospital and then drives them to their apartment. They have prepared for the baby and a cradle and baby clothes are already warm by the *Kachelofen*. They have food and Helen promises to bring champagne from the wedding feast to celebrate the birth. She returns to her own apartment and removes the soiled and damaged clothing. She hopes Edith will be able to negotiate a fair price as reparation for the ruined skirt. She takes cloths and water to the car and scrubs the seat clean of the birth fluids. When she is satisfied the car is in good order, she bathes and changes into the sweater and kilt *Maman* and Papa had brought from Scotland on their visit earlier in the year.

It is late in the evening when she returns to the wedding party. Erik sees the car arrive and comes to greet her and to take the keys of the car. He is delighted to learn of the safe delivery of the baby and asks her to pass his congratulations to Magda and Pavel. He will visit them as soon as he returns from his honeymoon. Suddenly she sways, a blackness surrounds her and she knows she is about to fall in a faint. He catches her and carries her to a sofa in an anteroom, the room where Traute will soon arrive to change into her "going away" outfit. He lifts her legs over the arms of the sofa and gets her a glass of water. He holds her hand and asks her why she may have fainted. She explains that she has not eaten since the previous evening as the nausea was so severe.

He looks at her and asks, 'Are you pregnant?'

'Yes, I believe I am.'

'Does Karl know?'

'I have not yet told him. He is much occupied with his work, and I was not sure until these past few days.'

'Is it possible that the child is mine?'

'Yes, it is possible, but I have also been with my husband since that day. I do not wish Karl to know of this pregnancy, not yet anyway. We have too many problems with our children.'

'I would wish to meet the child when he is born but I will be discreet. I love you too much to cause trouble in your marriage. And I have my own marriage to consider. But take care in this pregnancy; you are now even more precious to me.'

He kisses her softly on the lips and makes to leave. At that moment Traute arrives. She is not pleased to find Helen occupying the room where she is to change. Erik explains that Helen is exhausted from aiding in the delivery of Magda's baby. She is now leaving with her husband to collect her children from friends and return to her home. Erik ensures they leave with a bottle of champagne to toast the new baby.

Once their son has settled in his cot bed, they visit Magda and Pavel. Baby Josef is at Magda's breast.

She laughs. 'He is sucking the life out of me.'

Karl opens the champagne and all toast Josef and his happy parents. Róisín is not impressed by the mewling scrap that is getting all the attention and pulls at Helen's clothing to get to her breast. They leave soon after and settle Róisín in her cot. Karl takes Helen in his arms and holds her close to him.

'I missed your presence at the wedding feast today. It made me think we should have a German wedding. There is still the issue that our civil marriage is not recognised in Germany; your name on the register of marriages in Caen is Gabrielle Doucet. It is the same system in Germany as in France. There must be a civil ceremony. The religious ceremony is optional, but if you wish that as well, I am happy to do so. Perhaps now is the time to request the hand in marriage, not of Gabrielle Doucet, but of Helen Douglas von Werstein. If you like, I can kneel before you to request this.'

'And if you do, you will feel the full weight of my hairbrush. Of course I wish to be your wife. I love you more than you know. It is not necessary for us to have a wedding in a church, but if it would please Luisa and my parents then so it shall be. We will have the civil ceremony as soon as it can be arranged. Pavel will be happy to oblige as a witness, but the wedding should be as soon as possible as I am again expecting a child and do not wish to be the size of a whale when I walk up the aisle.'

Róisín stirs in her cot. Helen is sure she has heard every word that has been spoken and does not view the prospect of sharing her mother's attention with enthusiasm. She will have to be weaned from the breast as soon as Helen can persuade her to do so.

They decide that the wedding should be in December, as November is considered an unlucky month to wed, certainly in Scotland.

## 66

November 1947
Bonn, Germany

Helen is giving their son breakfast when they are disturbed by the concierge. On this occasion, she holds a letter bearing the stamp of the *Grand Chancery de France* and insists she had to pay the courier in order to acknowledge receipt of the letter. Helen relents and gives her a bag of sugar and half a kilo of coffee, which will mean no coffee for her and Karl until the following week.

Karl is still sleeping. He has been up during the night attempting to soothe Róisín and to encourage her to take the bottle of Nutramigen formula milk Edith has recommended to ensure that Helen is not exhausted feeding Róisín while carrying another pregnancy. This formula feeding has not been successful, at all, and Luisa is horrified by the concept. As Helen anticipated, Luisa has tales to recount of mothers in the family continuing to feed one child while pregnant with another. She recalls an aunt with an infant on one breast and a thirteen-month-old on the other. Both had grown into healthy children and fought for the Fatherland. As Luisa said this in the presence of Róisín, Helen feels this has played a part in her daughter's recalcitrance. While Róisín is content to eat mashed eggs and fruit and vegetable purees, she wants Helen's breast milk at other times, particularly during the night when her mother needs to sleep. Helen is certain that Róisín will prevail.

Helen's hands are shaking as she opens the letter. It informs her that she has been recommended by the French High Commissioner to the Western Zones of Germany, *Monsieur* André François-Poncet, to receive the award of the *Légion d' Honneur* "for extraordinary bravery and service during the time of war". The letter informs her that while there is no legal deadline for the ceremony to award her this honour, it is recommended that the decoration occur within the year following the date of nomination. She is informed that *Monsieur* André François Poncet himself has offered to be her delegate and present her with the award. If she is in agreement, she is required to inform the *Grand Chancery* that he be granted the power to represent the *Grand Chancellor* at the ceremony.

Helen finds it all very confusing. It is not clear where and when this ceremony will take place, and how she can reconcile it with her plans for the wedding, the birth of the baby and the completion of her medical degree. She shows the letter to her husband, who is in awe of the honour bestowed on his wife. He assures her it is well deserved and in no small way attributable to the impression she made at Major Mackenzie's supper party. All there had been aware of her courage and wartime exploits, even those Germans present who know that those exploits contributed to the defeat of their country.

She is astonished and overwhelmed by the honour and immediately composes letters to the Grand Chancery and to *Monsieur* François-Poncet accepting the award and thanking him for his nomination and his offer to be her delegate. She explains that she would prefer the award ceremony to be held in March of the following year as she has her medical degree exams to prepare for and is expecting a child to be born in May.

She bicycles to the Mackenzies' home where, after congratulating her, Edith arranges for both letters to be typed and addressed to the appropriate offices. Before she leaves, she informs Edith of the planned wedding. Major Mackenzie is at home and he immediately offers to be witness at the civil ceremony. He consults his diary and suggests that Monday the 8th of December would be convenient. Helen finds it difficult to express the gratitude she feels for the kindness they have shown her. She assures them that Karl will go to the *Standesamt* today to arrange the time.

The civil ceremony takes place on the 8th of December at 2 p.m. in the *Standesamt* in Bonn. Major Mackenzie and Pavel are witnesses to the vows Karl and Helen make, to love, respect and be loyal to one another until death, and sign the register recording the marriage. Helen considers the vow of loyalty and how flexible the interpretation of that vow could be with respect to her husband, and indeed herself, after all that has happened in the past year. But there is great love between them and it is love which will bind their marriage.

The wedding is held at Saint Remigius church in Bonn on Saturday the 27th of December. The church is full of friends old and new. *Maman* and Papa and a contingent of Douglas and Gordon cousins arrived on Christmas Eve. With the help of Edith, all have been found accommodation close to the church. The men in the family wear the clan kilts to the wedding. Damian and Amelie have driven Leah, Raisa, Ruth and Ellana to Bonn. They are to stay in a *Gästhaus* close to the church. Leah is now fully restored to health and looking forward to the birth of a great-grandchild. Ruth married the son of a camp survivor in February of this year; another happy reminder of Hitler's failure to annihilate the Jewish race. Iain and Morag are also at the church with their son, Jamie.

*Père* François had to decline the invitation due to his Christmas obligations at the church, but as he wryly put it, "It is enough that I have been at one marriage between you. I send my blessing for this one".

Hans and Jennifer are in the church. Hans had been much amused by Helen's suggestion to promote the Volkswagen Sedan as a proven maternity vehicle. Erik and Traute are also guests.

Lotti and Emilia are maids of honour. Their husbands are also in the church. Helen and Karl had been unable to attend their respective weddings on account of the circumstances of the past year. Edith and Tristan Mackenzie are present, as well as Colonel and Sybil Oakley. Edith suggested that it would be a tactical as well as a generous act to invite them and they had been pleased to accept. Magda and Pavel have brought baby Josef and, of course, there are their own children. *Maman* and Papa have taken charge of young Karl and Róisín, and Luisa arrives with the other children. Maria-Sophia and Johanna are bridesmaids, and Alexi, Leon and Felix are pages.

It has taken a great deal of bribery in the form of chocolate to persuade Maria-Sophia to agree to hold one side of the train of the wedding dress which had been Luisa's own and is a Von Werstein heirloom. Johanna had needed no such inducements and had quietly agreed to her role at the wedding, only requesting that the dog, Meg, accompany them to Bonn. Helen and Luisa worry about her; she witnessed the horrific death of her mother and her only comfort seems to be the dog. Nightmares and terrors, in which she screams for her parents, are becoming more frequent. The boys, by contrast, have settled well into the school in Lübeck and are as boisterous as all boys of that age. None of the children talk of their days in the institute but often speak of their time in the forests of Lithuania. In many respects, this has acquired a mythical significance in their lives, and their stories are often embellished with tales of "derring-do" against the Ivans and encounters with bears and wolves, which Maria-Sophia is quick to contradict, and another furious outburst frequently ensues.

Helen hopes that nothing at the wedding will provoke Maria-Sophia to any public displays of her temper.

Karl waits at the altar for Helen to arrive on her Papa's arm. He has not yet told her that as soon as her final exams are over, and she has received her licence to practise as a doctor, they will be moving to Berlin. That is for later. For the moment, he sees his beautiful wife walk up the aisle towards him carrying a bouquet of winter lilies and carnations, the swell of her pregnancy visible in the antique lace gown Luisa has adjusted to fit her. He loves her above all women.

As they kneel at the altar, the church doors open and four figures discreetly enter and take their seats at the back of the church. The nuptial mass is over and the priest gives his final blessing to Helen and Karl and the congregation. All has gone well; even Maria-Sophia sat quietly and in apparent awe of the event. They walk down the aisle, Helen smiling at her husband and at the guests on both sides.

As they reach the back of the church, they see Konrad and Auguste Adenauer and André and Odile François-Poncet sitting in the back row. All four stand up to congratulate the couple, who are delighted and honoured to see them. A crowd of well-wishers has gathered outside the church, and rice is thrown over Helen and Karl before they climb into the waiting horse-drawn carriage which will take them to the wedding feast.

# ACKNOWLEDGMENTS

I wish to acknowledge *The Guardian* newspaper article of Saturday 17th December 2005 by Ian Cobain titled '*The Interrogation camp that turned prisoners into living skeletons*'. In reading this article I first became aware of the camp at Bad Nenndorf. I recommend readers of my book to search for this article, and hope it will dispel the false perception that only the German Gestapo were guilty of torture and the incarceration of innocent people.

I would also like to acknowledge the following books which I found invaluable to my writing of *Restoration*, and thoroughly enjoyed reading:

*Ratlines* by Philippe Sands
*Berlin* by Sinclair Mckay
*Aftermath* by Harald Jahner
*Hunting Evil* by Guy Walters
*Checkmate in Berlin* by Giles Milton

# ABOUT THE AUTHOR

Jan Stirling Locke was both a trained registered nurse and teacher of English throughout her long working life in the UK and in a variety of countries around the world. As a young woman she travelled alone through Europe into former Iron Curtain countries, in the pursuit of love and adventure.

As a child of the '50s whose father, uncles and aunts had fought and/or played a role in the Allied victory, Jan grew up imbued with the concept that the Germans were the 'baddies' and 'all of them Nazis'. As an adult, during frequent visits to her cottage in Normandy, Jan attended the commemorative ceremonies of the D-day landings with her family, hosted veterans, and became an honorary member of the now sadly disbanded Grimsby Normandy Veterans Association. A walk along one of the lanes beside the cottage sparked her consideration for the German soldiers who had also died during World War Two, whose bereaved families would not be permitted to mourn their loss. They too were fighting for their country, albeit one ruled by Hitler. This prompted her to read about life in Germany in the 1930s, and to begin working on *Deception*.